"Lloyd Johnson has done an im_____ _____ _____ in bringing the reality of Israel and Palestine to the fiction reader. In *Living Stones* he shows us what most Americans don't see: the real face of Palestine and of life under occupation. Just as important, Johnson's strong faith shines through in every page. This is a story about crossing boundaries and about forgiveness. Don't pick up this book if you are not willing to have your assumptions challenged. But don't miss the opportunity—your faith will be strengthened and your horizons widened."

—Mark Braverman, Program Director of Kairos USA and the author of *A Wall in Jerusalem: Hope, Healing and the Struggle for Peace in Israel and Palestine.*

From his own rich experiences with the *Living Stones,* Lloyd Johnson weaves a story of intrigue and danger but also love, curiosity, forgiveness, and hope. *Living Stones* takes us as readers beyond simplistic understandings of Israel and Palestine. In this gripping novel, Ashley Wells' journey of discovery helps open minds and hearts—for others in the novel, but for us as well.

—Joan Deming, Pilgrims of Ibillin Executive Director

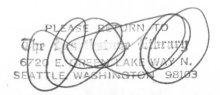

*Living Stones*
by Lloyd Johnson

ISBN 9781938467578

Published by

köehlerbooks™
an imprint of Morgan James Publishing

5 Penn Plaza, 23rd floor
c/o Morgan James Publishing
New York, NY 10001
212-574-7939
www.koehlerbooks.com

Publisher
John Köehler

Executive Editor
Joe Coccaro

In an effort to support local communities, raise awareness and funds, Morgan James Publishing donates a percentage of all book sales for the life of each book to Habitat for Humanity Peninsula and Greater Williamsburg.
Get involved today, visit www.MorganJamesBuilds.com

# Dedication

To my soulmate in life and in telling this story,

my best friend whose heart also yearns for peace

with justice in the Holy Land,

my beloved wife, Marianne.

# Acknowledgments

*"... If you can dream—and not make dreams your master;*
*If you can think—and not make thoughts your aim,*
*If you can meet with Triumph and Disaster*
*And treat those two impostors just the same."*

Kipling captured the calm through the ups and downs of life. Friends encourage when there's more disaster than triumph—whether in life or writing a story. Providing resources of knowledge, contacts and wonderful discussions around the tumult in the Holy Land, Sandra and Brad Gerrish stand out. I appreciate Bart Shorack for his counsel. Suzie Pham as a young adult, and Leonard Rodgers of Middle East fame inspired me too.

Friends in the Holy Land gave us insights as we visited them. Among many, Usama Nicola, Marwan Farajeh, Sami and Bishara Awad. Our hearts remain with all of them in their suffering. Knowing them, we've begun to understand and love our brothers and sisters there.

Through colleagues in the Northwest Christian Writers Association I'm acquiring the craft of writing a story, with much yet to learn. Particular thanks go to my faithful critique partners, Kathleen Freeman, Kim Vandel and Karen Higgins, whose suggestions have ushered me from drab stoicism to heights of emotion—something difficult for a platonic Swede.

For his patience and guidance, I thank my literary agent, Les Stobbe, whose experience and counsel have proved invaluable. Working with John Koehler, publisher, and his colleagues, Joe Coccaro, editor, Terry Whalin and Margo Toulouse, I've been pleased with their expertise and prompt skills in taking a story and producing a quality book.

And most of all, I appreciate my wife, Marianne, for her invaluable input sharing her heart, her perspectives and her faith. As in our own adventures in the Middle East, we've done this one together.

# Living Stones

## LLOYD JOHNSON

NEW YORK

VIRGINIA

He has showed you, O man, what is good.

And what does the Lord require of you?

To act justly and to love mercy

And to walk humbly with your God.

Micah 6:8

# Prologue

Ashley Wells crumpled on the sidewalk as the synagogue behind her collapsed in a cascade of debris and dust spraying in a thousand directions. The shock wave leveled everything in its path, including Ashley and her fellow graduate student, Najid Haddad, who had been standing on the sidewalk chatting on a sunny Friday afternoon. Ashley had noticed a young Caucasian man across the street in a hoodie staring at them, but she didn't think much of it. Other pedestrians had slowed to admire the magnificent stone Jewish house of prayer.

After their eyes briefly met, the man in the hoodie wheeled around and walked away. Ashley turned back to Najid. Suddenly a roar overwhelmed her and in the same second she was slammed to the ground. Next came agonizing pain, then blackness.

Najid stood unharmed except for minor lacerations on his arms. Ashley's body had protected him. He turned her onto her back. "Ashley, can you hear me? Ashley! Ashley!" Blood pooled on the sidewalk. She moaned. He felt a rapid pulse at her wrist. He waved his arms. "Help! Help!" His voice was just another in a chorus of screams as people scurried to the crowd gathered in the street. Then everything blurred as sirens screeched and police and Medic One ambulances appeared. Najid stepped aside, shaking his head, wide-eyed. He trembled. "Oh God, help Ashley! Make her live!"

Emergency personnel swarmed around her, quickly pouring in IV fluids. They moved her onto a stretcher and into a Medic One van, which then sped away with siren blaring and red lights flashing. Police, guns drawn, with helmets and flak jackets, rushed into the debris of the synagogue searching for other victims.

Najid gazed at the bloody sidewalk, shaking his head. His mind whirled and echoed with the explosion, unable to focus. It seemed unreal. He had fled violence in the Middle East for a peaceful education in Seattle. In a daze, he began walking slowly past large maple trees and older homes with wooden porches. Tears welled in his eyes. The prayer kept coming, "Oh God, please help Ashley. Don't let her die."

Still dazed, he heard staccato footsteps behind him and someone yelling. Suddenly a policeman yanked Najid from behind, clamped handcuffs on his wrists, and pushed him into a car with blue lights blazing. Najid shuddered. *This happens in America too?*

# Chapter 1

Robert Bentley, face flushed, stormed out of his father's dark-paneled home office, with Conrad Bentley close behind.

"Your life has been pretty easy. We've given you everything you could want. Half a million dollars in trust funds." The older man raised his hands palms up, shaking his head. "What more could you want?"

"I'm out of here, Dad. All you think about is money! You really could care less about me! Tell Mom goodbye when she comes home, if she still wants to live with you! Don't come looking for me. I won't be back!"

Conrad Bentley shouted back, "Don't act so indignant, son. If you're so high-and-mighty then why have you dabbled in drugs with Mark instead of studying at Cornell?!"

Robert raced across the mansion's patio and vaulted over the door of his red Corvette, which glimmered with its top down. Gunning the engine, the twenty-one-year-old jerked the car into gear. The tires screeched as he roared around the circular driveway, slowing only enough for the automatic gate to open. Knuckles white on the steering wheel, he flew down the street, suddenly swerving to miss a child on a bicycle.

He slowed, glancing in the rearview mirror for any police. The elegant Long Island community had proven generous with traffic tickets.

Robert seethed, gritted his teeth, and shook his head, fingers raking his dark hair. His dad had no clue! Of medium height and slender frame, shorter than his father, he scowled and hunched his shoulders over the steering wheel.

Robert heaved a deep breath and sighed, telling himself to *calm down* as he headed toward Mark's modest house. Talking to Mark might make him feel better.

One hour later, with Mark in the passenger seat and two backpacks full, they sped south down Highway 87 to the Bronx and then headed west, first on 95 and then Interstate 80. Robert's plan to flee his family's gilded emptiness was coming together perfectly. Mark always said he loved an adventure. He seemed to enjoy racing down the highway, top down, open to the sky above. Robert gripped the wheel, jaw jutted outward, teeth clenched. "I just told my dad what I think of him. You know, it made me feel good to tell him off."

"Cool, dude. Sometimes a guy's got to do it. OK, now tell me why you want me to go way out West with you." Mark rolled up the window. It was a sunny day, still warm for October. "I don't get you. Like ... you kept leaving our hangout every afternoon to go to that mosque. A mosque? What's up with that?"

"I'm not sure you'd understand. I'm sick of the way America works. It's all about money and superficial stuff, like scrambling up the corporate ladder and stepping on everyone else in the fight to the top. New York is run by financial phonies, man, and controlled by the Jewish businesses and press. My family is into it big time, you know, but it's not for me."

Mark stretched with his hands behind his head and gazed at the world flying by. "They say Wall Street runs on fear and greed, and I believe them. Your family has done pretty well though."

"I don't care. My dad had me in business training at Cornell, and man, I hated it. I figured maybe we Westerners have it all wrong. Maybe I needed a whole different perspective on things. So I found a mosque and dropped in to hear what they had to say. It changed my life and gave me some direction and a reason to live. It's been awesome!"

"You mean, like you had no direction for your life?"

"Yeah." Robert shook his head and shrugged. "None. But in the mosque they have a plan. They have five pillars in their belief system and they pray to Allah, five times a day."

"Dude, no way! Five times every day?"

"Yeah, really. They face Mecca in Saudi Arabia and bow clear to the floor, touching their foreheads. Strange, man, at first. There are lots of rules, including stuff you can't eat or drink. It's like hard, but it's challenging."

"So what does that mean for you? Sounds difficult."

"Well, for one thing, the word 'Muslim' means submission to Allah. So I'm learning to submit."

"You're crazy, dude!"

"Well, at first I attended a mosque once in a while, but then I found the Salaheddin Islamic Center, and now I see the world as it really is. True believers see what is really happening."

Mark turned toward Robert, grabbing the backrest behind him, frowning. "What do you mean, 'true believers' and 'what's really happening'?"

"OK, it's how the U.S. attacked the poor people in Afghanistan and Iraq, and the Jews cop the land in Palestine. The Zionists and the United States are conspiring to destroy Muslims, Arabs, and Palestinians. So, you know, we've gotta help them resist and fight back."

"How do you do that?" Mark suddenly stiffened in his seat.

"Well, look what we are doing in lots of places in the world, with the Taliban and other groups, and of course al-Qaeda. I don't know much yet about the Salafi-jihadi ideas, but their goal is to establish ruling caliphates with sharia law in a bunch of countries, not just Saudi Arabia or Afghanistan."

"I don't know much about that stuff, but it sounds bad. Like, what are you planning on doing?"

"Jihad."

"So you're learning about jihad?! Did you get all this in New York?"

"Oh no. Now I have a bunch of friends around the world on the Internet who are far ahead of me. Like I've found a ton of websites and chat rooms. That's why I'm going to Seattle. A group there is interested in jihad, and they have invited me to join them."

Mark frowned. "Hey look, I just came on this outing for a fun road trip. I had no idea that you are considering Islam and jihad. That's serious, dude."

"It's, like, the only thing that makes sense to me now. It's us or them in the world, and I want to be on the winning side."

"Well, if you're on the 9/11 side, I'm outta here."

"That American conspiracy of our own government, you know, played nicely into the West's anti-Islam prejudice. Man, don't you see? It amounted to a clever ploy by the CIA to turn the nations of the West against us, against Muslims."

"You gotta be kidding! Like you actually believe 9/11 was an American government conspiracy?"

"It's clear that our government did it!"

"Robert, I don't think I belong on this trip. Let me off at the next exit, dude. I'll find a bus or train back to town."

They coasted to a stop at a strip mall just outside the city. Mark clapped Robert on the back as he reached for his backpack to leave.

"You're going to miss a real adventure, you know."

"I hope you survive!" Mark replied over his shoulder as he hurried out of the car.

# Chapter 2

Most considered Ashley Wells beautiful. She was tall and slender, with long blond hair and sparkling blue eyes that squinted when she laughed. But when she looked beyond the mirror each day, she saw a serious young woman deep in thought about world affairs, helping animals and healing people.

Ashley had moved from her home state to get an advanced degree in zoology at the University of Washington in Seattle. She loved animals, but decided to apply to medical school after she finished the zoology master's degree program. She had some catching up to do, including studying for the rigorous MCAT entrance exams.

As a doctor, she could serve humanity in a more forceful and meaningful way. She had grown up in a conservative Christian family in Oklahoma and the idea of service was instilled deep within her social conscience. Her parents were delighted when she decided to go to medical school.

Their support for Zionism had transferred to Ashley. She too believed that Israel should possess the Holy Land at all costs. God promised it. It should be its own state and be staunchly defended by Christians because of hostile Arab neighbors. And she followed events in the Middle East with interest. She saw them as the fulfillment of Biblical prophecy.

That was one reason Najid Haddad interested her. She had never met an international student from the Middle East. Both graduate students were also lab assistants for the beginning zoology classes. "Come in. Please, come in," Ashley beckoned to the tall young man with black hair and a swarthy complexion who stood in the doorway. She had noticed him coming down the hall. He reminded her of one of the international soccer players on the Seattle Sounders. The small-windowed break room for graduate students contained a couple of tan lounge chairs and an old print sofa—but most importantly, a coffee maker and teapot. Two other young men sprawled in the chairs seemed indifferent, lost in their reading. "Please, come in," she said with a broad smile. "I don't want anyone to feel left out. Coffee or tea?" She patted the sofa next to her, indicating where he could sit.

"Tea would be fine," he said softly. "I did learn about American customs, that it's all right to accept a cup of tea on the first offer instead of waiting for the third one. But I don't know if it would be acceptable to sit so close to a young woman."

With that, one of the American grad students looked up. "She won't bite." He resumed his reading.

Najid sat next to Ashley, who rose to bring him a cup of tea. "Thank you. I didn't worry that you would bite."

"Bad American joke," Ashley said. She pondered this athletic-looking guy who seemed mild mannered and reserved. It would be good to learn more about him. *Maybe he's just unsure of this new American culture.* "Where are you from? It's Najid isn't it?"

"Yes, and I'm from Israel, near the town of Nazareth."

"Really? And how long have you been here?"

"Three weeks."

"Awesome! What do you think of Seattle so far?"

"It's beautiful, but very busy. Everyone seems to be in a hurry. I don't know any Americans yet. My two housemates are from Libya."

"Your English is great. Where did you learn to speak it so well?"

"We studied it in school starting from the sixth grade."

"So was that in Nazareth?"

"Yes. But we studied in English at the University in Haifa."

"Is that where you got your zoology degree?"

"Yes. But then I had another year in graduate school while applying here at the University of Washington."

"Are you on a scholarship?"

"Of course. I could not come on my own. My father works in the olive groves near us and has to support my mother and their six younger children. So I applied for a Fulbright Scholarship and here I am." Najid smiled for the first time.

By this time the two other grad students perked up. "I'm Brandon," one said. He put his papers aside and stood to shake hands. "You know Ashley here, and this is Ethan."

Najid stood and returned the handshakes. "I didn't know her name, and I am so pleased to meet all of you."

"So you live in Israel, not the West Bank?" Brandon asked.

"Yes, my family has lived there for generations—over three hundred years." He sat down, sipping his tea.

"So you're Jewish then."

"No, but we have many Jews in our town. We are Palestinians."

"So let me get this straight." Brandon look puzzled. "You are Palestinian and your family goes back three centuries in Israel?"

"Probably longer than that, but we have no records older than about ten generations."

"So you speak Palestinian?"

"No." Najid laughed with a twinkle in his eye. "We speak Arabic."

"Oh." Brandon furrowed his brow. "You mean that you are a Palestinian Arab but you live in Israel? I thought all Palestinians stayed in the West Bank."

Najid chuckled. "No, we have lived there always, before Israel existed as a country. But many of us do live in the West Bank or Gaza."

"Do you speak Hebrew?" Ethan inquired.

"Oh yes. I played with Jewish boys growing up and learned it from them, but also at school."

"So you must be Muslim," he replied. "Which branch are you with, Sunnis or are you Shiite?"

"Neither. I'm a Christian."

Ethan looked surprised and rose to pour another cup of coffee. "More tea?" He gestured toward Najid, who held out his cup for more tea. "I don't get it. I assumed all Palestinians are Muslim."

"Oh no." Najid shook his head. "I come from a long line of Christians dating back two thousand years. So I am a Christian by birth … but also by choice."

"Okaaay …" Ethan paused, gazing out the window. "So you're telling me that many people in Israel are not Jewish, but Palestinian. And some of those are Christian and not Muslim? I've never read that."

"There are five million people in Israel and about a million are Arabs," Najid said.

"So how many of the Palestinians in Israel are Christian?"

"About two hundred thousand."

"Poor Najid," Ashley intervened. "He came here for tea and ended up getting grilled."

"What is grilled? You mean like a sandwich?"

"No," Ashley said with a laugh. "That's an English idiom that means you had to answer a lot of questions."

"Oh, I don't mind them at all. I love to talk about my country and our history."

Ashley looked at this shy young man, feeling strangely attracted to him. He came to a new world, far from home, unsure of America's informal culture and direct speech. He struggled to know what was acceptable behavior. She had never heard of Palestinian Christians living in Israel playing as children with Jewish neighbors. He didn't fit her picture of a Palestinian terrorist. She hoped they could get better acquainted. He sparked a sense of adventure in her, as though he might open her eyes to new things, and she wondered where it could lead.

"Well, we better get back to work." Ashley stood. "Those freshmen students won't know a frog's liver from its spleen."

# Chapter 3

Robert found his Internet friends in Seattle. Most had emigrated from Muslim countries within the last few years, but several were born in the U.S. of immigrant parents. Ali Shakoor, a Pashtun, born in America to a Pakistani family, became his close friend. Ali spoke Urdu, Arabic, and English.

"Why don't you come to live here with the group, Robert?"

"Maybe I should." So he moved in, but still kept his own place in an old home nearby. Both houses occupied part of an old neighborhood on Capitol Hill.

Ali walked into the sparsely furnished kitchen with white painted cupboards. Robert had just finished his bean soup.

"Why did you come to room with jihadists, Ali?"

"Lots of reasons," he began. "For example, I don't like the U.S. for its strong support of Israel and its invasion of the Muslim world of Afghanistan and Iraq. What makes America think it can dictate to other countries what they can or cannot do?"

Ali grew passionate, "And I hate the secular government of Pakistan."

"You do? Why?"

"Pakistanis are not Salafis. Sharia law does not exist there. Now, Pakistan has switched from supporting to persecuting my Pashtun Taliban brothers in South Waziristan along the Afghan boarder. I want to learn what I can do about all this.

"How about you? Why did you come from New York?"

"Good question, Ali. I guess I had nothing to live for there. Then I wandered into a mosque one day and met people who lived by a strict code and knew what they believed."

"Really! Never been in one before?"

"Never. I learned a different way of looking at life and what is going on in our world beyond just making money. Then, you know, I found you guys on the Internet and decided to come here to put to work what I was learning. I've finally found a cause I can live for ... and maybe die for if it comes to that."

Over the next few weeks, Robert joined Ali on an intense religious quest. They prayed at the Masjid Al Farah Mosque in Central Seattle and heard readings from the Qu'ran—the Holy Book—and Hadith, and the Traditions. While they sat in a semicircle on the carpeted floor facing the front, the imam sat on a chair near the stand holding the Holy Book. He would take the Qu'ran, slowly turn its pages, and begin reading in Arabic that to Robert, sounded like poetry.

One Friday evening he explained jihad as the mystic Sufi Muslims believe.

"Jihad is a struggle in life to please God since you can never be sure your good deeds will outweigh your bad ones. But some see jihad as Islam taking over the world. They're trying to establish Muslim rule in many countries of the world. But these are the radical fringe of Islam. And some are terrorists."

Robert glanced at Ali, who was scowling.

The imam continued: "The vast majority of Muslims are peaceful and just want to live their lives like everyone else. We respect others, including people of the Book, Christians and Jews. Those extremists, the radical jihadists, they pervert our religion. What they do has nothing to do with true Islam."

As Ali and Robert walked home that night, a crescent moon

seemed to float in the southwest sky.

Ali shook his head. "This imam doesn't know what is going on in the world! He's weak and naïve, too 'otherworldly.' He's a mystical Sufi. Too few Muslims see things as we do because of people like him. He never spoke of revenge for what the West is doing to the Muslim countries."

"Well, maybe he does know but he doesn't care. Anyway, I think we should go somewhere else."

The sidewalk shone wet in the streetlight as they approached a traffic light on Broadway in the Capitol Hill district of Seattle. Robert stopped walking and grabbed Ali's arm. "I heard of the Islamic Center that meets on Fridays not far from here. That may be just what we want. One of the guys in the house told me about it. He goes, you know. The imam there knows what's going on. Jabril Safar teaches real jihad!"

The following Friday afternoon, Robert and Ali stepped up the hollowed-out wood steps onto the broad porch of an old house with peeling paint outside. They entered a large front room with front and side windows, carpeted, similar to that in the previous mosque, plain and unfurnished except for the Qu'ran stand. To Robert it smelled old and musty but with an odor of curry as well. They sat in a circle with others before the prayers would begin.

Imam Jabril Safar launched his sermon with a few introductory remarks and then gradually raised his voice. "The Qu'ran teaches us about jihad. Fighting for sharia law against the infidels in this world is our religious duty. That struggle, the jihad, is the best way to please Allah!"

Jabril expanded on the spiritual basis for jihad and the wonderful benefits of sacrificing one's life in the struggle for pure Islamic rule for all nations. *Heaven and seventy virgins await such a soldier. This should be the goal of every Muslim man.*

"Dude, that's what I've been waiting to hear!" Robert punched the air as he and Ali walked home after evening prayers in the mosque. "I would give everything to be able to fight in jihad!"

"Maybe we can, but how?"

"Let's make an appointment to talk with Imam Jabril to see what he says."

The following Wednesday afternoon at the Islamic Center, Robert and Ali sat on the floor with Imam Jabril over tea and a plate of dates, pear slices, and crackers. The imam, in his turban and glasses, gazed at the two young men through fierce dark eyes.

"Asalaam alekum. What brings you here?"

"Asalaam alekum, Imam Jabril. I am Ali and this is Robert. I guess Allah, through Mohammed—peace be upon him—called us to the Islamic Center and to you. We believe in Salafist jihadism. We come to learn how we can involve ourselves in jihad."

That began a long interrogation of the two young men, their backgrounds, understanding of Islam and jihad, motivation, and seriousness of their intentions. The imam finally asked, "Do you understand what you are requesting, involving yourselves in jihad?"

Robert trembled at the question as he sipped his tea. Was he prepared to give his life in the Jihad-Salafi cause to bring Muslim rule to the nations of the world?

"Are you really willing to live in that cause?" the imam asked. "Are you ready to die in it? Would you be willing to carry a bomb into a crowd?"

With wide eyes, Ali looked at Robert, whose hands shook. Robert studied the two windows across the room, his mind in turmoil. A test question or was this for real? To see if they were serious about learning how to be a jihadist? Or was the imam asking whether they were actually up to being suicide bombers? If they said no, what would he think? That they were chicken or didn't really believe in jihad? If they said yes, did that mean that he would arrange a suicide bombing and they'd have to do it or offend Allah?

Ali swallowed and nodded his head. "Yes, I would do it." He turned to Robert, his eyebrows raised.

Robert's heart pounded and he began to sweat as he thought, *Man, I guess I should be willing to die myself if I agree to plant a bomb in a crowd of infidels. But I would have to think about it further, you know, because remaining alive means you could do it again. And which would be better?* His hands began to tremble.

"I need time to consider this," he replied.

"Of course. Such things can be decided later," the imam said as his frightening gaze seemed to penetrate right through Robert.

Robert exhaled, not realizing he had been holding his breath. He shifted his uncomfortable crossed-legged position, not used to sitting on the floor. *This guy doesn't fool around.* He got right to the point. "So what do you suggest we do?"

"You need intensive training, and the best place to get that is overseas, but first …"

Ali suddenly spoke in Urdu, and then translated for Robert. "I recognize you as being a Pakistani brother, Imam. Do you have connections to a madrassa there?"

"Yes, I do, but I think it would be dangerous for you to go to North Waziristan," he replied in English. "We need to prepare you here before you go." He paused, nodding his head. "But I can introduce you to some brothers in an Afghan camp near the southern border. You could fly to Quetta in Pakistan and take ground transport from there. We have Taliban friends in Quetta."

That began a long and friendlier conversation, the first of several planning sessions over several weeks. They learned the first weeks there consisted of paramilitary training like Marine boot camp, followed by weeks of instruction in creating and using explosives.

The imam seemed pleased to have recruited Ali and Robert. "I won't tell you the name of the camp or the names of any contacts, for security reasons." He leaned forward, handing Ali a piece of paper. "But I am providing you with an address in Quetta. You must destroy it on arrival at the safe house there."

With that one simple piece of paper, Robert realized he and Ali had launched into a world of intrigue and danger, with no idea what was ahead.

# Chapter 4

The flight from Seattle to New York and then Karachi took more than thirty hours with a stop in Abu Dhabi. Robert traveled separately and would rendezvous in the Karachi airport. They both used Pakistani tourist visas. After clearing customs with a pat down and search of his backpack and carry-on bag, Robert found the line for domestic flights and bought two round-trip tickets. Ali appeared after a wait of several hours. Then they flew north to Baluchistan province and its largest city, Quetta, near the Afghan border.

From a small dilapidated cab, Robert, wide-eyed, saw colorful painted buses and trucks competing with cars and animal-driven carts in the crowded streets and roundabouts. People and honking horns were everywhere. He looked around, smiling at Ali. There were men in long shirts and pajama pants, beautiful women adorned in bright sari-like dresses. The young ones wore jeans, most without head coverings. Small shops bordered the streets, open in front and busy with people. He'd never seen such markets.

They sped on a hectic cab ride into a residential area with houses all behind high, painted walls. The community apparently contained the safe house Imam Jabril described. The cab eased up to a concrete wall ending in a metal locked gate that slowly opened in response to the cabbie's horn. Two tall guards with beards pointed AK-47s at the car then motioned for Robert and Ali to get out.

Robert stared at the guns and raised his hands. His heart raced and he began to tremble. "Why are they doing this Ali?" he whispered. "Didn't they expect us?"

Ali shrugged. "They want us to get our packs out."

Ali paid the cabbie, and then they raised his hands up again. The cab quickly backed out while the gate banged shut, and one of the guards spoke in broken English.

"Where your papers?"

Ali answered in Urdu, nodding at the smaller of his two packs. A third guard appeared and found Ali's U.S. passport and Jabril's sealed envelope. He tore it open and read something out loud to the two other guards. They all nodded. They opened and inspected all the bags, found Robert's passport, patted both men down thoroughly, and asked Ali in Urdu for the name of their gardener.

"Abdul-Alim Kalb." He said it proudly, just as Imam Jabril had instructed. The guards suddenly dropped their weapons, smiled broadly, and welcomed both men with a handshake and kisses on both cheeks. Robert's face, which had turned ashen, regained its color, and he took a deep breath.

"I guess we passed the test, Ali."

For the first time he noticed the tan painted house with its metal roof, window bars, and green metal door. Entering the house, they removed their shoes and walked to a back room. It looked empty, except for mats stacked near the walls and a tablecloth in the center of the carpeted floor. A platter contained dates, figs, pomegranates, nuts, and bread. A short Pakistani brought tea and cups. The guards quickly surrounded the tablecloth with large, colorful, one-inch-thick mats, and the new guests sat down on them, legs folded under as did their three hosts. Robert had learned you don't show the bottom of your feet. A fourth man appeared, bald and with a gray-streaked beard, and all stood up. He shook hands all around, first with Ali and Robert, and spoke English clearly.

"Welcome! I am Hamid. Please sit down. How is my friend Jabril?"

"He is well," Ali replied in English, "and sends his greetings."

"Ah, good," he said nodding. "He is a fine man. We attended school together many years ago in Peshawar. I apologize for our reception of you. But these days you can't be too careful."

After eating, Hamid interviewed Robert and Ali separately for three hours to determine their goals and level of training. Then he asked a sequence of questions. He probed into the level of risk they were willing to take, how they felt about working with dangerous materials, and whether they were able to work alone. Then he explored how they handled fear and whether they were willing to sacrifice the innocent in order to convey a message to infidel governments. Would they be willing to carry out acts of holy war anywhere in the world? Were they willing to give up their lives for jihad?

Robert had steeled himself for these questions. He knew they were coming. If he couldn't answer yes, why had he come?

By the fourth hour, Hamid seemed satisfied with the answers they had provided. "We will take you north just over the Afghan border, where you will receive training in the things you need to know for jihad. The test explosions you will carry out will be back in Pakistan for security since foreign troops are still in Afghanistan and get curious. Be ready in the morning."

# Chapter 5

Robert and Ali sat quietly in the old tan Toyota 4x4 behind the driver, one of the guards from the gate. The paved road wound north from Quetta through apricot orchards.

Soon the cultivated landscape transformed into scrub brush only. Deep in thought, they silently watched the now barren desert slip by as high hills increasingly loomed on either side. Robert looked at his passport. A loose page with some writing on it had been inserted. It looked like a foreign script. He studied it for any English. It appeared official. "What does this page say, Ali?"

"It's your Afghan visa, written in Pashtun, identifying you as a tourist. That number at the bottom seems to be our identification with Hamid's program, so they'll know we are the ones he sent. It's loose because once you take it out you'll have no permanent record of ever being here."

Robert suddenly sat up tall, eyes wide. He'd never thought of that. He started to talk as he turned to his friend. But Ali stared ahead, apparently lost in thought.

Robert remembered he could be questioned about this trip, and he'd have to insist he came only as a tourist. Then he wondered how Ali would handle any questions. "Does it feel right to return to your family's country?" Robert asked.

"Yeah, but I'm scared. I don't know where they'll send me after the training."

"Man, I hadn't thought that far ahead. Like, I just assumed they will send me back to America. Now you have me worried."

"They probably will since you look European. But me, I could be from anywhere, from Indonesia to the Middle East to London in the Asian community."

At the border Robert stared wide-eyed at dozens of trucks lined up with appliances, computers, and other electronic equipment. He wanted to ask their driver about them, but he was busy talking to the Afghan soldiers who gathered around the car. Many men in turbans and long shirts stood around the numerous shops. Robert noticed several military vehicles in various states of repair, including a couple of army tanks with broken tracks and blown-off turrets. After Robert, Ali and the driver showed their passports, and the soldiers waved them on. In five minutes he suddenly veered off the main road heading east. For an hour they followed a two-rut track through desolate dry-brown rolling hills to the outskirts of a village where some low, unpainted, wooden buildings matched the surrounding brush. A guard appeared with an assault rifle. He grinned when he saw the driver and spoke a few words.

Ali reached for Robert's passport. "They want to see our papers." After appropriate scrutiny the guard ushered the two men with their packs into a room with a bare wood floor and mats for sitting. Shoes remained at the door. Robert scanned the metal roof above and the concrete block walls painted white. No chairs. They joined three other men who Robert guessed were Central Asian or Pakistani. They shook hands all around, silently without smiling.

In walked a tall, turbaned Afghan, his skin dark from the sun. He stood ramrod straight, slender, with an intense gaze. His long Pakistani shirt extended to his knees, while loose cloth pants and sandals showed below. They all shook hands and then sat down on thin mats around a central tablecloth. Robert tucked his feet in, cross-legged, uncomfortable. His new comrades seemed to sit easily that way. He wondered what was coming. No one spoke. Soon a turbaned man appeared with tea and dates. He set them on the tablecloth and disappeared through a back door.

"Welcome," the head man spoke in Pashtun. "Can anyone translate into English so our American friend can understand?"

Ali nodded and spoke briefly to their host in Urdu and Pashtun. The three IMU young men also spoke to him in another language Robert did not recognize. "Who are they?" Robert whispered to Ali.

"They are speaking Dari, the language of northern Afghanistan—like Tajik, Persian-based. They're members of the Islamic Movement of Uzbekistan, the IMU. It's a fundamentalist Islamic group active here and in other countries of Central Asia," Ali whispered. "One guy is Uzbek, but the other two are Tajiks."

Robert felt strange, the only white guy, the only one without Asian roots, singled out because he spoke only English. He'd never heard of the IMU and wondered how they linked with the Taliban. He felt so out of place, as though he didn't belong here. He began to wonder whether he should have come. The realization that this choice could lead to his death or imprisonment struck hard. He glanced at the door. The driver had gone back to Quetta, so there was no escape. *Man, what am I doing here?*

With Ali's translation, the Afghan head man began to speak. "You have been carefully screened and chosen to learn to fight in the worldwide jihad to free our Muslim brothers and sisters. You will become jihadis, Salafis, to establish caliphates in many countries, obeying sharia, the correct path. During the next two months you will learn many skills."

Robert's heart raced. *No backing out now. I know too much already. It would be crazy to even try.*

The leader continued, "But first, security. You will not know my name, but call me 'leader.' We will not know each other's names, but refer to each by Pashtun number."

The five trainees counted off, "Silfer, Yow, Dwa." Ali would be "Dre," and then the leader pointed to Robert, "Salor." Number five. Ali helped Robert pronounce his new name.

"You will not know the name of this place or its telephone number or e-mail address. Now give me your cell phones and computers.

You will get them back at the end of the training. When you do, you are never to mention or write about anything you have done here, anyone you have met, or where this camp is located."

The leader held out a box. The five students rose to turn in all their electronic equipment, including cell phones, cameras, and laptop computers.

"It will be as if this experience and the people you meet never existed. If ever arrested, no record exists of your being here, and you will deny ever being here, meeting us and receiving training. We do fear the enemies' learning of this place and our mission. They have been using drone airplanes, targeted bombs, and rockets to kill our people. Any questions?"

There were none. Sweat trickled down Robert's temple. His heart raced. He knew the U.S. drones killed Taliban brothers on both sides of the border. Now he was in a target site himself. And were his tracks covered well enough? The airlines could document his arrival in Quetta and return to Seattle, but otherwise no one knew his travels except Ali. *OK, Imam Jabril.*

Robert had thought of taking an Arabic name to identify with his fellow jihadis, but realized he would maintain his security better by staying with "Robert," at least at home. No one in the movement, even in the U.S., would know his last name anyway. He looked at Ali, who didn't seem to be worried, sitting with a passive expression as though he was back in school.

"Allow me to outline the program's schedule," the leader continued. "Part one includes conditioning and teaches you military skills. Some of you will be fighting with our brothers in various parts of the world. You need to learn to be a soldier, to fire weapons, to handle explosives. We will toughen you up. After three weeks of basic training, those interested in fighting in the Middle East, here in Central Asia, and in Pakistan, will continue to acquire advanced military skills. That includes tactics, how to blend in with civilians and so on. You will get some training in creating bombs.

"For those with American passports, Dre and Salor, you will break away after three weeks and focus on the manufacture of explosives and how to conceal and use them. These skills are necessary since the only tools you will have for fighting our enemies may be weapons you create yourself. It is now nearly impossible to return to the West with explosive material, even in shoes or underwear!" Ali looked at Robert with a whimsical smirk at the failure of their predecessors. And now they knew that they could return to their homeland or at least to Western countries.

# Chapter 6

Ashley couldn't get Najid out of her mind. She was attracted to him, but there was something about his conversation in the coffee room that bothered her.

Ashley called her new friend in Seattle, Jim Swain, a young associate pastor at the church her father had recommended. He had found it on the list of "Churches United with Israel."

Entering his carpeted office she noticed pictures of his attractive wife and two small boys on his desk, and a number of certificates and athletic trophies. Tall with dark hair, he extended his hand to shake Ashley's and then gestured toward a large overstuffed chair across his desk near a floor lamp. A Bible rested on an end table close to the chair, along with a box of tissues.

"Welcome, Ashley. How's school going?"

"It's OK, but it doesn't rock my socks. You know I'm in graduate school and a teaching assistant in zoology, but it's just a stepping stone on my way to medical school."

"So, what's up?"

Ashley paused. "Uh ... I've been raised in church all my life, and I became a serious Christian in high school. Our church in Oklahoma

teaches that God brought the Jews to Israel in my grandparents' lifetime. And we believe that fulfilled Biblical prophecy, right?"

"That's correct."

"I just know bits and pieces of Jewish history, mostly from Bible
stories. But I understand they've gone through a lot of persecution."

"Incredible amount!" Pastor Jim leaned forward and spoke
rapidly. "Just think, Ashley. They had no homeland. Remember the
pogroms beginning in Russia and Europe in the 1800s, like in 'Fiddler
on the Roof'? That's why Theodor Herzl began the Zionist movement
in Europe in 1897 with the slogan about Palestine, 'A land without a
people, waiting for a people without a land.'"

"But weren't people already there in Palestine?"

"I've always understood no one lived there," the pastor said.
"Ashley, we're talking about the persecutions of the Jews over centuries. Think of the big one, the holocaust during World War II ..."

"I've read that some people now deny that ever happened."

Pastor Jim shook his head. "Six million Jews, Ashley, slaughtered
by the Nazis. It happened. Remember, and never again. But now
these suffering people who brought us Leonardo da Vinci and Albert
Einstein have a land they can call home."

"Da Vinci was a Jew?"

"Yes, Ashley. Scholars believe his mother was a Middle Eastern
Jewish slave who converted to Christianity. There are still many
anti-Semites who deny this or any fact that reflects positively on the
Jewish people."

"Why are Jews still being persecuted? Why do so many hate
them?"

"Well, there have been several wars, and the Palestinians are
trying to keep Israel from expanding into the promised land that God
gave them. Many world forces want to keep the Jews contained—or
even eradicated."

"That's what's bothering me right now, Pastor Jim. I have heard
for years that the Palestinians, and the Muslim countries surrounding
Israel, are trying to push it into the sea."

"And they are, Ashley. By the way, just call me Jim."

"That's what I learned, and I have always believed." Ashley
frowned and squinted her eyes. "So two weeks ago I met Najid

Haddad, who just joined us in the graduate program in zoology at U Dub. We learned that he is Palestinian. And ever since, I can't get our conversation out of my mind."

"Did he talk Middle East politics?"

"Oh no! He's such a gentle guy, extremely polite, wanting to get acquainted, and eager to please. He only shared a bit about his family and background in response to our questions."

"So why were you so surprised with what he said?" Jim asked.

"Well first, he lives in Israel proper, near Nazareth. I always thought the Palestinians were in the West Bank and Gaza only. He says there are over one million Palestinians in Israel, about twenty percent of the population."

"Huh." Jim paused, frowning. "I didn't think there were that many."

"So, we asked whether he was Sunni or Shia Muslim, and he floored us by saying he is a Christian, by birth *and* by choice, and that there are at least two hundred thousand Christian Arabs in Israel itself. Christian Palestinians! I thought the Palestinians were all Muslims."

"So?"

"Then he went on to say that his family had lived there for at least three hundred years with records showing that."

Jim looked pensive, chin in his hand, and gazed at Ashley without saying anything. Finally he asked, "So what do you make of his story?"

"That night I couldn't sleep thinking of Najid. Here is such a gentle, refined guy with no apparent political agenda. He was just answering personal questions honestly and seemed quite free to respond to us."

"So what kept you awake?"

"Jim, don't you see that Najid doesn't fit our Palestinian stereotypes? I had no idea that so many Palestinians actually live in Israel, and they apparently have lived together peacefully with their Jewish and Muslim neighbors for many years. Najid learned Hebrew from growing up playing with Jewish boys. He doesn't seem to have a chip on his shoulder for Israelis. I've learned that out of the heart the mouth speaks, and there has been nothing so far to make me believe he hates Jews."

"Do you think he is a real Christian?"

"He says he is, both by birth but also by choosing his own faith. Plus I had no idea that ancient churches exist there."

"I must admit I don't know much about them either," Jim added. "So does the fact of Christian Arabs in Israel bother you?"

"No. I can accept that. What amazes me is that these people have been there for centuries—it's their home. And they're not Jews. Do the native people have a right to live there? Is it supposed to be a Jewish country exclusively?"

"But Ashley, don't you believe God promised the land to Israel in the Bible?"

"I do, but I don't understand just how these promises apply to the Christians there. Or Muslims for that matter. Should they be able to live there as they have for centuries?"

"Ashley, let's talk again when you have had time to think and study the Bible about the significance of God's special people of Israel. You have lots of questions, but don't be influenced by anti-Israeli views. There's a lot of anti-Semitism out there. Just keep an open mind to what you have learned your whole life."

# Chapter 7

Climbing out of bed in the dark, Robert moaned to Ali, "I didn't sign up for Marine boot camp." Up at five, fifty push-ups, and a five-K run all before breakfast. Then more exercises. Climbing wood walls and slithering under barbed wire on his belly with live machine-gun fire overhead, followed by target practice—lying, sitting, standing, and on the run using AK-47s and live ammunition. More push-ups, sit-ups, and weight lifting. Finally Robert sat down as an instructor demonstrated how to break down their assault rifle and put it together again. Robert's hands shook from fatigue, and he came in last in accomplishing that task. Lunch came in somewhere during the torture, and Robert could hardly remember the rest of the day when he crashed onto his mat at seven just after dinner.

"Ali, I didn't know what we were getting into!"

"Neither did I. They seem to want us fighting tigers."

"I think the IMU guys are in better shape than us. Dre and Salor always come in last."

"Maybe we're smarter."

"I doubt it," Robert said. "Silfer, Yow, and Dwa seem to know several languages, and all I speak is English."

"You don't need any other language. They have to get along in different countries of Central Asia. They must know Russian as well. Remember they used to answer to the Soviet Union."

"I'm too tired to understand all that. Tell me tomorrow. I can't even remember your Pashtun name. I'm not using it when we're alone. I'm almost asleep."

The next morning Robert could hardly move. He couldn't understand any of the shouting except Ali's scream, "Robert, on your feet! The leader's coming!"

The torture continued day after day. By the third week, he and Ali could keep up with the IMU guys, and they seemed to bond during the difficulties of the program. Robert sat with Ali on the floor at lunch. "It's funny, man, that I could get so attached to a bunch of terrorists."

"Look, Robert, you're a freedom fighter in the cause of jihad, for freedom from Western domination. Don't use the term 'terrorist.' That's Western. We fight for noble causes, to free the Palestinians and to force the Israelis to return the land to our brothers and sisters, that is rightfully theirs."

"That's what I want to do, Ali. I hate Israelis, and the United States for supporting 'em! If I could get a bomb in a synagogue, I'd shock 'em all the way to Jerusalem."

<hr />

Robert noticed Ali's upper body filling out, and then his own arms and torso looked more powerful than he had ever seen them. His beard grew a bit scraggly. He would get rid of it on the way home.

They still had morning calisthenics, but the second leg of their training concentrated on chemistry and the production and handling of explosives. The leader ushered Dre and Salor into a large room in a concrete block building several hundred meters from the main camp. Filled with glassware, bunsen burners, and scales sitting on concrete counters, it reminded Robert of his chemistry lab in high school, even the smells of chemicals.

"This lab is far from camp for safety reasons. We have never had an explosion and we don't want one now, so pay close attention. You are going to learn to work with concentrated nitric acid and hexamine to make RDX. That's the explosive used commonly by armies and our brothers around the world. It produces a blast more powerful than TNT." The leader continued, pointing to each of the terms on the blackboard.

Later the IMU men would join them. They would not participate in the chemical creation of RDX, but just learn how to use it. Except they did learn to add the plasticizer, making pliable the final product, C-4.

# Chapter 8

The next five weeks flew by for Robert as he became more comfortable both with the procedures the leader had outlined and the lab. Finally the day came for testing the students' C-4 cocktails. Robert had formed his bomb into several bricks, which he stacked just like those in a brick wall. Ali had shaped his into triangles to make a circle of C-4 explosives. The five students, with their detonators, cords, and timers, set off with their leader. They placed all of the bombs and detonators into separate padded boxes, which fit into an underfloor compartment of the leader's Land Rover and drove away.

Robert looked at Ali. "I know this stuff needs detonators to explode, but I still wonder if all this bouncing on the road will set it off."

"It might," Ali chuckled. "I'm looking forward to the seventy young ladies."

With his friends waving him across the border, the leader drove back into Pakistan. After going several kilometers toward Quetta, he turned onto a faint two-rut path heading west and drove overland for what seemed like forever to Robert.

The hills hid them, and the barren, arid land was uninhabited and remote as Robert could imagine. They finally stopped and carried all the boxes and detonator cords for a quarter-mile to cliffs rising one hundred meters out of the desert. In their shadow the students set out their bombs against the rock walls about seventy-five meters apart. The men placed detonators into one of their bricks of C-4, connected the cords with the timers, and set each timer to trigger at the time prescribed by their leader. Then they all walked back to the Land Rover and stood behind it.

Robert's heart pounded as he awaited the first explosion. The blast came with a force that shattered the cliff above, showering large rocks far out into the desert. He felt a compression wave against his chest and an explosive roar echoed in his head. Each succeeding blast proved equally dramatic, including his own, number four. The cliff cracked just above the fireball and released an avalanche of large rocks that crashed down with a deafening rumble. Finally Ali's went off with a shock wave and intense crack that echoed off the cliff and shot rocks upward over the top of the cliff.

With ears ringing, they all beamed and shook hands at the most unusual graduation Robert had ever imagined. He would actually become a jihadist.

Salor became Robert again as they returned to Quetta. But where and how could he ever acquire the equipment and material he had used to make such a successful bomb? He would have to depend on Imam Jabril to guide him. That remained in his head on the long flight back to Seattle. Robert experienced no trouble getting through customs in New York. Neither did Ali a day later, who explained he had gone to visit his cousins in Karachi.

# Chapter 9

Robert and Ali wasted no time making arrangements to visit Imam Jabril.

"Hamid in Quetta returns your greetings and asked about you," Robert began.

"Good man, Hamid." The imam smiled, but still looked fierce under his dark eyebrows. He led them out to the backyard without explanation. They sat on plastic chairs under a large tree, continuing the conversation. The imam had several questions for both Robert and Ali, who related their experiences in the Afghanistan camp.

"But graduation provided the highlight of the trip, Imam." Ali beamed. "You should have been there. With five students setting off five bombs, the sky nearly fell in! We became real jihadists in the desert of northern Baluchistan."

A long discussion covered many ideas, including, as Robert expected, the difficulty of acquiring bomb-making equipment and material.

"The Bureau of Alcohol, Tobacco, Firearms, and Explosives registers and controls RDX and even the chemicals to make it," the imam explained. He smirked with a mischievous look. "But I may have a possible source of bomb material for you."

Robert's heart raced as his eyebrows shot upward. The imam explained that he could put Robert and Ali in touch with a person in Butte, Montana, who worked in the explosive department of a large mining company there. "They use C-4 in their open-pit mining operations. Some shipments of material actually contain a bit more C-4 than their paperwork shows. Their shipments also include detonators, detonator cords, and timers. My friend has been able to collect some of this extra C-4 and accessories over time, and I just learned that he has enough hidden away now to make a powerful bomb."

Robert with Ali noted the distance from Seattle to Butte, Montana. Six hundred miles. "Should take less than twelve hours."

Ali had never traveled in a red Corvette let alone one with the top down. He seemed to revel in the experience as they cruised through the warm wheat fields of Eastern Washington. Robert glanced at his friend, who smiled as though they were enjoying a Sunday afternoon drive.

Guided by the security measures they learned in Pakistan, they made contact with the imam's friend without even knowing his name or seeing his face. They paid for and then found the materials as directed in a note. The C-4 and accessories lay in a flat box hidden under a large box behind a bulldozer. Robert's mind whirred as they spent the night at a motel in Butte.

"Man, that's incredible!" Robert said, shaking his head as they headed toward the western Montana mountains. "Really, too easy. I couldn't imagine, you know, how we'd ever get the chemicals and lab equipment along with a place to put everything together without arousing suspicion."

"All six bricks of C-4 look just like what we created in Afghanistan," Ali remarked. "They should make for quite a blast. Where are you thinking of putting them?"

Robert had considered this for a long time, discussing target selection with his Afghan leader as well as Imam Jabril. He wanted to make a statement to the U.S. government and to American Jews to quit bankrolling the Israeli government in their oppression of the Palestinians. But more than that, he wanted America to stop dominating Muslim lands, including the two countries they had just left— and Iraq. He believed his choice would shake up the establishment in the West. His act must speak to the world. "I'm putting the bomb in a synagogue to make my point."

"Awesome! Will it to go off with lots of Jews in the synagogue?"

"No, Ali. You can't blame the little people. I'm just after the leaders and the rich. I hate 'em. If there is a rabbi or two that gets in the way, well that's OK. It's not my fault. It's the U.S. government who caused it. So I think it would be best to have it go off maybe like an hour before their Sabbath service on a Friday afternoon."

"Do you have a synagogue in mind?"

"Yeah, there's one just north of the university. People around there see lots of students from many parts of the world carrying backpacks, you know, and I wouldn't arouse suspicion carrying a student backpack. Like, I'd wear a hoodie anyway. The synagogue would be open just before people come."

"So when do you think you would do it?"

"I'll need to scout the territory. But I think within ten days. Maybe the second Friday of May."

⸻

Ali and Robert stashed the C-4 and accessories in a rarely used room in the basement of their house. Concrete, dank, musty smelling, and dark. No windows. Perfect place, Robert decided. On Wednesday they chatted after dinner when the others had left.

"Are you still planning on a couple of days from now?"

"Yeah. I checked out the synagogue last Friday. I didn't see anybody around at five p.m. in the main auditorium or the vestibule just inside the front door. I'm thinking I can get the detonator and cord into the C-4 bricks and tie them together. I'll carry it ready to go in my backpack. Then I'll just have to activate the timer for five thirty and, you know, it'll be a breeze." He shrugged his shoulders. "The whole thing will be hidden in the backpack sitting out of sight in the corner of the vestibule behind a bookcase."

"Aren't you scared?"

"Yeah, I am, but I'm also determined. It'll echo around the world and be heard by the leaders I want to get to. I'll teach 'em a lesson!"

"How will you get away from the synagogue without raising questions?"

"I'll just walk down the street. I want to be close by when it goes off, but maybe a block away so I can see the results. It should at least blow the front off the synagogue, and maybe bring the whole building down."

"Cool! Do you need me to pick you up in your car?"

"No, it'll be better to be on foot and just be one of the startled people who come running to see what happened. I'll hang back from the crowd, you know, and disperse with them when the police barriers go up."

"Sounds like you have the bases all covered. So Friday at five-thirty it is!"

"Right, Ali. I'm ready!" It suddenly hit him. He would actually do it. An explosion that would reverberate around the world.

Ali rose from the table, shaking his head. "I can hardly believe you really are going to be the next jihadist in America after 9/11. Allahu Akbar!"

# Chapter 10

The campus burst with color in the Seattle spring. Following an afternoon lab session, Ashley approached Najid, who seemed to be adjusting very well to his teaching role in the zoology lab. He stopped collecting a few dissecting instruments left on the black soapstone counters as he chatted with several students who had stayed behind. She waited as they finished their conversation and left.

"Hi, Najid. How about going to the HUB for some tea?"

"Sounds good. You know, no one has explained why it is called 'the HUB.'"

"It stands for Husky Union Building, I think. You know the meaning of Husky?"

"Is it a dog from Alaska?"

"Yeah. We call it a mascot ... um ... it's hard to explain. Every college has one, usually an animal, like the Texas Longhorns. Uh ... longhorns are cattle with big long things on their heads. You probably have them in Israel."

"I've never seen one."

"I'll show you a picture sometime. Anyway, let's walk to the HUB.

It's so pretty with the red and purple rhododendrons in bloom."

"They are wonderful. I've never seen any plants like them."

"They don't grow very well in Oklahoma either. They need cool weather and lots of rain."

As they strolled by lawns and gardens resplendent with color, Ashley inquired about Najid's family, their church, and their living situation. Sitting down in the HUB Café, filled with students at both long and short tables, Ashley enjoyed the view beyond the large windows looking east toward the Cascade Mountains. With their tea, Najid opened up a bit.

"My father is a farmer ... but, ah ... we don't have a farm anymore. But he still takes care of an olive grove. My mother—"

"Why doesn't your family have a farm anymore?"

"It is a long story, Ashley. It happened many years ago, and I can't tell you now."

"So where is it that you live?"

"Outside a town called Genigar, not far from Nazareth. Most people know about Nazareth in Northern Israel. We live in a small house now, three bedrooms."

"Do you have Jewish neighbors?"

"Not close now. They live on a hill above us. It is hard to explain to you, but they live on the top of the hill with a wall around it. A highway separates us, and we can't be on that road. But my friend David, who lives there, used to come down to spend time with me since I couldn't go up to his house."

"How did you get to know each other?"

"We both went to a Christian school because that was the best school in the area. Palestinian schools are struggling. But you could pay to go to the Christian school no matter what religion—Muslim, Jewish, Druze, or Christian. And both our parents wanted us to get the best education."

Ashley stopped asking questions long enough to sip her tea.

"Where in Oklahoma do you come from, Ashley?"

She still had a hundred questions to ask Najid, but realized she should share a bit as well. "Oklahoma City. We are not popular here in Seattle. We just stole the local basketball team called the Sonics. They are now the Oklahoma City Thunder."

"Oh! Did you come in with guns firing like thunder, like the western movies?" Najd's eyes twinkled. "With horses?"

"Right, Najid, like thunder and lightning. We had a shootout and dragged the team away."

They both laughed, lightening the mood. He told her of the young lady in the freshman lab who couldn't find the frog's heart. Ashley enjoyed Najid's sparkle as he tried to keep a straight face describing the lab adventures. He seemed to enjoy talking to her, and told stories of his own foibles in Haifa. At least she had learned a bit about Najid and his family.

The close ties of Christians with the Jewish people and their common heritage in the Bible had stirred Ashley. Most early Christians were Jews. She had cried repeatedly while reading "The Diary of Anne Frank" and Corrie ten Boom's account of her family tragedy in Nazi concentration camps, killed for their sin of hiding Jews from the Nazis. Ashley grew passionate about the Jews as her heart ached for their suffering and for their contributions.

Najid and Ashley walked to the "Ave" for lunch, and while waiting for the traffic light to turn green on 15th Avenue, she began. "Najid, have you ever been to a synagogue?"

"Oh yes. We have them in Nazareth."

"Do you understand Hebrew?"

"Sure. I have no trouble understanding them."

Ashley shook her head and chuckled to herself. *How many languages did he know?* She steered Najid to a Greek restaurant, a small well-lighted two-room place on University Avenue. The garlic and cumin smell tantalized her. "Oooh, I love Greek food!"

As they settled down over lunch, she asked him, "What would you think about going to a synagogue here in Seattle?" Her eyes twinkled and she cracked a smile.

"I've never thought about attending one here. Why do you ask?" Najid moved his glass to allow the waitress to bring his lunch plate. The cucumbers showed at the ends of the pita bread enclosing them.

Ashley furrowed her brow. "Well, I've been doing some studying about how we Christians owe so much to the Jews for the past—all they gave through the Ten Commandments and the prophets. But such terrible things have happened since then. It gets confusing. Particularly in your part of the world."

"I agree. It is—"

"But Najid, the trouble now, the unrest in the Middle East that you personally face, doesn't that bother you?"

"Yes it does." He paused and tightened his lips. Then he looked at Ashley and nodded. "But I've decided to put that aside here in America."

"If I told you that our church supports Israel one hundred per-cent in the current conflict, what would you think?"

Najid stared silently out the window as they both started eating. He began slowly. "That is a choice people make. I hope your church is well informed with the facts. Sometimes I see tour groups of Americans in Israel visiting the historical sites where Jesus lived and worked. Most of these shrines have beautiful stone churches, but tourists don't connect with the people who live there. They get back on their bus and go to their hotel. I think of how Peter once called Jesus's followers 'living stones.' The tourists see the dead stones in many shrines in Israel but don't meet the living ones."

"A lot of Americans tour the Holy Land," Ashley said. "You mean they never get to hear the experiences of people who have actually lived there for a long time?"

"I think so, but I'm not sure. You'd have to go yourself to deter-mine that."

"I'd love to. You make me want to go there."

"Ashley, you would be most welcome to stay as a guest in my family home."

She remembered Najid's mentioning their small house and understood the generosity of the offer. Ashley smiled and nodded. "Thank you. Maybe someday. But right now, I want to know more of what the Jewish people think. How do they feel about the generous support Israel gets from people in some of our American churches?"

"So that is why you want to go to the synagogue?"

"Yes, but also just to learn more about them. I've never been to one."

"I would be glad to go with you sometime. I could translate the Hebrew for you so you could understand the rabbi."

"Oh, Najid, that would be awesome! There is a synagogue not too far from the U-district, and we could meet there. Maybe on a late Friday afternoon just before their Sabbath, toward sundown. I looked it up on the Internet, and this particular one has their Kabbalat Shabbat at six p.m."

He pulled out his smartphone and studied it for a moment. "Next week I think would be fine."

"Great, let's plan on that unless your schedule changes. I'll confirm with you on the day before and text you the address if we don't meet in the lab. We can get together in front of the synagogue at five-thirty on Friday, that's the second Friday in May. You better show up now that you promised." Ashley chuckled, raising her eyebrows, eyes dancing. "You know that ninety percent of life is just showing up!"

"Really?"

"Could be true, Najid," Ashley said with a wink. "At least Will Rogers from Oklahoma thought so."

Ashley left the freshman zoology lab at ten-thirty for a coffee break in the grad student lounge. She found Najid huddled in deep conversation with Ethan over his cup of tea. He looked up and grinned.

"Did you get my text message about the address?" she asked.

"I did, Ashley. I'm looking forward to it. That's today, right?

"You got it. I'll plan to meet you in front of the building at five-thirty so we can talk a bit about what to expect before we go in."

"OK." Najid seemed to enjoy talking like an American. He resumed his conversation while Ashley turned to get her coffee.

# Chapter 11

The plan flowed without a ripple. No one appeared as Robert, heart pounding in his chest, walked in the front door of the synagogue toward the right-side corner at the front of the building. He found the vestibule empty, decorated in muted tones, lighted by several stained-glass windows, and brightened by a menorah holding seven scented candles on a nearby table. Very quiet, the space had a pleasant smell. He strolled toward a large bookcase filled with books along the front wall and stood between it and the side wall in the corner, well hidden. Easing out of his backpack, he put it down gingerly. Hands shaking, he adjusted the timer for five-thirty p.m. and connected it to the detonator cord inside the backpack. As he slipped out the front door unseen, he heard someone walking in the rear rooms of the building.

Robert, forcing himself not to run, strolled casually to the nearby sidewalk and across the street, stopping under a large tree in front of a modest 1930s house. His dark-blue, hooded sweatshirt hid all but his eyes, nose, and mouth. He waited for three minutes. At five twenty-nine he watched as two young people walked toward each other. They met and stopped to talk directly in front of the right corner of the building, separated from it by a narrow garden of bushes and small trees. The girl, blonde and pretty, stood with her back to the building. She looked up and caught Robert looking at her. He quickly averted his gaze. The young man from the back reminded him of Ali. He shrugged. They'd just be part of the collateral damage.

Robert turned and walked away at a normal pace, face flushed, determined not to panic. When he had reached the middle of the next block, a huge explosion ripped the air around him. He felt the blast and turned to see the synagogue come down in a huge gray plume of dust and debris. Flames shot from the rubble. Robert's heart pounded with excitement, hardly able to take in the phenomenal success of his mission. He had never experienced an adrenaline rush like that, even when he'd tried crack cocaine.

The blonde girl lay on the sidewalk as the man kneeled over her and waved wildly. People rushed from their houses and soon chaos enveloped the scene. Within moments sirens screeched as the fire grew higher. Robert followed the crowd, drawn like a magnet, pressing in closer to the site then finally making a path for the police and fire trucks. A Medic One van raced forward as the crowd parted, stopping where the girl lay. Paramedics transferred her within a minute to a stretcher, IV running, and drove away, sirens blaring.

Robert watched as firemen controlled the flames and began with police to search the cooler rubble for victims. Smoke and dust filled the air. He smiled, taking in a deep breath at the smell. The bomb succeeded beyond his expectations. All the training and careful planning had paid off. He felt his face flush and heart race. It would make world headlines. Jihad once again in the United States, this time on the opposite coast from New York. He hadn't done well at Cornell, but at slipping past Homeland Security, he had excelled when others couldn't. He would be honored by brother jihadists around the world, admired for his exploit even if they didn't know who did it.

He saw the young man get up from the bloody sidewalk and begin to walk toward him. His arms looked bloody. A policeman raced after him, clamped on handcuffs, and forced him into a police car.

Robert turned back, away from the scene, and walked casually up a side street against the human tide of people swarming to the site wondering what had happened. He continued to walk for two hours, over the University Bridge, hearing incessant sirens and people gathered on streets far removed discussing what they had just seen on local television.

He reached the house on Capitol Hill and entered to find his puzzled but excited jihadi friends gathered around the TV in the front room. They stood around the screen watching wide-eyed at the worldwide reaction to the bombing, asking each other, "Who could have succeeded in doing the impossible?"

Robert stared at the screen. It felt like an "out-of-body" experience, as if he were looking on a triumph someone else had done. The president spoke, vowing to bring the terrorists to justice, and the Prime Minister of Israel expressed his condolences to victims and their families.

Ali flashed a quick thumbs-up at Robert, confirming their secret would remain hidden, even from the brothers in the house. In fact, it seemed like the perfect jihad event. Imam Jabril, he trusted. He obviously risked arrest with his complicity. Their C-4 provider in Butte had no idea who they were except friends of the imam and would have hidden his own participation. Any fingerprints would be burned up along with the backpack. And no one saw him. Well, no one except the girl, and then only a bit of his face. He frowned with some nagging concern, but put it out of his mind. She probably died from the blast or would have no memory of the event if she lived.

# Chapter 12

With siren screaming and red lights flashing, the Medic One van charged into the ER receiving area and backed up to the door. The medics rushed Ashley on their wheeled stretcher into Harborview Medical Center, oxygen mask covering her face and IV solution pouring in at a rapid rate. She lay on the gurney under a large light in a treatment room with a tile floor and glass cabinets lining the walls. Several people in scrub clothes gathered around her. A nurse and physician stripped off her bloody clothes under a hospital gown and began to examine her injuries while hearing the medics' story of the explosion and finding her on the sidewalk, bleeding.

While examining Ashley, Dr. Eric Thompson shouted orders: "Stat blood draw and emergency lab profile! Type and cross-match six units of blood, stat chest and abdominal X-ray! Push in lactated ringers' solution as fast as possible. Bring me a central venous catheter kit and a chest tube insertion tray and water seal with pump." A team of several nurses and two surgical residents sprang into action. An X-ray tech and lab person appeared.

"Alert the OR," Dr. Thompson ordered. "Any family with her,

Melanie?"

"No, she's by herself. I'll check her purse here on the stretcher," the nurse responded. She found Ashley's wallet, which contained emergency contact information—Mr. and Mrs. Frank Wells in Oklahoma City, with their phone number.

"Get them on the phone and I'll talk with them. Stay on the line, Melanie, to monitor the conversation and verify permission to take her to the OR."

Melanie grabbed two wireless phones and soon had Mrs. Wells on the line. She handed one to Dr. Thompson, who stripped off his bloody gloves.

"Hello," Mrs. Wells answered.

"Mrs. Wells, this is Dr. Thompson at Harborview Medical Center in Seattle. We have your daughter here in the emergency room. She's been injured. Our nurse Melanie is also on the line."

"Oh, no! What happened? How is she? You sound so calm. Is ... is she OK?"

"We hope she will be, Mrs. Wells. But she has multiple injuries and—"

"What kind of injuries? Frank, get on the line!"

"Frank Wells here. You're saying that Ashley had an accident?"

"Yes, sir. Pieces of a building from a bombing struck her in the back, breaking some ribs, causing a collapsed lung and bleeding into her abdomen and chest. She does not seem to have a severe head injury or any brain damage as far as we can tell. But she needs a chest tube to re-expand her lung and blood replacement. Then—"

"Oh God, help her! Will she live, Doctor?"

"We think so, sir, but she needs to go to the operating room. We suspect she is bleeding from a ruptured spleen, and if so we'll probably have to remove it. There could be other injuries, including in the chest, that need repair as well. So we would like to have your permission to move her to the OR and take care of any problems we find."

"Can she get along without a spleen?"

"Yes. There is a small increased risk of some kinds of infections in the future, but they are rare and can be prevented for the most part with an immunization. Right now she needs an operation, and she could have complications, further bleeding, infection, and she could die. Do you understand?"

Dr. Thompson waited for a reply. Finally Mr. Wells spoke. "Yes, we do. Does Ashley understand the situation?"

"No sir, she's in shock and doesn't know what has happened."

"Do what you need to do to save her life, Doctor. Do you agree, Dorothy?"

"Oh yes! We'll be praying for you and her. We'll fly out there as soon as possible." Mrs. Wells broke into sobs.

"Did you hear that, Melanie?"

"Yes, Doctor. We have permission from Ashley Wells's parents as next of kin to take her to the OR for an abdominal procedure and whatever else is necessary."

"Do you understand that you have given us permission for Ashley's operation?"

"Yes, Doctor." Frank Wells sighed.

"I'll call you when we finish."

# Chapter 13

Najid could not fully grasp what had happened as he sat locked in a cage in the back of a Seattle police car. The explosion had stunned him. He had tried to help Ashley and then they took her away. He had walked away in a daze after seeing her blood on the sidewalk. His ears still rang.

The policeman had said he would return in a few minutes and that they would go to the station. Najid didn't understand what *station* meant. Did he mean jail? Would he be beaten? And why did the officer need to put the uncomfortable handcuffs around his wrists and push him into the car? Did they think he blew up the synagogue? Did they think he would run away?

And what about Ashley? His special American friend. He'd never met any girl like her, so friendly, so bright, so open and fun. They took her somewhere to a hospital. Was she still alive? *"Oh heavenly Father, be with Ashley right now, and keep her alive and give her doctors' wisdom to know what to do."*

He sat for what seemed like an hour, waiting, for what? He didn't understand why, of all the people gathered around the scene, he should be picked out. What had he done wrong? Should he have stayed by that bloody sidewalk after they took Ashley? It must have been wrong to leave. What could he have done to help with all the police and firemen arriving? If he were still in Israel, he would probably be stripped and beaten now, to get information. Finally two police officers arrived, removed the handcuffs and drove him away.

The officer in the right front seat turned to the back. "You are being detained as a person of interest. You are not being arrested at this point. You have Miranda Rights. You have the right to remain silent and refuse to answer questions. Do you understand?"

Najid did, and he nodded. "Anything you do say may be used against you in a court of law. Do you understand?"

Najid thought a moment, and then nodded. The policeman continued explaining the rights he had.

Najid trembled. The reality of being in a foreign land and not understanding the system or why they should think he was a terrorist suddenly hit him. If he insisted on getting a lawyer, wouldn't that make them think he was guilty? Would he have to stay in jail longer? Would the police be angry if he wouldn't answer questions? Would they beat him to get him to talk? What should he do? Maybe he should answer their questions. He had nothing to hide.

"Well, what is your answer?"

Najid swallowed and took a deep breath. He sat up straight. "I am a foreign student here from Israel. I did nothing wrong. We were talking in front of the synagogue we were about to visit when the explosion happened. I will answer any of your questions. How long will you keep me?"

"Save your explanations and questions for the detective at the station." With that the policeman turned around and chatted with his fellow officer as they drove downtown.

A policeman led Najid into a bare room with only a desk and two chairs. The florescent lighting glared from the ceiling. No outside windows. The detective sat down behind his desk, looked briefly at some papers, and then stared at Najid. "Please, sit down." A dark interior window faced him. Najid sat, looked back at his inquisitor, and did not avert his unblinking gaze. Finally the detective spoke.

"A terrible crime occurred today. A rabbi died and a young lady suffered severe injury. This happened because some criminal terrorist or group exploded a powerful bomb in a synagogue. We have the right to investigate any crime and detain anyone we have reason to believe might be involved."

Najid shifted in his chair. *They must think I did the bombing.*

"We found you at the scene, injured a bit, and walking away. You come from the Middle East and are from an Arab background, and although we don't hold that against you, it does increase our need to check you out. We are not saying you are guilty at this point. You are what is commonly called 'a person of interest.' We can lawfully hold you without any charges for twenty-four hours. During that time we will investigate to determine whether any formal charges are justified. Do you understand?"

"I think so. Formal charges mean what?"

"That would be taking the step of accusing you of being a suspect, possibly involved in the crime. Then we would arrest you, take pictures and fingerprints, and keep you longer pending further investigation, although you could be free on bail. You would eventually face a trial if the prosecutor or grand jury thinks you could be guilty."

"So you are not arresting me? Will I be beaten? I am willing to answer any questions. I have nothing to hide. I am so sorry the rabbi died and my friend got injured. We had planned to go to the synagogue service and talk with him afterward."

The detective smiled and shook his head slightly. "We understand that you are willing to answer our questions without a lawyer present. No, you will not be beaten. However, because the investigation will last until tomorrow, we will have to lock you up overnight."

"Jail?"

"Yes."

That began a long series of questions about Najid's background, his coming to the USA, and his work at the university. Then they focused on what he did during the time leading up to the blast. The detective wanted to know why he and Ashley planned to visit the synagogue, who his friends were here, and what kind of Muslim sect he favored. The officer seemed surprised when Najid explained his Christian faith. Finally he served Najid with a search warrant and asked for keys to his house and room. The detective explained that this was normal investigative procedure to check out his paper records, passport, and computer files. They would also be inquiring with the U.S. Immigration Office and the University of Washington.

Najid complied and walked willingly into a holding cell where he sat on the metal bench, exhausted. He surveyed the metal bed and toilet, the sink on the wall, a few paper towels, and waste basket ... and the wall of bars between him and freedom. He thought of the dead rabbi and his family. And his dear friend could be dead. Could she have lived through the blast? Who could have done such a thing in America? No terrorist had succeeded since 9/11. His parents wouldn't know he had landed in jail. He thought of them, struggling to survive on such a meager income while supporting his six siblings. It all piled up for Najid. The tears came. He couldn't control them.

# Chapter 14

Ashley awakened in the recovery room. She moaned with pain both in her chest and abdomen. "Where, where am I?" She looked up into the face of a young woman in scrub attire.

"You're in the recovery room in Harborview Medical Center," the nurse replied. "You had a bad accident and an operation."

"I did?" Ashley grimaced with pain. "What happened?"

"We'll talk about it later, Ashley. Do you need more medicine for pain?"

"I think so. My chest and stomach really hurt every time I take a breath."

With the IV morphine, Ashley drifted back to sleep.

Frank and Dorothy Wells eased open the door of Ashley's room on the surgical floor and tiptoed in. The sound of the footsteps brought her out of the medicated sleep she'd been in since yesterday's transfer from the recovery room. She watched as their eyes widened approaching her bed and all the tubes. A monitoring screen showed a moving cardiogram and several numbers.

"Mom and Dad!" She winced with pain. "What's going on? Nobody tells me anything except that I'm doing great and it won't be long before I'll be out of the hospital ... I don't even know how I got here, or how I got hurt."

"Ashley,the whole world knows what happened."

"Well I don't. C'mon you guys. Clue me in on what's going on!"

"Dr. Thompson will explain your medical situation, your injury, and what they did to treat you."

"I have a vague memory of the recovery room. I know I had an operation, but not much else. What's this tube coming out of my chest?"

"You'll need to ask your doctors, Ashley. It seems that you were out in front of a synagogue yesterday when a horrible explosion occurred. You were injured"—his voice broke as he swallowed several times— "and they rushed you to the hospital emergency room."

Ashley pushed her medication button again. As another small dose of morphine soon eased her pain, Ashley's mind focused and she found it easier to talk.

"Yes, I met Najid and we were talking on the sidewalk before going inside. But I don't remember anything after that."

"Apparently a terrorist bomber targeted the synagogue. You just happened to be in the wrong place at that moment ... But you're going to be OK."

"Oh my gosh! But Dad, what happened to Najid?"

"Who's Najid?"

"He and I talked out in front of the synagogue. He's a friend. Oh no! Did he survive? Is he in the hospital here? Where is he?"

"I don't know, Ashley. We haven't heard anything about a young man being hurt or killed. Unfortunately, they found a rabbi's body in the rubble of the building. It sounds like he died under the falling structure."

Ashley stared wide-eyed out the window, shaking her head. "We had planned to visit that rabbi, attending their Friday evening service. So he is dead. And you don't know what happened to Najid?" She began to nod, staring vacantly as the tears finally came.

# Chapter 15

Friday night passed slowly for Najid on the thin mattress. He couldn't get comfortable. Hot and stuffy, with no fresh air, it smelled musty. He dreamed of the bomb and that he had tried to run into the synagogue to defuse it, but couldn't. He woke up before it exploded. Who could have escaped all the security measures in place in the United States?

He lay awake thinking about Ashley. She had made him feel at home, like he belonged, like an American. She just naturally brought people together. Was she even alive? He shook his head.

What would his parents think if they knew he slept in jail for doing nothing wrong? Just like home. Why would they put him in jail with no evidence and no charges, like "administrative detention" in the West Bank? At least here they must let him out after twenty-four hours—instead of six months.

His watch moved slowly. Finally, at 7 a.m., a black lady dressed in dark slacks and a crisp white shirt appeared, clipboard in hand. She stopped to chat. "I'm LaTisha. I supervise the jail cells and all the inmates in the holding area."

Najid explained a bit of what happened. LaTisha mentioned

people's shock and their sudden crisis of confidence in United States security measures.

"People have flooded the telephone lines of the Congress and the White House. The bombing news flew around the world, with al-Qaeda claiming responsibility for it."

Najid stared at LaTisha. "Then they'd look for the bombers in the Middle East as well."

"Probably," she said. "They're leaving no stone unturned. Local and federal law enforcement officers have combed Seattle and the entire state. A national alert has shut down all international flights for twenty-four hours until the FBI and other federal agencies have time to check the Terror Watch List for any links to the Seattle bombing. They say that list contains over ninety thousand names!"

Najid stared wide-eyed at LaTisha.

"Thank you for giving me all this information. I hope you realize that I am telling the truth. I am a victim myself." He showed her his arms, still bloodied from multiple small lacerations. "And I don't know what has happened to my friend. Her name is Ashley Wells. Do you know if she is alive?"

LaTisha gazed silently at Najid, and then smiled. "They would take her to Harborview Medical Center ER since it's the major center for trauma in Seattle. Let me call there when I have the chance, and I'll get back to you."

"Oh, thank you." Najid's eyes misted.

⸻

The detective came after a cold breakfast of eggs, toast, and coffee. He asked Najid for additional information about his life near Nazareth, travels from Israel, and entry into the United States. They had searched his room, his papers, passport, cell phone records, and computer. The man never introduced himself, and left.

The hours dragged on interspersed with a sandwich for lunch. Najid longed for some hot tea and naan with hummus. The coffee tasted stale and cool. He lay down, waiting, waiting, waiting. No one appeared. Finally he heard footsteps approaching. LaTisha had a broad smile and laughed out loud, breaking the awful silence.

"Najid … this is your lucky day!"

"I don't feel very lucky right now."

"Well you should. Ashley is recovering nicely after her operation at Harborview. They wouldn't give me anymore details over the phone except that she is doing well."

"Oh, thank God! And thank you, LaTisha!" She reminded him of his mother. "You have been such a help. What can I do for you when I get out?"

"Nothing! That smile is my reward. If I can brighten your day, it makes my day. God bless you, Najid. I hope I don't see you here tomorrow!"

She moved to the next cell, chuckling.

# Chapter 16

The black sedan's tires screeched as it skidded to a halt outside the police station, where Najid languished in boredom and fear. A very tall, well-built man in a dark suit hurried in, flashing his card to LaTisha before stepping into the detective's office. "Gordon Appleby, FBI." He realized they had expected him. The man behind the desk rose slowly, extending his hand without smiling.

"I'm Richard Hunt, detective for Seattle Police, assigned to the synagogue bombing."

After a perfunctory handshake, Hunt began:

"About Najid Haddad, we've checked everything we can: university records, his advisor there, his computer, and his cell phone. We've sacked Najid's apartment for paper files, talked to his roommates, Libyans. Nothing, squat, no evidence of anything suspicious." The detective threw up his hands in a gesture of futility. "I'm not sure why we're keeping him."

The FBI agent frowned. "We have nothing either. We've checked the Watch List for terrorists, contacted U.S. Immigration, and even called the Israeli intelligence service for Northern Israel where he lived. State Department and Homeland Security have nothing on him. They don't think anyone shipped in explosives."

"So where could the bomb material have come from?

"Good question. We know it's similar to what has recently been used in bombings in Europe and India. But no tips, no unusual events on the airlines. Where could whoever bombed the synagogue have gotten the C-4? We've checked the markers on the explosive residue in the synagogue and traced it to a manufacturer on the East Coast, but their company has no knowledge of any missing explosive material. They supply legitimate needs to a number of companies like mining outfits, and we are checking each of these for evidence of missing material. That hasn't finished yet."

"Actually," Richard shrugged his shoulders, "Najid seemed like an innocent man in my interrogation yesterday. We have no evidence to charge him even as an accomplice. So he remains a person of interest only. As you know, by law we can't hold him any longer than twenty-four hours. We've got to let him go. We know how to reach him if needed."

"I'd like to meet him. That would help in my report to FBI headquarters. Impressions can be valuable."

"No problem. I'll take you back."

"Oh, one more thing," Gordon added. "I could recommend to FBI headquarters that they contact the State Department to put a hold on Najid's passport for sixty days if he's at risk to flee the country. But assuming he's innocent, it could trigger airport security computers long into the future."

Richard bit his lower lip, shaking his head. "He's here on a Fulbright Scholarship in graduate school at the University of Washington. We can check on him periodically. I think he's clean and I would rather not do that to him. Let's go." They walked to the hallway and the holding cells.

Najid lay on his bunk, staring at the ceiling. His arms were folded over his chest. Time passed so slowly. He had nothing to read, no radio, no contact with the outside world. He wondered what it would be like to remain in jail for months, or years. Several of his West Bank friends had spent years in "administrative detention" just for throwing a stone at an Israeli army tank. Now what would they do with him as a foreigner? His eyes closed. Then he heard footsteps. Najid rose on seeing two men opening his cell door.

"Najid, I'm sorry. I didn't introduce myself when we first met. I'm Richard Hunt, Seattle Police Detective, and this is Gordon Appleby, with the Federal Bureau of Investigation."

Najid extended both hands to shake with each man, bowed slightly, and said nothing. His hands clammy with cold sweat embarrassed him. *Had they found something to make them charge him with the crime?*

"I'm pleased to meet you, Najid." Gordon Appleby smiled. He towered over Najid's six-foot frame. "I hope you understand that we in the United States have experienced another terrorist attack and are quickly investigating every possible lead to find who did it."

"I understand, sir." He looked the FBI agent in the eye and shook his head. "But I didn't do it."

"I sympathize with you. It must seem very unfair to you to be singled out for incarceration when you are a guest in our country and a Fulbright Scholar. I would like to hear a bit of your story, how you happened to come to America, and what you are doing at the university. Please, sit down."

Najid wondered what they were trying to get out of him. But his best defense seemed to be the truth. So he began his story, including how he came to be standing in front of the synagogue when the bomb went off. He told of his friendship with Ashley. And he detailed everything he remembered about what he'd seen and heard before the explosion, which wasn't much. He desperately wanted to help them find whoever hurt Ashley. He shook his head and grimaced. "I wish I had been paying more attention."

The FBI agent then had a few questions. After several minutes he seemed to be satisfied and Najid began to relax.

"Well, Najid, we appreciate your being forthright with us."

"Forthright? I don't know that word."

"Honest," Richard spoke up. "You have cooperated fully with us, and now we have some good news for you. We have found nothing to incriminate you and are not bringing any charges. You are free to leave, and I will drive you home."

Najid sighed, his shoulders and head dropped. He closed his eyes to blink back the tears, shook hands with both men, and walked out to the car into freedom.

# Chapter 17

Robert had rarely used the room he still leased in a small Victorian home on Capitol Hill. He decided to move back to his room quietly and gradually. None of the brothers, including Ali, knew the address. The large bedroom up the narrow stairs served as a studio apartment. It looked and smelled old, with faded floral wallpaper. But it would do to keep him out of view. He would show up at the brothers' house occasionally to not arouse anyone's suspicion. But he'd gradually disappear, even from Ali. His plan included taking classes at Seattle Central Community College so he would have student credentials. He decided to stay away from the Islamic Center or any other mosque that could be targeted for investigation.

So Robert moved back, out of the brothers' house, to his rented room. His jihadist fervor and hate of the establishment was tempered by a constant nagging fear of discovery. That the country boiled with anger didn't help. No effort would be spared to find him. He rehashed the scene of the bombing in his mind, going over and over it, trying to remember all the details. He had briefly exchanged glances with the girl. She probably couldn't see his face with the hood covering some of it, or the red birthmark on his forehead. Too far away. He still didn't know for sure whether she survived and had no way to learn that since she had dropped out of the news.

History and psychology interested Robert, so he asked whether he could pay to audit courses already underway for spring quarter at the Seattle Central Community College on Capitol Hill. He began to sit in on two classes. The first morning he sat next to a girl in the psychology class and struck up a conversation. That led to an invitation later in the week for coffee in the student cafeteria. He led her to a table in the corner, away from most of the students. The noise of conversations seemed loud. Jenny, a short, dark-haired girl with a pixie haircut, smiled a lot. She seemed quiet, but friendly. Robert learned that she wanted to transfer to the UW next year when she completed her associate degree.

"What then, Jenny?"

"I'm thinking of a counseling career. But that takes years of training, so I don't know. God must have something in mind for me."

"You must be religious."

"Oh, maybe. But I do believe that God leads us somehow. Do you, Robert?"

He thought for a minute. What to reply? Didn't he try to fit into Allah's plan? "I, um, guess I do. You probably go to church somewhere."

"Yeah, I do. It's one I've discovered that is quite interesting. Partly because they teach about Israel and believe that we are close to the end times."

"I don't get it. Why would they care about Israel? And what do you mean, 'end times'?"

"Oh, that's easy! They believe that Israel becoming a nation in 1948 represents the beginning of the end, you know, when Messiah returns." Jenny smiled, but with a quizzical furrowed brow.

"So they are all supporters of Israel?" he asked.

"Right. We even wave Israeli flags once in a while. There is an association of churches who support Israel in every way they can. They are all over the country."

"I had no idea churches like that existed."

"Would you like to come sometime? I'd be glad to take you."

"I guess it wouldn't hurt, you know. Why not? I'll look at my calendar and get back to you."

Watching television news in the living room of his landlord's house, Robert realized the intensity of the national frenzy. He understood the corresponding determination of the FBI to find the bomber. What should he do to lie low? No way could he get out of the country without raising suspicion, not with a Pakistan visa in his passport. They would have that in their computers even in the process of getting a new passport.

OK, he would avoid any close contact with anyone. He would not even eat dinner at the brothers' house. The FBI could be tracking them, or Imam Jabril. He would miss seeing Ali, but it would be better that way. With his small refrigerator and stove, he'd cook his own food in his room or eat out occasionally.

Then he thought of Jenny's invitation to visit her church. He smiled. What could be better for his cover than attending a church that is known to be pro-Israeli? What a great idea for a jihadist looking for a place to hide.


The psychology lecture droned on, explaining the significance of conditioned responses. Robert had learned of Pavlov's dog in junior high school. He spotted Jenny across the lecture hall, and she smiled when their eyes met. After class, they spoke in the hall, revisiting her invitation to church. Her eyes sparkled.

"Next Sunday will work for me," Jenny said.

"Sounds good. Where do we meet?"

"How about right in front of the college where the flag and benches are located? On Broadway. Maybe nine-thirty in the morning? You driving?"

"Yeah, I'll be there. I'll pick you up and you can show me how to get there."

# Chapter 18

Najid listened to the news on his radio while he hurried to dress. It felt good to be home and showered, and he was anxious to see Ashley. He had solved the puzzle of riding the buses in Seattle and had no trouble arriving at Harborview Medical Center. He checked at the nurses' station on Eight North before tiptoeing toward Ashley's room. The door was partially open, and Najid eased his way in to find Ashley asleep. Beeping monitors and the screen showed changing numbers. Fluid ran into her arms through the IV tubing. He didn't know what he should do. He didn't want to hurt Ashley by waking her. So he sat down in a chair by the window to wait.

He watched over Ashley, beautiful and almost smiling in her sleep. His heart ached as he saw her, so open, generous, and loving—so seriously hurt. He wanted to hold her hand, to kiss it. He found a recent newspaper from Oklahoma City on the sill with headlines about the bombing in Seattle and immersed himself in it. So he didn't notice when Ashley opened her eyes and turned her head toward the window.

"Najid, Najid! Oh, you're OK!" She flung her arms upward,

forgetting about the IVs and cracked ribs. Najid leaned over the bedrail to join in the hug. "I'm so glad to see you." She jerked and grimaced with pain suddenly. "It seems like every time I move, my chest hurts. They tell me I have some broken ribs. I asked about you but no one seemed to know if you survived the blast."

"And I didn't know about you after they took you away in the van with the flashing lights. You were bleeding on the sidewalk and couldn't answer me. I didn't know what to do except shout for help."

"Did you get hurt too?"

"Just scratches on my arms. You took the force of the explosion and I was behind you." Najid's voice broke. "You ... protected me." He swallowed several times and couldn't speak.

"I did? Well ... that's good. But tell me exactly what happened and what you did, where've you been. Nobody tells me anything, and I have so many questions."

Najid stood by the bedrail and looked into the eyes of the most beautiful person he could remember meeting outside his family. He shook his head and smiled. Their eyes met as his face flushed and his eyes filled with tears. "Ashley ... I prayed for you to live." He became silent, nodding as she smiled. Then he began to grin. "So you want to know everything?"

"Everything, Najid."

That began a long account of all that had happened to a bewildered foreign student in a faraway land who had become a terrorist victim along with Ashley. She had additional questions about his confinement as a "person of interest" and legal questions, many of which he couldn't answer.

Then Ashley asked about the bombing itself: What had happened? She continued, "I don't remember much at all. Being at the synagogue is a big fog. I must have been stunned if not knocked out. A policeman came briefly yesterday asking about what I remember, and I'm afraid I wasn't much help. He said that people who lose consciousness in an accident often have no memory of the events just before it happened. The doctor confirmed it and called it 'retrograde amnesia.'" She grew silent for a moment. "Maybe it's best that I can't remember anything." She seemed to gaze beyond the opposite wall in silence. "But what about the reaction in the United States? I'm too sleepy to watch the news on TV."

"I know a bit about that. It's international news as well. I've been isolated too, Ashley. But I did hear a bit on the radio this morning. And I found a paper from Oklahoma City just now with a lot of information. Someone must have left it."

"Oh, that would be from my parents. They flew in to be with me. They should be here soon. My dad is a news junkie, and he'll know the latest."

"Junkie? Is he on drugs?"

"No," Ashley laughed. "My dad getting high? No, he's just hooked on news. Junkie's another American slang word meaning he's addicted, in this case to reading the newspapers."

"I'd like to meet him."

"You will. Both Mom and Dad should be back soon."

"OK. Now tell me how they treated you here in the hospital. You could have died. I thought you might not be alive."

So Ashley related all she knew of her injuries and what Dr. Thompson told her about what had happened in the OR. Her memory remained clouded for most of the time after the blast, until today. "Pain medicine, I guess. I keep falling asleep."

Ashley answered a soft knock on the door. "Come in. Oh, Mom and Dad! I'm so glad you came so you can meet Najid. You remember we spoke of him yesterday, and we didn't know whether he survived the bombing. Najid, these are my parents, Frank and Dorothy Wells."

Najid bowed slightly and shook hands with both parents as they approached Ashley's bedside. "I am so happy to meet you. You must have been very worried for your daughter."

"We were," Dorothy said. "But I'm pleased that you both survived. It must have been a frightening experience for you."

"Yes. But especially seeing Ashley lying on the sidewalk, bleeding and unable to speak. She protected me from the blast."

"Really? Did you escape any injury?" Frank asked.

"I have a few scratches on my arms, that's all. But I didn't know what happened to Ashley. We are friends and classmates in graduate school at the University of Washington."

"I understand that. So what have you been doing since the explosion?"

Najid briefly described his detention as a "person of interest" and then asked Mr. Wells for any current information from national or international news.

"You would be blown away by what is happening around the world. Ah ...," he paused, "that's probably a bad phrase to use."

Dorothy grimaced at her husband's choice of words.

"Anyway, intelligence agencies all over the world are investigating to determine where the explosives came from and who might be involved. It has triggered alarm also in Europe and of course, Israel."

"It clearly targeted Jewish people," Ashley said.

"No question, Ashley. Jewish organizations are up in arms. Everyone in the country wants to find the bomber. The departments of Homeland Security, the State Department, the FBI, and the White House started taking hits for not detecting the plot before it happened. They seem to have no idea who or what organization perpetrated the bombing."

"It's no wonder you were detained," Ashley added, looking at Najid. "The authorities are desperate to find who did it."

"Al-Qaeda has claimed responsibility, but the intelligence people in the United States doubt that," Frank continued. "It could have been a homegrown terrorist or organization as they have not been able to identify anyone from overseas. They've poured over the Watch List here in the U.S. to find leads, but that has proved a huge undertaking and takes time."

The conversation turned to other subjects, including how Najid came to U Dub. He realized Ashley needed to visit with her parents. "I'll come back tomorrow after classes." He shook their hands, walked out, and tried not to wonder what Ashley's parents might think of him. For some reason, their opinion mattered ... a great deal.

# Chapter 19

So, how are you feeling, Ashley?" her mother inquired after Najid left.

"I hurt, but the pain medicine is enough. I have a little button here I can push when the pain gets worse ... every ten minutes if I need it. I'll be upright tomorrow and start walking, they say." She chuckled and then winced, eyes closed. "Sounds impossible right now."

"How long will you be in here, assuming everything goes well?"

"About a week total, Mom. Dr. Thompson says I'm doing fine. The ribs should feel better by that point. By the way, you don't need to stay here since the crisis is over."

"We'll decide that later, Ashley. Tell us more about Najid. He's not an American is he? He has an accent I can't place."

"He's from Israel, here on a Fulbright Scholarship, a graduate student in zoology, finished in Haifa at the university there. I asked him to go with me to the synagogue to go to a Shabbat service. He speaks Hebrew, so he could translate for me. That's how he happened to be with me when the bomb went off." Ashley sighed. "We both could have been killed."

Dorothy Wells shook her head, gazing out the window. After a moment she said, "I didn't realize he's Jewish. That's great, Ashley. We're so pleased that you're making international friends from Israel. They are such wonderful people who have gone through so much difficulty."

"He's not Jewish, Mom. But he's an awesome guy."

"I thought you said he's from Israel."

"He is, from a town near Nazareth."

"So if he's not Jewish, what is he?"

"He's Palestinian, Mom. But he's a Christian."

"Wait a minute!" Frank Wells said. "I've never heard of a Palestinian Christian. Are you certain about his faith? His name sounds Muslim."

"Dad, he's part of an ancient church, the Melkites, who trace their history back to the first gentile church in Antioch of Syria. The one Paul taught. And his name is an Arabic name, not a Muslim one. Their family can trace their history in that village back three hundred years."

"How do you know he's really a Christian, Ashley? Besides, some of those very old churches are dead and formalistic from what I hear."

"How does anyone know another's faith, Dad? I take Najid as his word. His life is consistent with what he says."

"Yeah, but he could be talking a good line and you'd never know it. He could be here on some kind of mission, posing as a 'Christian.' I would wonder with his proximity to the bombing, whether he might even have had some involvement in it unknown to the police. Anyway, I think you should stay away from him. I don't trust him, Ashley. I don't trust Palestinians after what they have done to the Israelis!"

Ashley lay silent in bed, overwhelmed with her dad's tirade about Najid. She didn't know about other Palestinians and generally trusted her parents' beliefs. But Najid would not lie to her. What would she tell him on his next visit? She hoped her parents wouldn't be around. *But what is the truth? Is Najid not who he says he is?*

"I think you're tired, Ashley," her mother said. "You need to rest, so we'll be going now and come back tomorrow. Have a good night and God bless." She and Frank leaned over to kiss their daughter good night.

"Good night, Mom and Dad. See you tomorrow." But Ashley couldn't go to sleep despite the morphine. And not because of pain.

# Chapter 20

The next afternoon her parents came and sat with Ashley, sometimes chatting and other times reading as she slept. She had been up and walking in the hall and wanted to rest. She awakened and began to talk.

"Do you know why we went to the synagogue in the first place?"

"No, you haven't explained that," Dorothy replied.

"It's because of the Seattle church's support of Israel, just like ours in Oklahoma City. I wanted to find out how Jewish people understand the situation, particularly the active way that we help them. They must question our motivation. They certainly don't believe as we do, and yet there is a common background in the Old Testament. So I wanted to get it directly from them. But I've never been to a synagogue and so really don't understand. That's why I invited Najid. He speaks Hebrew and has close friends who are Jews."

"We won't discuss Najid anymore," Frank Wells said. "But we have Jewish friends, as you know, and have helped fund projects for new European Jewish immigrants now living in Israel. It would be good for you to get involved a bit here, as you have time."

"I'm also thinking of taking time off from school to go to the

Middle East. There are a number of tours offered at reasonable prices. Our church has one coming up to see the places where Jesus walked. I'd like to do that."

"Do you think you'd be well enough?"

"It's not until July, Dad. I should be fine by then. I'll take the MCAT in June, and I don't need to take anymore classes to apply for medical school, so I can skip summer quarter and still get my master's degree by finishing my thesis."

"It sounds like you've thought this through. Touring Israel would be a good education for you, and you could use the funds you've saved up that would have gone for tuition. But perhaps you should see how you are recovering before making definite plans. Do you agree, Dorothy?"

"I think so." She looked at her watch. "Ashley, we'd better be going. We'll be flying home tomorrow and want to get some good sleep. You seem to be recovering well and ..." She stopped and looked at the door opening slowly.

"Najid! Come in. My parents are here. Sit down and let us know how school went today."

Najid put out his hand, but Frank shunned him, looking the other way. Najid looked puzzled and nodded a greeting to Dorothy, who dipped her head slightly without saying anything or extending her hand. Ashley forced a smile and a nervous laugh. "Najid, did our friends discuss the bombing, and did you tell them in the lounge about what happened to us?"

"Yes, I did."

"Well, how did it go?"

Najid gazed at the floor. He shifted in his chair and cleared his throat. "They wanted to know about your injuries, so I told them." He stopped talking. Ashley sighed, shifted in bed and turned to her parents in the awkward silence. They both looked away and said nothing. Finally Frank got up and retrieved his wife's purse from the windowsill.

"We should be going now, Ashley," he said.

Her mom had tears in her eyes as she kissed her daughter goodbye. "We'll be in touch by phone when we get home tomorrow."

Frank leaned over to kiss Ashley, while Ashley fought her own tears and didn't smile. They left without speaking to Najid—as though he didn't exist. She shook her head. She couldn't believe it.

After an awkward silence, Najid looked up at Ashley. She saw a pained expression on his face she had never seen before. He didn't speak.

Finally Ashley shook her head. "I think my parents are tired with all the events that have happened, Najid."

"Yeah," he said with a nod. "I suppose that is true. I think you are tired too, Ashley. Why don't I go now and let you rest." He gave a perfunctory wave of his hand and tiptoed out the door.

Ashley burst into tears and sobbed. Everything seemed too much. The bombing and nearly dying, the pain of recovery, and now her parents' rejection of Najid. Why was being Palestinian so bad? Would Najid think she didn't want to be his friend? How could she deal with her parents' strong feelings against him? She didn't know. What should she do?

As her tears dried, Ashley looked up. *"Oh God. Please comfort Najid right now. And my parents, God, I know they want the best for me. Please help me to know what to do."*


Each day Ashley grew stronger. Dr. Thompson freed her from her chest tube. She began to eat and changed to oral pain medication. Walking in the hall, she met other patients and families. They all seemed glued to the TV news to learn the latest in the hunt for the terrorists. Despite the intense manhunt all over the world, nothing turned up.

Dr. Thompson came in to check Ashley and view the computer monitor with all the day's lab and clinical information. He tweaked her toes with a hint of a smile. "You're my most popular patient."

"What do you mean? I still look like I've just crawled through a knothole."

"The news media are clamoring to interview you, Ashley. Lots of national reporters, cable news people. We've kept them away. You need time to recover before they pounce on you."

"Thanks, Dr. Thompson. I couldn't tell them much anyway. I really don't remember what happened except that we planned to meet at the synagogue."

Later a police detective did come to her room to quiz her about what happened leading up to the bombing.

He introduced himself briefly, but Ashley couldn't remember his name. She explained her interest in visiting the synagogue and her discussions with Najid, her friend and would-be translator. She remembered planning the visit, but had little memory of the hour prior to the blast, nor of the explosion itself, or being rushed to the hospital. The detective thanked her and left.

Several of her new friends at church and her housemates came to see her. She received a card and flowers from her grad school colleagues. Najid had signed the card, but he didn't come to visit her again. *After what we've been through together, why does it have to end like this?*

# Chapter 21

A week to the day after the bombing, Ashley's friends drove her home. Signs over the front door welcomed her. Walking into the living room with its dark-blue rug, walnut paneling, and white ceiling, she sat in her favorite chair, a comfortable recliner. She could smell the curry and soon learned her housemates had put on a special dinner for her.

Two days later she appeared in the zoology department lounge. "Welcome back," read the sign. Then she noticed the bottom line, which said, "to our colleague, famous for two days!" Soon her fellow students gathered, and Najid appeared. She greeted them with a smile and then gazed at Najid, who looked at her blankly and nodded. He didn't speak.

"Tell us about what happened," one of them insisted. "We've tried to get the story out of Najid here, but he won't say much." Najid looked out the window and remained silent. "We read in the paper that he tried to help you before Medic One arrived."

"I really don't want to talk about it now. It's true that Najid tried his best to help me right after the bombing." Ashley smiled at Najid, but he didn't notice. She walked over to the coffee urn to fill her cup as the conversation drifted to other subjects. She tired of the constant news and the obsession with catching the bomber, apparently on everyone's mind.

After a week Ashley returned to studying for the MCAT exam, her full schedule of classes, her work on her master's thesis, and her lab assistant duties. She did have an hour with reporters and TV people, but they seemed dissatisfied with the little she could remember.

Rabbits had replaced frogs for dissection, and she enjoyed the eager freshmen, so anxious to play doctor even though their patients had been euthanized.

She saw Najid occasionally in the department or during coffee breaks, but they rarely spoke, and then only briefly. Finally, unable to stand their distance any longer, Ashley made a special effort to track him down in the Suzzalo library.

"Najid, we need to talk."

"About what?"

"About you and me."

"I've recovered, Ashley, and it looks like you have too."

"It's not about recovery. I want to talk to you because I have hurt you deeply."

"I don't blame you for asking me to go to the synagogue. I chose to go."

"You don't understand, Najid. It's about feelings. We Americans can't just sweep all our feelings under the rug. We need to talk them out and reach an understanding. Otherwise they keep festering—I mean ... they continue causing problems in relationships."

"I don't understand the rug part."

"That's just an idiom. What I mean is we try to hide our feelings and not deal with them."

"Oh." He nodded. "I learned long ago in Nazareth that when people don't like you, you just be quiet and move on with your life. There is nothing you can do about it—except talk to God."

"And I've done that too, Najid. But now it's time for us to talk. When can you do it?"

Najid grew silent for a moment and gazed at the bookcases lining the walls and in aisles too numerous to count. "I guess I have no choice. You and I have been through so much together. Maybe lunch tomorrow, at the HUB?"

"Let's meet at the lounge and we'll walk over together."

                           

Ashley noticed Najid seemed to be enjoying the special of the day, a rice pilaf with lamb. She finished her salad at their table in the corner. Students filled the cafeteria and the noise level made it hard to hear Najid's soft voice. They started tentatively on safe topics, such as what their students were learning. Najid talked about the embryology of the brain and his increasing amazement that such a complex computer could develop out of two cells coming together. He had challenged his students' thinking. "What genes direct that process? Who builds them and why does it work so well?" He smiled for the first time since the bombing.

"I don't understand the process or the genetics, Najid, but I do know who got it going."

Najid nodded. "Macs and PCs don't just happen either. Or smartphones."

"And relationships can be complex, like the brain, and they also don't exist without a reason."

Najid flashed a knowing smile. "So what are you trying to say, Ashley?"

"Well, first of all, Najid, I want to say I'm so sorry for the way we treated you during that last hospital visit. I still feel terrible about it. You did not deserve it. You came into the room as a friend, and we were rude to you and made you want to leave."

"It's OK, Ashley. I didn't know what I had done wrong. It must have been something I didn't even realize. So I thought it best to leave."

"Oh, Najid! You did nothing wrong." Ashley had tears in her eyes.

"Are you sure? After that I didn't know whether you wanted me to visit anymore, so I just signed the card instead."

"No, no!" she said, shaking her head and grabbing his arm. "I did want you to come. And I do want us to be friends just like before!" She squeezed his forearm and then let go.

"So then if I did nothing wrong, why the trouble?"

"We have a saying in America that some things are like an elephant in the living room. It's huge, but we don't want to deal with it or admit it exists, so we walk around it as though it's not even there. Some subjects are like that. They are very big, but we never talk about them. They're too painful. So we pretend that they simply don't exist."

"I like that example. I'll have to remember that. We have lots of 'elephants' in our living rooms at home."

"One of yours may be here as well, Najid. I'm going to come right out with it so we can deal with that huge creature. Some Christians in this country believe that God has ordained that Jews return and take over Palestine, even the West Bank and Gaza. They believe this began with the establishment of the state of Israel in 1948. So helping the Jews will speed up the return of Jesus in our own time."

"I didn't realize that Christians here actually believe that."

"There are a lot who don't. There are all kinds of speculations and beliefs about what might or might not happen, and when. That's why I wanted to go to the synagogue."

"I don't understand that." Najid looked puzzled.

"I wanted to go because I need to know how Jewish people feel about Christians supporting Israel all the time. Jews don't believe like we do about Jesus as Messiah, so how can they possibly understand why we send them so much money and support them? They must wonder."

"OK. Now I understand why we were there at the synagogue."

"Good. We in the church I attend generally believe that Palestinians hate Israel, and that Israel should rule all the Holy Land. Then there is the Muslim thing. Like most Americans, we don't know that there are many Christians in the Middle East, in lots of countries. In our church, we never talk about Palestinian Christians even though they're our brothers and sisters."

"I didn't realize that we Arab Christians are so unknown here."

"It's sad but true, Najid. You probably picked that up when we first talked in the lounge and our friends assumed you were Muslim. Many Americans seem to think all Palestinians are Muslim. And then some people lump all Muslims in with the terrorist fringe of Islam."

Najid paused, nodding. "Terrorists are bad; therefore, all Muslims are bad because they're all the same and they want to harm you. And since all Arabs are Muslim, they are bad too, even though some of us live in Israel?"

Ashley looked puzzled. Was he kidding or serious? "Hmm ... yeah ... correct. Now, not all Christians in this country feel this way. Not all Americans do. But our church does and many hundreds of evangelical churches in the U.S. seem to. These beliefs and attitudes vary a lot. It's hard to explain, Najid, but most of us don't even realize how we naturally champion one side only."

Najid shook his head. "I didn't know that. You don't care about justice for our people?"

"We mostly don't even *know* about your people. We hear only about Israel and the occasional rocket attack by the Palestinians from Gaza."

Najid sat staring out the window, shaking his head.

"So, Najid, put yourself in my parents' shoes. You have been brought up to believe this way and never question it. It's right out of the Bible, or at least the best interpretation of it. So when your daughter is nearly killed in a synagogue bombing and seems to be drifting toward friendship with a Palestinian 'bad' man, you object. You are rude to him and pay no attention to him—almost like he isn't even in the room. You don't want him in your daughter's circle of friends."

"I had no idea that is how they felt about me or why! Now I understand, Ashley. We can't be friends anymore?"

"Oh, no, no, no! You are my friend and always will be, Najid. You saved my life. You are a real gentleman, and one of the nicest men I've ever known."

Najid gazed silently out the window. Finally he spoke softly. "But can we be friends if your parents don't approve of me?"

"I'm a grown woman, Najid, and I will do what I think is best. And you are the best." She reached out to squeeze his left hand.

Najid placed his right hand over his heart and nodded his thank you.

# Chapter 22

Robert enjoyed driving his red Corvette with the top down in the late May warmth, past parks with rhododendrons still in bloom. Nine days after the bombing, it seemed safe. No one would link such a car with jihad. Jenny chatted about her classes as she directed Robert to the church. They had to cross Lake Washington on a floating bridge. She pointed out Mount Rainier to the south, shining white and huge in the morning sun, and Mount Baker far to the north.

"Our church is in Bellevue."

"What's it like, Jenny?"

"It's hard to explain. Do you go to any church?"

"I went once; you know, for a funeral, with my parents."

"Well, you'll find this quite different."

Robert drove on in silence, wondering what he had agreed to do. But strange or not, it would provide good cover. At least it got him out of his room.

Robert stared at the front of the auditorium as they walked into a row near the back with comfortable-looking upholstered dark seats. But they didn't sit. Hundreds of people, standing, sang and clapped rhythmically to the music of a band on stage. It had drums, guitars, electric bass, a keyboard, and big speakers, just like any rock concert. The three leaders stood and sang into microphones as everyone followed words to the song projected on large screens on both sides. Jenny sang along. A large empty cross covered the back wall. Wasn't Jesus supposed to be on it? Then he saw the two flags on either side of the stage: one American, the other Israeli. He shook his head. He didn't know whether he could handle this.

Finally after more songs and a prayer, to Robert's relief, they sat. The pastor stood behind the lectern and told the people to turn in their Bibles to Genesis chapter twelve. Jenny reached for one in the rack in front of them and quickly found the passage. Everyone dropped their heads to read along.

The text said something about Abram, later called Abraham, and some special blessing of God for him, and even curses for his enemies. All nations would be blessed through Abram.

The minister closed the Bible and explained that this applied to Israel today since Jews traced their ancestors back to Abram. He moved to a high stool and sat down. He said this special Sunday honored Israel, and that they support Israel because "it heralds the soon return of Jesus." Robert couldn't understand how Israel fit with Jesus. *Didn't he start a different religion?*

Pastor Tom Evans shared his compassion and respect for Israel for enduring all its suffering at the hands of the Palestinians, and explained that it fulfills God's plan for this time in history. "We must support Israel's survival," he said. Then he recommended ways to contribute money to Israeli projects. Robert almost walked out, but realized it wouldn't look good and would upset Jenny.

Robert seethed inside, trembling as they drove home, but said nothing. Jenny remained quiet for several minutes. Finally she spoke.

"What did you think, Robert?"

He couldn't tell her what he really thought. Would he have to go through this again next Sunday?

"Is this, like, what you do every Sunday?"

"No. We are strong supporters of Israel, but you got in on a special Sunday today when we honor them. It happens fairly infrequently."

Robert felt nauseated and terribly agitated. His hands shook on the steering wheel.

"Will you be coming next week?" Jenny added a musical lilt to her question.

He wondered why women talked that way, high notes and low notes. He liked being with her. But was this worth going through just for trying to cover his tracks? He could stand it for an hour, he supposed. Or maybe he could put up with that stuff just to be with Jenny. "Yeah, I'll pick you up at the same time and place."

# Chapter 23

Ashley recovered fully over the next few weeks. Najid had found a group of international students, Christians, several of whom had Muslim backgrounds. Their group met on Friday evenings. He and Ashley discussed many of the issues between Muslims and Christians over coffee, and she learned a great deal from Najid's experience. She began to attend her own church again.

On a Sunday in mid-June during the sermon, her eyes wandered to a young man with black hair sitting next to an attractive young lady. He slouched in his seat, head down, not asleep, but possibly reading. Ashley couldn't tell. He didn't seem to be interested in the sermon and stood up very slowly at the end of the service. He didn't sing the last song. She could see that he grimaced a bit at the final words from the pulpit. Ashley then filed out into a crowded foyer near the entrance where the people gathered to talk and greet the pastor. She met friends and chattered about her upcoming trip to Israel.

While mingling she found herself within a few feet of the young man she had noticed. He seemed anxious to leave, with the girl behind him not happy with his pushing people. Ashley answered her friend's questions about the planned trip. She had to almost shout because of the crowd noise. She looked up finding the young man staring at her. He had a distinctive red birthmark above his left eye. He quickly moved and shoved his way out the door, turning away from the pastor's extended hand.

Heading out to lunch with several friends, Ashley wondered aloud who that strange person could be. She couldn't remember ever seeing him before. And yet his gaze and the red mark on his forehead triggered the thought that she had seen him somewhere in the past. Maybe at church. He had seemed both bored and nervous, certainly anxious to get out the door. Later at home she got out her maps of Israel and Palestine and began to trace the itinerary of their tour. She could hardly wait to go.

Jenny climbed into the passenger seat after church and Robert took off, tires screeching. It put the exclamation point on how he felt.

"You're going to get a ticket driving like that," Jenny cautioned.

"Yeah, you're right, Jenny." Of all things, he didn't want a confrontation with the police and getting back into their computer database. He didn't know what was in there, but he'd had some previous traffic experiences and investigations by police in New York. So he slowed the car and drove her home sedately.

"You pushed your way right out of the church, Robert. You were rude. Why?"

"I needed to get out of there, Jenny." He didn't mention the real reason: that blonde. After dropping Jenny off at her rooming house, he decided to drive top down up to Snoqualmie Pass. He had come in on I-90 on his way to Seattle both times and wanted to see the mountains again. Robert stopped at a drive-in for some fast food, put the top down, and punched cruise control for sixty miles per hour so he wouldn't have to worry about police. He grabbed his cheeseburger, held the steering wheel with his left hand, and put his milkshake between his legs. A cloud shadowed his mind on the beautiful sunny day in June.

His mind raced. *That blonde at church. She looked familiar.* He had seen her somewhere. Robert needed to find the answer, but how? He had heard a bit of her conversation over the crowd noise, and even been close enough to hear something about her recovery and a trip to Israel with a group from the church in July. When she glanced up she had looked into his eyes. Just for a moment. *Oh no, the synagogue!* His eyes widened and mouth dropped open. "Shit!" he shouted, banging on the steering wheel. "No! Yes! She's the one."

He was certain that was the girl he had exchanged glances with at the synagogue bombing, the girl across the street who saw him. Their eyes had met then, just like today. Just before the explosion. He had seen her on the sidewalk, bleeding, he had assumed to death. But she had dropped out of the news after a week or so. She obviously had recovered, and that's what she spoke about. But also about a trip to Israel sponsored by the church.

He had looked away quickly today, but maybe not quickly enough. She must have recognized him! The more he thought about it, the more sure he became. He knew now that she would remember him. No doubt about it. She would go to the police and tell them. But she didn't know his name or anything about him. If he never went back to that church, she'd never see him again. Thank Allah he had never signed a visitor's card. He had better lie low and hide in his room. No, that would be too obvious. He should continue attending Seattle Central Community College as though nothing had happened. He would see Jenny and tell her no more church. She would understand. It would be natural since she already knew he didn't like it.

By the time he passed Denny Creek Campground, Robert had a plan worked out, but he had to get more information.

On Monday after class, Robert found an empty office at the college. *Maybe it's good they don't have pay telephone booths anymore,* he thought. Too easy to trace. He called the church office and asked to speak to someone about the trip to Israel coming up. The operator rang another office, and a lady informed him she volunteered on Monday and didn't know very much about the trip, but would be happy to answer any questions she could with the information available. She didn't ask his name.

"It's a great opportunity for you," she said. "The cost is only nineteen hundred dollars for ten days there, and that includes airfare, hotels, transfers, and some meals. That's what it says here on the brochure."

"That's a good price," Robert said. "What are the dates of the trip?"

"Let's see ... you would leave on July tenth and return to Seattle on the twenty-fourth."

"Where generally would it go?"

"It looks like the first few days are in Bethlehem and Galilee, then a trip to the Dead Sea and Qumran—you know, where the scrolls were found. Then Masada, then north to Jericho, and the last few days in Jerusalem."

"Do you know how many are going?"

"Looks like eleven people are signed up with their deposits, according to a list printed on Friday."

"Could you tell me who they are?"

"I'm not sure I should release the names. Are you interested in going? I can send you a brochure."

"I'll think about it, you know, and maybe get back to you. Thanks for the information."

He had just found the key to eliminate the final threat.


Robert could hardly wait to get home to his room. He had saved lots of news feeds about the bombing on his computer, including on Facebook. He scrolled back to the day after the event and sure enough, there was her picture. Ashley Wells. He stared out the window, gritting his teeth. She'd seen him again, at church.

# Chapter 24

Robert rehashed memories of Imam Jabril as he parked his Corvette a few blocks away from the Islamic Center. He found the imam alone in the kitchen of the mosque at three-thirty, following afternoon prayers, preparing tea. He looked at Robert with those piercing dark eyes. Like a scowling Ayatollah Khomeini.

"Tea?" he said, offering the cup to Robert. "Where have you been?" He changed to a soft whisper. "We haven't seen you since the bombing. I haven't seen Ali either. You both just disappeared."

"I've been changing my routine."

The imam put his index finger over his mouth. "Security," he whispered.

The imam continued, his voice barely audible. "You succeeded. Congratulations. Allahu akbar."

"Only with your help, you know. And now I need it again."

"Come," Jabril whispered. "We'll go out in back to the chairs under the big tree. The police drive by here sometimes, and I'm suspicious they may have a bug in the main prayer room. We are careful in what we say out loud now."

Robert drew up a chair outside, opposite the imam, and sipped his tea. He told Jabril about going to the Seattle Central Community College, not far away from the Islamic Center. Without mentioning the church, he shared about Ashley Wells, about seeing her initially across the street at the synagogue, and that she saw him just before the explosion.

"I've read the articles on my computer right after the bombing. Did she survive?"

"Yeah, she did. She dropped out of the news after about a week. She wouldn't do interviews, so I guess they left her alone."

"Are you sure she saw you at the synagogue?"

"Yeah, I am. You know, our eyes met, like just momentarily before the bomb went off. Then she collapsed on the sidewalk."

The imam nodded, stroking his beard. He picked up his cup and sipped. "Have you seen her since?"

"Yeah, that's the problem. We were fairly close in a crowd, and she saw me looking at her. At first I didn't recognize her, but I know she recognized me, probably by the red birthmark above my eye."

"Are you sure the girl you saw in the crowd is Ashley Wells?"

"I went home and looked up her picture on Facebook. Same girl."

"Have you seen her since then?"

"No, and I don't want to. That's why I'm here. She is the only one in the world who could identify me as the bomber ... besides you and Ali."

"Wasn't there a man with her?"

"Yeah, but the guy had his back to me."

"So what do you want from me?"

"Imam, I need your help to eliminate this threat." Robert told him about her impending tour with the church group to Israel without relating how he learned of it. He didn't want anything to happen here since the police loomed everywhere. Could the imam help with his international contacts, to have something happen to her in Israel?

"How do you know she's going to the Zionist Entity?"

"I've checked it with the church by telephone and confirmed it on their web page. I know exactly when they are leaving, which airline. Destination: Tel Aviv."

"You want me to arrange with my friends there to trail her and find some opportunity to get rid of the infidel?"

"Yeah." Robert nodded. "I can make it worth your while. Also for your friends there."

"How much?"

"Thirty thousand up front, and another thirty when the job is complete."

Imam Jabril gazed off toward the house, which needed repair. He nodded. Several moments passed. Robert wondered what he was thinking.

Finally he spoke. "Do you have that kind of money?"

"Yeah, family trust fund. I can bring you a bank check tomorrow."

The imam nodded. "I'll see what I can do. I have secure e-mail so I will check with my friend in Jerusalem. Then we'll see if he can help. Come back day after tomorrow."

Robert couldn't keep his mind on the lectures. He met Jenny after class.

"Hey, Jenny, I won't be going back to the church, but we can see each other at school and have coffee together once in a while."

She frowned and sighed. "I guess I'm not surprised. OK then."

He liked her, but didn't want to get close. She shouldn't learn any more about him. Distance equals protection.

He couldn't think of anything except his meeting with Imam Jabril tomorrow. The financial transaction had been a snap at the bank. He'd mentioned buying a new car, and the teller handed him the bank draft for thirty thousand dollars without any questions, based on his large amount in their money market fund.

The imam had their tea ready, and they walked out to the white plastic chairs under the big tree. Robert noticed the whole place needed fixing up, inside and out.

"Did you hear from your friend?" Robert didn't wait for any greetings or small talk.

"I did." The imam nodded and continued. "He has people there who can help with the project. And yes, he is interested ... for a price."

"How much?" Robert asked.

"Fifty thousand if they succeed. But I have to share the up-front costs with them, so I'll need more as well."

Robert stopped to consider that. If they didn't get rid of her, he'd eventually be dead meat. "Fair enough. I'll also provide another thirty to you on proof of success. Here's the down payment." He handed Jabril the bank draft for thirty thousand dollars noted to "Cash" and a flash drive. "And here is all the information you will need on Ashley Wells. You know, picture of her, flight information, itinerary with departure and return dates from Tel Aviv. It's all on there. Are we in full agreement?"

"We are. You are well prepared," Jabril said, nodding his head. "And you can count on my friend in Jerusalem. He has men who are skilled. He will succeed." They shook hands. "Allahu Akbar."

# Chapter 25

Ashley looked out the window at the white beaches rapidly approaching as they glided silently, descending over the blue Mediterranean into Ben Gurion airport near Tel Aviv. The flight attendant announced the time: three p.m. With a short day and night, Ashley found herself too excited to sleep. She would crash in the hotel later. Her new friend and seatmate, Marie, a quiet, single woman in her thirties with short brown hair, shared her enthusiasm. "Look at all the people on the beach. The tall buildings must be hotels," Marie said. "It looks like Waikiki."

Ashley leaned toward the window, next to her conservatively dressed friend, who she couldn't imagine frolicking on the beach in Honolulu.

"I've never been to Hawaii. I've been to northern Mexico, but that's it."

"Well, we're in for a treat, Ashley."

The bus trip to Bethlehem took only one hour, with traffic. Thirty miles sounded like nothing in Oklahoma. Ashley had studied Bethlehem and couldn't wait to see it. The pictures on the Internet didn't suggest the "little town of Bethlehem" she sang about every

Christmas. They ascended on the highway winding through hills and forests, getting higher all the time. Scattered farms and large collections of white towers on the tops of hills looking like condos gleamed in the sunshine.

They pulled to a stop at a low building with a roof that crossed the highway. Ashley saw an armored personnel carrier and a uniformed man armed with an automatic rifle approaching the driver. He showed the soldier some papers and all of the team's passports. Jim Swain, the young pastor and team leader, had collected them. After several minutes, the Israeli soldier waved them through. Jim stood in the front of the bus and explained as they turned onto a smaller road toward Bethlehem.

"This is just a security measure, routine, don't worry. We are now out of Israel proper and in the West Bank. We will encounter several checkpoints during our trip, but as Americans, we'll have no problems."

Ashley sighed. She hadn't been afraid. The stark reality of checkpoints simply surprised her. She began to notice apartment buildings, some with holes in the walls. Small shops appeared as they drove. The city appeared shabby and old, mixed with some attractive buildings, churches and mosques with their minarets. She turned to Marie. "Bethlehem doesn't look like I pictured it in my mind."

"Are you surprised?" Marie asked.

"Yeah, I guess I am. I had envisioned a quaint large village with all kinds of open shops."

"Well, remember that the Israeli Defense Forces raided the city in 2002 looking for terrorists."

"Really?"

"Yes. Some of them fled into the Church of the Nativity and became hostages for about five months. The soldiers killed several, deported others. Bethlehem became a war zone."

"That accounts for the holes in the apartment buildings?"

"I presume so. You can't have a war without damage to the city."

Marie seemed to know the recent history of Bethlehem. Ashley had read mostly of the area's ancient past and felt embarrassed that she knew so little of current events.

The whole team streamed into the hotel and rested before

dinner. Ashley and Marie asked to room together. After eating and visiting with the eleven team members, Ashley escaped to their room and crashed into bed. Though her watch read nine at night, her biological clock said it was midday. She finally slept and dreamed of soldiers and artillery firing on people in their apartments who then ran into the Church of the Nativity. A soldier came out of an armored vehicle with an assault rifle and demanded her passport. She woke up relieved she'd been dreaming.

The next morning Ashley and Marie stepped off of their tour bus along with their team and other tour groups. Jim led the way past a large open square with shops and a mosque.

"This open area is called 'Manger Square,' and that very old building ahead is our goal."

The group approached a historic church built of ancient carved stones with a flat front wall, very plain and deteriorated with age. They bowed at the low doorway to get into the Church of the Nativity, the oldest standing active church in the world. It seemed unreal to Ashley to be in a church building seventeen centuries old.

Crowds of people swarmed the open areas. Some other tourists kissed the raised stones on the floor. A line wound down the stairs to the "cave." Jim explained that this was thought to be the actual site of Jesus's birth, commemorated by an ornate silver star in the floor. It had a hole in it that visitors could peer through to the cave itself where the birth occurred. Ashley dropped to her knees. She couldn't see much. *Imagine, the King of the Universe, born in a dark cave used to house animals!*

Ashley found Marie, and after looking at some paintings, they stepped quickly out into the sunshine. "I'm confused. I should be more thrilled to be standing where people over many centuries commemorate the birthplace of Jesus."

"It's hard, isn't it," Marie replied. "There's no magic in stepping where Jesus came to our world. But it does make me realize that it actually happened. History verified. Our faith validated. Maybe it's the press of the crowds that bothers us, or the confusion. But that's what he experienced, many times."

"That helps." Ashley gazed at the crowds of tourists pouring out of their buses. She remembered that Jesus quieted throngs of people, fed them, healed many, and taught them. He had compassion. He didn't seem to get frustrated. She needed to see beyond the chaos too.

But that proved hard, particularly since she couldn't shake the odd feeling that someone was watching her. A ridiculous thought in such a crowd. She probably just noticed one of the guys in another tour group looking at her.

# Chapter 26

The next morning, the Shepherds' Fields just outside Bethlehem appeared smaller than Ashley had envisioned. She walked into several cool open caves in the rocky hillside, escaping the hot sun. Stones and dry grass seemed to blanket the hills overlooking the city.

"So this is the site where the angels terrified the shepherds, Marie." They walked across the hill where the shepherds probably slept when the angels came. "I wish these dead stones could tell the story of discovering that baby."

"But Ashley, dead stones endure. And the church buildings they form do tell his story.

After lunch in the air-conditioned hotel, most of the team decided to rest in their cool rooms, Marie included.

"Ashley, I'm going to give in to jet lag. I know you're supposed to stay up and fight it through until nighttime, but it's so cool and nice in here."

Those who wished could take a short trip, only seven miles south of Bethlehem to Herodion. Herod the Great's "illusion of grandeur" comprised a palace and fortress built around 20 B.C. They passed the ruins of the palace pools on the flat area, and then walked up the adjoining conical hill rising two hundred feet above the desert floor.

Jim and five others, including Ashley, strode up the steep and narrow rocky road in the heat of the early afternoon. It spiraled upward around the partly man-made cone. Too hot for most tourists, apparently. She saw a lone man behind them, but otherwise no one besides their small group. Ashley remembered Kipling's assertion that only mad dogs and Englishmen go out in the noonday sun.

Coming to a rest plateau with tables and benches, Ashley decided to stop at the small kiosk for a soda. The others of the group kept climbing. "Go ahead," she said, waving them on. "I'll meet you at the top."

She could see the ruins down below on the flat desert outlining multiple rooms and pools. It must have been magnificent. Looking up she glimpsed the man she had noticed before staring at her. He sat with arms folded; a hat and visor shielded his face. She could just see his eyes behind shaded glasses—dead eyes, expressionless, fixed on her. He quickly glanced away. A chill ran up her spine. She sensed something was wrong.

Suddenly Ashley felt like running. She looked around for other tourists. None. Maybe she should stay near the kiosk attendant? Or should she run down to the bus? It would be locked. No, she should find her friends as quickly as possible. They would be only five minutes ahead of her. She had to get away. So she took her drink and started up the narrow road, which spiraled around the cone to the top.

She heard the man get up and walk after her. She picked up her pace, and he sped up as well. Her eyes widened and her hands shook. Ashley started to run uphill. Rounding a corner, she glanced back to see him coming about thirty feet behind. Walking fast. She thought of screaming. Where were they? Another turn in the spiral road. Short of breath, she didn't know how long she could keep up the pace, still not fully recovered from her wounds

Finally she saw them, walking on the rim of the ruins at the top. Her team. She waved. Should she shout to them? Looking back, she saw him turn and walk back down the hill. Ashley drew a deep breath and sighed.

The team had moved on, listening to their driver explain the spectacular ruins. Ashley joined them without a word about her panic. She felt rather foolish. The man was probably just another tourist who happened to be behind her, perhaps looking for someone else. Her mind was playing tricks, and she refused to be paranoid. She'd made the promise after the bombing not to let fear get the best of her.

Still, she had trouble concentrating on the driver's explanation of the complex ruins of baths and pools and courtyards. He pointed to the remains of a synagogue and an underground passageway. Ashley tried to digest what he said, but wanted to get back to the bus. She stayed close to the driver and Jim.

# Chapter 27

Ashley returned to the hotel, found Marie gone, and sat in their room to collect her thoughts. She rehashed what had happened with the man who seemed to be following her. Coincidence maybe? Probably perfectly normal for him to look at a girl with curiosity and then try to go up to the top but turn back in the heat.

She spoke out loud, "Come on, Ashley, get a grip on yourself. First the church, then the Herodian. This is getting ridiculous. You're being paranoid." She refused to let fear ruin her trip.

Soon Ashley became restless. She didn't like inactivity when she could explore. Four o'clock, no problem. She had several hours before dinner at seven.

Ashley walked north one block, then west crossing Manger Street, making a mental note of her turns so she could find her way back. Across another street busy with cars and taxis, she saw a complex of three one- and two-story buildings and a sign that read "Bethlehem Bible College." Most signs used English and Arabic. Up on the hill above and off to the east, a large number of elegant apartment towers crowned the top of the hill, contained within a high wall. Around the perimeter, a highway encircled the complex.

Three blocks north of the Bible College, Ashley approached another wall that blocked her way and that turned ninety degrees to extend along a narrow street. She stopped and stared at it, mouth open. It rose forty feet into the air, concrete, with multiple glassed-in guard towers on top of the wall. She wondered whether it contained a prison right in the middle of Bethlehem. Painted prominently on the wall, she read "Nakba." Other graffiti read "Shame." On one section someone had painted a soldier with a gun and a fifteen-foot-long U.S. dollar bill. As she paused to study the wall and read more of the graffiti, a young man approached carrying books. He greeted Ashley in English. "Are you from America?"

"Yeah. I just arrived last night. Do you live here?"

"We live in Beit Jala, a town next to Bethlehem. But I attend the Bible College here."

"Really? You must be a Palestinian Christian."

"I am now. But my family is Muslim."

"Oh, I'd like to chat with you sometime. I want to learn about this part of the world and the people in it. Are there many Christians here?"

"There were thousands in Bethlehem, but many have left."

"Why is that?"

"Lots of reasons. Like this wall here." He gestured toward the wall. "We are trapped, since 2002. Many families and young people used to work in the city."

"You mean Jerusalem?"

"Yes. Now we can't go. Even people who were born there but live here are not permitted to return to see their families in Jerusalem. Many jobs there are gone to us."

"What does your father do?"

"Construction—when he can find work. We have twenty-seven percent unemployment. It's from the wall of separation of people. This one," he said, glancing up at the wall. "'Apartheid,' they called it in South Africa."

Ashley frowned. "I didn't know that." She gazed quietly at the tall stranger, reminding her of Najid. "Oh, I have so many questions, but I mustn't keep you. Just tell me what *Nakba* means. I see it on the wall here and down there a ways," Ashley said, pointing to the wall fifty feet down the narrow street.

"It means 'catastrophe.'"

"What is the catastrophe?"

"It's the tragedy of one government forcing hundreds of thousands of people from their homes and lands. It began in 1948. It's still going on. I doubt whether you Americans understand what is happening here. I've read you refer to the wall as a 'fence.'"

Ashley looked down, shaking her head. "You are probably right. We don't understand, but that's one reason I'm here."

"Good. I'd be happy to talk with you some more. I'll be back at the college tonight." He pointed back the way Ashley had walked. "We have a small discussion group to practice our English, and you would be welcome to come."

"Oh, I'd love to come ... a ... I don't know your name."

"Gamal. And what is yours?"

"I'm Ashley."

He didn't seem inclined to shake hands.

"What time this evening?"

"About eight. Come in the south door. The Bible College is just three blocks south of here. We'll enjoy having you, a native English speaker as our guest."

<hr />

Ashley took the right angle bend with the wall and wandered down the small side street along it, reading the graffiti, much of it in English. The unmanned guard towers continued along the top. She felt uneasy and began reading another painting in large letters: "KNOW" and below that "HOPE." She pulled out her smartphone to snap a picture of the graffiti, then she noticed someone behind her. Ashley turned quickly to see a large man staring at her, dressed in dark clothes. Her eyes widened. Same guy as on the Herodian. The brim of his cap covered his forehead. Heart pounding, she nodded an acknowledgement of his presence, smiled briefly, and noted his menacing expression. He gazed at her from behind his tinted glasses.

She looked up but could not see a guard in the nearby tower.

The man said nothing and began to walk toward her, right hand in his pants pocket. Ashley's face drained of blood. She broke out in a sweat. Looking around she saw no one either behind the man or back the way she came. He kept coming, slowly. She trembled.

"OK, OK! What do you want?"

He glanced around silently and up to the guard tower, apparently to confirm they had no company. He drew his hand out of the pocket, revealing a small pistol. Every muscle tensed. She stared at him as he approached. Paralyzed as in a nightmare, she could not run.

"I'll give you all the money I have!"

He raised the gun, covering the small pistol with his left hand.

Ashley screamed loudly enough to raise the dead. Then, "Oh God, please help!" A taxi she had not noticed coasted to stop just behind the man, and he quickly concealed the gun in his pocket. The taxi door opened to let out three passengers. Ashley ran to the front door of the cab, jumped in the front seat, and slammed the door closed. She tried to catch her breath.

"Please take me to the Bethlehem Inn! Quickly! That man is trying to kill me!"

The car sped away, tires squealing, and Ashley broke into tears. The beginning of her trip of a lifetime, and someone was trying to kill or kidnap her!


The short ride to the hotel took three minutes. She paid the driver and fell into a lobby chair, still breathing deeply. She didn't want to panic in front of her teammates. Should she call the police? Should she tell Jim Swain? It might jeopardize the team's schedule if she should be delayed for questioning.

Could it be that the man wanted to rob her and didn't understand English? Would he have had a partner in a car drive up to kidnap her for ransom, rape, or murder? Did she wander too far off the beaten track for safety? Did he intend to kill her in the open on that side street? Why? No one knew her here. Who would do such a thing?

Ashley calmed herself. She wouldn't tell anyone of her experience.

It would frighten them. Ruin their trip. She would not let the experience spoil hers either, this visit of a lifetime. She'd go to the police.
No, she had no evidence and they'd think she was some frightened
woman tourist imagining trouble. She wished Najid were here. He
would know what to do. He'd protect her. He always seemed so calm
and thoughtful. She'd stuff her fears for now and not dwell on the
incident. But she would be more careful in the future and not go
out alone.

# Chapter 28

Ashley felt safe in the hotel lobby with others around. The large windows provided lots of light and she could see anyone coming. Despite the danger, she wanted so much to go to Gamal's group at the college after dinner. If only she had an escort ... then she opened her eyes and saw Jim Swain walking in the lobby.

She ran to catch Jim. "I had a wonderful chance meeting today with a student from the Bible College. He invited me to join them at their English Club meeting tonight, as a native English speaker. I'd love to go, but it might get a bit late, and I need someone to go with me. Would you be interested? It would be a chance to meet local students who are Christians. It's at eight."

"Great idea, Ashley. I'd be delighted to go. I had hoped for a cultural experience like that. We could walk over while it's still light and take a taxi back. I know where the college is. Let's meet right after dinner here."

Ashley could hardly wait. She ambled to the bar to get a Fanta and noticed a young woman with a Muslim head covering, studying. Ashley didn't want to be alone and needed someone to talk to besides her fellow tourists. She walked to a chair opposite her and sat down, enjoying her drink. She tried to relax. The girl looked up from her notebook with a smile that lit up her beautiful face.

"You look American. Did you just arrive with a group?" She spoke English well with a charming accent.

Ashley noticed a Bible among her books. "How could you guess? But you're right. There must be something about Americans. Maybe the way we walk."

The girl laughed. "My name is Fatima. What is yours?"

"I'm Ashley. And I'm very curious."

"I don't know 'curious.' What does it mean?"

"It means I'd like to ask a question."

"So, ask it."

"You are wearing a Muslim head covering and yet I see a Bible with you. I don't understand."

Fatima smiled. "I'm a student at the Bible College. I'm studying while waiting for a ride home."

"So, are you a Christian?"

"No. But I'm a follower of Jesus."

"But you look Muslim."

"I am. I grew up Muslim. My family is Muslim. I first learned of Jesus in the Qu'ran. But I began to follow him when I learned about him in the Injil ... ah, the New Testament. And in it didn't he say to follow him? He never talked about becoming a 'Christian.' That's a different culture. My culture is Muslim."

Ashley frowned and shook her head. She had never heard anything like that.

Fatima continued. "So we stay inside our own culture and talk about the love of Jesus with our friends and families in a natural way."

"Do your parents approve of your going to the Bible College?"

"Oh yes. They see how I have changed. And the college has a good reputation for giving us a good education in Bethlehem."

"That's wonderful, Fatima."

An old Fiat pulled up to the hotel entrance. "I have to go home now," Fatima said. "But we have an English Club at the college tonight at eight. Could you come? We like to have native English speakers to help us talk correctly."

Ashley laughed. "Gamal already invited me. My friend Jim is coming with me, and I am absolutely delighted to come tonight."

Ashley and Jim looked for the students as they walked in the entryway of the college with its tall ceiling. Fatima appeared and, after introductions, she led them past the library with its glass doors and into a classroom. A beautiful girl, Ashley noticed her shining, long black hair, uncovered by a headscarf. Gamal rose to greet them as did the other ten students, who shook hands with Jim and Ashley. Fatima brought out a tray of dates and olives with flat bread to go with their tea.

Gamal smiled and wanted to know about Jim and his work in America. Jim mentioned that he, as a pastor, cared about people. An eager student, Majid sat on the edge of his chair, waiting to ask a question.

"How do you work with Muslims in America?"

Jim looked surprised. "I guess I don't since I don't know any."

"Oh. We live and work with Muslim people every day and live in peace together. In Israel and the West Bank, eighty percent or more of the people are Islamic. We don't have any problem with them because we're Christians. We both suffer from the military occupation and it draws us together. We become friends."

Ashley couldn't contain her curiosity any longer. "Fatima, I notice you are not wearing your headscarf here. Why not?"

"It's not needed in here, Ashley. I wear it outside for modesty in public. That is important in our Muslim culture. The hijab stands for modesty. I am still a Muslim in my culture. In my faith, I love Jesus. The two are different. I have not taken on the Christian culture of the West as that would terribly upset my family and tear us apart. So I don't embarrass my father by going out without the scarf. My parents ask what I am learning here. I tell them about Jesus. Remember, he was born here."

Jim looked stunned. "So are you are still a Muslim?"

"In my culture, yes," Fatima smiled. "'Muslim' means to submit. So I submit to my heavenly Father and to my earthly one. It pleases both, I think. Didn't Saint Paul become all things to all men? He kept being a cultural Jew all his life, going into synagogues, entering the temple, and taking a Jewish vow at the end, right near here in Jerusalem."

Jim shook his head and laughed, turning to Ashley. "Fatima just scrambled my whole theology."

"What do you mean, 'scrambled'?" Fatima asked. "I thought that's what you Americans do to eggs."

Back in the hotel lobby, Jim and Ashley sank into the overstuffed chairs. Jim shook his head with a chuckle. "It could have gone on all night. We had so many questions. My brain is loaded with still more."

"I found Majid's story sad," Ashley said. "He and his parents, like so many of the students and their families without work, live in these tiny apartments referred to as 'refugee camps.' I didn't realize what all these shabby buildings really represent, some with holes in them from the war."

"Yeah, he called it 'Ayda camp.' Majid said it's one of three camps here in Bethlehem. And Majid's father is an unemployed engineer, Ashley. He explained it while you chatted with the girls. He can't get into Jerusalem to his former company. They have exhausted their savings and live on what they can sell in the open markets. Majid, fortunately, is on a scholarship."

"Did you realize, Jim, that one of the girls we met is Jewish?"

"Really?"

"Yes, she lives in that beautiful settlement off to the east, high on the hill overlooking Bethlehem. It has a wall around it and the highway below that you can see from the street."

"How does a Jewish girl happen to come to the Bible College?"

"She met Fatima somehow."

"Her parents let her come?"

"Apparently they don't mind. Her father's a wealthy businessman in Jerusalem, and her mother is a busy socialite. So they're too busy to object. They're not 'observant Jews.' Besides, Adala says they have a Palestinian nanny who really takes care of them. Their gardener drives her to the college every day."

Ashley checked the time—midnight. "I'm not even sleepy. Too revved up I guess."

"We'll be having breakfast around eight. Then the team will have time to explore Bethlehem and visit the college. It would be good for them to meet some of the staff and students. We'll leave on the bus after lunch. It's only about one hundred miles to Galilee."

"I won't be at breakfast, Jim. Fatima invited me to meet her parents at nine, for breakfast. But I'll check out early and meet you all here at least right after lunch."

# Chapter 29

Ashley watched the small Fiat drive up to the hotel with a distinguished looking gray-haired gentleman at the wheel. Fatima jumped out, her head covered with a lovely red-flowered hijab. Ashley realized she should have one ready to throw over her head, particularly when visiting a church or a mosque. Fatima introduced Ashley to her father, Saleh bin Tariq.

He bowed, but didn't extend his hand. Ashley understood that Muslim men would not touch a woman outside the family.

"Asalam alekum," he said, smiling.

Fatima explained: "That means 'Peace, to you.' You can address him as Saleh. That's his name. The 'bin Tariq' means son of Tariq, my grandfather. I can translate for you."

"Asalam alekum, Saleh. Tell him I am delighted to meet the father of such a lovely daughter."

Fatima blushed and laughed. She said something more than that to her father in Arabic, and he laughed. "He says I kept you up too late last night."

"Well, it was great fun. I enjoyed the Church of the Nativity earlier in the day. But you know what I loved even more?"

Fatima repeated Ashley's question to her father.

"I loved being with you students. You are the hope of your people of Bethlehem and the West Bank. I am so excited about what I am learning. I couldn't sleep much last night trying to remember what you all shared with us about reconciliation."

Fatima placed her hand over her heart, while translating for him. Then her father spoke. "He wants to know what you do in America."

Ashley explained her role at the University of Washington, and then asked about Saleh.

"He manages a company here that distributes food and sells cooking ware. I think that's the right English word," Fatima explained. "He used to manage a large import-export company in Jerusalem, but since 2002, he is not allowed into the city."

Saleh swung into a parking area on the broken-up asphalt road, passing a large pile of stones and broken pieces of concrete blocks.

Ashley furrowed her brow and pointed to the rubble. "What is that, Fatima?"

"That used to be our neighbor's house. Israeli soldiers demolished it."

"Why."

"We never know. Another family a few hundred meters from here have a demolition order on their home. They are trying to fight that in court. But it's expensive, and they usually destroy the house anyway."

"I'd never heard of such a thing, Fatima! What gives them the right to do that?"

"We don't know. Israelis are not allowed to come to the West Bank in Area A, except for the settlers on their own highways. But soldiers come, every night, and sometimes during the day. They drag young men out of their houses and take them to prison."

Saleh cleared his throat as he stopped the car, getting out to open the car door for Ashley. Fatima's mother opened the door and smiled broadly. She wore a lovely hijab of tan and purple, her head covered with the scarf extending under her chin. Two younger sisters, bareheaded, dressed in jeans and looked like typical pre-teens. Fatima presided over introductions with the mother and daughters.

They sat on plain chairs around a low table. The room contained a low sofa and a bookcase. Windows opened on the two outside walls, both covered with a steel grate. Her mother spoke to the young girls, and they disappeared into the kitchen bringing back platters loaded with fruits and breads of a wide variety. Ashley had not tried pomegranates. Naan and hummus, dates and figs followed, along with tea. Then the youngest daughter brought out a "dallah," an Arabic coffee pot steaming hot. The coffee was rich and strong.

Fatima chuckled. "We don't usually drink coffee, but we made it just for you. We have water again."

"What do you mean 'again'?"

"Oh that. We get used to it. The Israelis turn off the water, sometimes for weeks at a time. We don't know when it will happen, so we store water. But it's hard to wash the clothes."

"Why would they do that?"

"We don't know that either. My friend in the settlement on the hill up there tells me they have plenty of water for their swimming pools."

"It's water from here, from the Palestinian territory?"

"Yes. We have underground water, but Israel takes eighty percent of it. It's part of the 'Nakba.' Do you understand that term?"

"Gamal explained that as 'catastrophe,' right?"

"Right. Maybe it's to punish us or just make our lives difficult. We don't know."

The conversation grew animated. Ashley wanted to know how they survived the war in 2002. Fatima translated for the family. The younger girls understood more English than they spoke. Being Saturday, they had no school. Fatima's mother spoke no English, and her father seemed to understand some, but spoke only Arabic. But they each talked excitedly and all at once, apparently to be sure to get in their account of the war into Fatima's summary.

"Our young men threw stones at Israeli tanks that moved into Bethlehem, with IDF soldiers behind them."

"IDF?"

"Israeli Defense Forces," Fatima explained. "There had been several incidents of suicide bombings in Israel by radical Muslim terrorists. Prime Minister Sharon forced his way up the Temple Mount with many soldiers, to the Dome of the Rock, insulting Islam. Those incidents, along with failure of the Oslo peace talks, began Palestinian resistance, mostly throwing rocks at soldiers and tanks. This second intifada began in Jerusalem.

"The riots spread. Israeli troops invaded Bethlehem and other West Bank towns. Our people had almost no weapons. When soldiers came into Bethlehem, our young men threw rocks to try to stop them. They turned off everything in Bethlehem. For weeks we had no water, no electricity. With the curfew lasting for forty-two days, we couldn't get out for propane or food."

Ashley sipped her Arabic coffee, surprised it tasted so good.

Fatima continued as the family all contributed their accounts to her. "The helicopter gunships came first, then the tanks with big guns. Bulldozers blocked the road to Jerusalem at Rachel's Tomb. The soldiers invaded homes to imprison 'terrorists.' My father fled. He ran with crowds of men to Manger Square, fearing death. They escaped into the Church of the Nativity, and the Israelis then shelled the square and even the shrine itself. They said the men must be terrorists. They seemed to use that term  for most Muslims."

"So what happened?" Ashley asked as she scooped out another spoonful of the colorful red pomegranate seeds.

"We had some fighters with guns. Most of them died. Others threw stones and were shot. Israeli snipers shot anyone walking out on the street. Several priests and nuns died from bullets fired into churches. Bethlehem was surrounded. Israeli soldiers blocked ambulances from getting to the wounded, even women and children."

Ashley had never even heard of this war before Marie had mentioned it. "How long did this last, Fatima?"

"Father survived somehow in the church for over one hundred twenty days. They killed some of the men. The Israelis finally deported several of the men they called terrorists to Cyprus or elsewhere. Others were released.  We didn't dare go out for many days. We lost count how many.  Then they built the wall and our people lost their jobs in Jerusalem. It separates us from Israel, but also from each other in many places."

The family kept urging Ashley to eat. She didn't fear missing lunch at the hotel but realized she needed to get back in time for the bus trip to Galilee. Her head swam with impressions of life in

Bethlehem. She tried to answer their questions about her life in Oklahoma—for them a world away. She remembered the words again: "Oh little town of Bethlehem, how still we see thee lie." Not anymore.

Fatima's father presented Ashley with a carved wooden replica of the Church of the Nativity and drove her back to the hotel. She wished she had brought a gift for the family. He took her on a short tour with Fatima explaining the sights. Just prior to a checkpoint with an Israeli armed soldier blocking the way, Saleh turned off to a back road, bumpy and with twists and turns that made the journey interesting for Ashley.

Fatima apologized. "We are not allowed to drive on the highways reserved for Israelis."

After saying goodbye at the hotel, Ashley stopped in the lobby, staring blankly, shaking her head, having no idea how to put what she had just learned into the context of her belief system.

# Chapter 30

On the small bus traveling north to Galilee and its largest city, Nazareth, Ashley leaned her head back and tried to sleep, but couldn't. She opened her eyes at a checkpoint, re-entering Israel from the West Bank. The green countryside of hills and valleys with farms of olive groves and various citrus trees flew by out the window. She turned to Marie.

"My brain won't slow down. I've had so many experiences in Bethlehem that I didn't expect. They don't fit with the mindset I've always had."

"What doesn't fit, Ashley?"

"Well, for example, Palestinians and Muslims as our enemies." She paused. She had forgotten momentarily about her experiences on Herodian and at the wall. "I met a beautiful student, Marie. She and others follow Jesus without leaving their Muslim culture."

"That sounds pretty controversial. I think many converts close the door to their past when they become Christians."

"I suppose," Ashley said. "But Fatima enjoys such a great relationship with her Muslim family. She wears the hijab when out and about to not offend her parents. She doesn't take on the culture of 'Western

Christianity." The family expressed such hospitality, such gentleness, such kindness."

"What else doesn't fit your usual thinking?"

Ashley paused and shook her head, gazing out the front window of the bus. "Demolitions of houses. No water for weeks. Curfews. Arresting young men. Soldiers shooting civilians."

"I remember your saying you had not heard about Israel's incursion to find terrorists in 2002."

"No, I hadn't, Marie, and certainly not from the Palestinian point of view. I've only read and heard of 'Palestinian terrorists,' rockets that Israel's Arab enemies shoot from Lebanon and Gaza, suicide bombers of a decade ago. They claim they built the wall to stop them. Perhaps, but it seems to be incomplete. And now Palestinians promote non-violent resistance to the military occupation. What really stopped the bombers from Gaza?"

Ashley paused to ponder and visualize the city they had just left. She felt sickened by the contrast between the partially destroyed buildings they called refugee camps and the spectacular Israeli settlements on the top of the hills. And roads on the Palestinian land reserved for the exclusive use of Israelis. And demolitions and curfews. "So much is new to me. We never hear any of this in our church ... or in our news media for that matter."

"You have a lot to process, Ashley."

"I do. Do you suppose we'll have a chance to hear what the Israelis think of all this? I hope we can make some Jewish friends and learn what they are thinking."

# Chapter 31

Ashley used her cell phone with the new SIM card for Israel to call Najid's family from the Nazareth Tourist Hotel.

"Hallo," a man's voice answered.

"Hello, this is Ashley Wells, Najid's friend—"

"Ah! Mo-ment." Then Ashley heard a shout: "Sami!"

After a few seconds and sounds of footsteps, a male voice came on the line.

"Hello. This is Sami. Welcome, Ashley." He spoke just like Najid and even sounded like him. "Where are you?"

"I'm at the Nazareth Tourist Hotel. It's so good to hear your voice. You are Najid's brother, right?"

"Yes, he's number one; I'm number two. My English used to be better than his, but not anymore. Can you come visit us?"

"I'd love to, Sami. Maybe tomorrow. Najid said he arranged for you to come pick me up. Is that correct?"

"That's right, Ashley. We have a car and I will come and pick you up after church tomorrow. How about at eleven? We have early morning mass."

Ashley joined the team in a room off the lobby. The planning discussion faded in and out of her head as she thought of connecting with Najid's family. She did hear a bit about Tiberius and Capernaum on the Sea of Galilee, and the mountain where Jesus preached his famous sermon. She chatted with Marie about seeing some of the sites. "I'll miss visiting some of them, but it will be worth it. I'm not sure how long I should stay in Najid's home. They didn't say. I'll have to play it by ear." She thought how good it would be to be safe in a home of friends, in a totally different area of the Holy Land, far from any crazies.

⚬

Ashley watched the red Ford Pinto station wagon pull to a stop in front of the hotel. It was just like her grandfather's 1980 Pinto, which collected rust behind the barn at home. Najid's father, behind the wheel, smiled as Sami jumped out to greet Ashley and grab her carry-on bag.

"This is my father, Rafiq." Ashley nodded and smiled. She climbed in the back while Najid's father said slowly, "Welcome. How are you?" She realized he probably spoke most of the English he knew. He beamed.

She used about all of the Arabic she knew. "Asalam alekum."

"I'll be your translator," Sami offered as he slid into the front passenger seat.

They passed a number of shops and apartment buildings on the narrow streets of Nazareth as they drove. Ashley noted the light tan buildings with houses and apartments extending up a large hill. "You look and sound very much like Najid, Sami. Have you been in touch with him? And how is your family?"

"We are well. Yes, we talked with Najid on Skype early this morning and told him you will come today. He said the tea at school doesn't taste as good without you. I didn't understand what he meant."

Ashley smiled. They began passing orchards out of the city. "What are those trees?" They were not large, but had thick trunks, with heavy foliage of small gray-green leaves. They looked old.

"Those are olive trees. Some hundreds of years old. We grow mostly olives."

Ashley smiled. She remembered singing *Wind Through the Olive Trees* as a child at Christmas time, but they were around little Bethlehem. "Sami, say your father's name again so I get it right. And I don't know your mother's name."

"His name is Rafiq. He understands a bit of English."

Rafiq smiled and looked at Ashley in the rearview mirror.

"Tell him that he smiles just like Najid."

Sami laughed and translated for Rafiq. "And my mother's name is Farah."

"Oh I like that name. I can hardly wait to meet her. She has done such a good job in raising Najid. And I understand you have other brothers and two sisters."

"Yes, three younger brothers, Talib, Waleed, and Hassan. My sisters are Hana' and Jamilah."

Rafiq peppered Ashley with questions about Najid and his life in America and about Ashley and her family in Oklahoma. He wanted to know about her studies, and then approached the bombing with hesitation.

"We were so sorry to hear about your injury and operation. But you look fine now. Have they caught the terrorist who did the bombing?"

"Thank you, Rafiq. No, he must be very clever to escape the police net they say covers the entire United States ... and the world. We haven't kept terrorists out."

"We haven't either," Rafiq said. He explained first Jewish terrorism: "Menachim Begin bombing the King David Hotel, killing ninety British soldiers. Then Israeli soldiers terrorized over five hundred Palestinian villages, even now in East Jerusalem. And now Palestinians, crazy guys mostly from Gaza, fire an occasional rocket. We believe in nonviolent resistance to the Israeli occupation of the West Bank. We have many friends here in Israel—Jews, Muslims, Druze. It doesn't matter. There is room for all religious groups. Not one exclusively. We are Christians, a minority, and just want to live in peace."

Ashley smiled. Who doesn't want to live in peace? She tried to speak slowly so Rafiq could understand directly. "I would love to hear your family story. And I want to learn more about your church. Najid tells me it is very old. But he wouldn't tell me what happened to cause you to leave your home of many generations. I understand your home and orchards were beautiful."

"Yes," Rafiq replied, "they were. I will tell you what you want to know, Ashley, after some tea."

The house seemed too small to contain the energy of so many children. The living room had only a table set up with several chairs and benches on a small colorful rug. A door led to a hall leading to bath and bedrooms. The smell of naan, the delicious flat bread, wafted in from the kitchen. Through that door, Ashley met Farah and the two girls. Sami introduced everyone. He called the boys in from their soccer game. The boys nodded to Ashley and tried out their English, while Hana' and Jamilah smiled shyly and wide-eyed, watching Ashley's every move.

Ashley inquired about Farah. She listened as the soft-spoken woman shared how her family had fled their home to Jordan in 1948 but were not welcome there. The term "dirty Palestinians," used even by fellow Arabs, revealed the attitudes that made life difficult. "So we lived in a refugee camp provided by UNRWA, the United Nations Relief and Works Agency, in southern Lebanon for many years. We survived the bloody Shatila massacre of 1982 by Phalangists, aided by Israeli soldiers."

Farah paused with a wistful shake of her head. "Now we just want our children to have a normal life and a good education. We'd like to have freedom. Particularly for our relatives and friends in the West Bank. They live one hour's drive from the ocean but have never seen it."

"Why not?"

"Because they are not allowed to. No Palestinians in the West Bank can travel into Israel."

The girls brought two plates of fruit, melons, grapes, and flat bread with hummus, insisting Ashley begin eating. "My father found a job near their home in Israel. We were allowed to return, but not to our home or farm. The Israeli government had sold our property to an immigrant family from Poland. They lived in town and didn't know how to farm. So my father worked as a laborer in the orchard we once owned. I met Rafiq, married, and now we are happy to have work near Genigar."

Throughout the meal the children tried out a few English words, encouraged by Ashley, who asked them about their classes at school. They tried to answer in English and then would look to Sami for translation. They whispered to Sami in Arabic asking if most women in America were beautiful. He laughed as he translated when Ashley blushed. Hana wanted to know what it was like for a girl to grow up in America and whether girls actually wore jeans to school. Ashley nodded, having seen pictures of the girls in their school uniforms.

As the meal concluded, the younger boys left and the girls helped Farah clean up. Ashley's pent-up desire to hear the story Najid would never tell her, about his father's history, burst out. "Rafiq, tell me your story now."

# Chapter 32

Rafiq smiled and began. Ashley took detailed notes with Sami's translating, stopping Rafiq occasionally to ask questions to be sure she understood. That night she didn't fall asleep until she had written the entire story as accurately as possible:

*You must remember that my memories are those of a child, aided by what my parents told me.*

*In the quiet village of Irgit near the Lebanese border in Northern Israel, where we had lived for generations, olive orchards and fig groves provided a peaceful home for farmers like us and their families. We weren't rich, but our home was large and comfortable, five bedrooms. Our orchards surrounded the house, ten acres. So we had a comfortable life. We Christians lived with many others—Jews and other Arabs who were Muslims. We had no problems.*

*In 1948, my father heard rumors of soldiers coming to nearby towns and villages making the people leave their homes. The soldiers were from the new state of Israel. Trucks arrived in Irgit filled with soldiers who carried guns. My brothers and I looked at them with fear and fascination. We had never seen soldiers or guns before. Our parents told us to go into the house. Soon soldiers came to the door and our parents invited them in as guests. They told us they would stay for a while, and we fed them for several days. Other families did the same.*

*We had to sleep on the roof when the soldiers came. They took the bedrooms. One day Father had to go with the other men of the village to the town square, where an officer told them that there would be trouble soon and the safest thing would be for us to leave and camp out in the hills, just for a few days. Rumors flew around the village, but we had no choice, and left with our neighbors to camp out in our own orchard. Our soldier guests said they would take good care of our house. They would come to bring us back when it was safe. It rained and I remember being cold.*

*After many days with no word from the soldiers that it was safe to return, my father and other men did return to the village only to be met by armed soldiers who told them to get out. Our men protested, and the soldiers pointed their rifles, ready to shoot, and accused my father and others of being terrorists. Father returned to us in the orchard and said we would have to find other homes. We couldn't survive out in the open in the winter, which would be coming in a few months. So we walked with nothing but the clothes we had on for many days, trying to find a place to live. We found some villages that had been taken over by soldiers with few residents left. One nearly empty village had houses occupied only by elderly people who couldn't walk easily. The soldiers had let them stay. We wintered with them, finding food where we could. But the soldiers came back and we had to leave.*

*Finally we headed across the border into Lebanon along with many other refugees. The United Nations had set up tents where we could stay, and provided food. As a child, I didn't understand what had happened to our home and land, only that we were in a neighboring country in a camp, surrounded by the people of the land who didn't want us there.*

*After many years my father and mother learned that many of our orchards had been sold by the Israeli government to foreign settlers from Europe. Some farms collected into what they called a 'kibbutz.'*

*Other immigrants settled in the towns and villages and didn't know how to farm the orchards, nor wanted to live in the countryside. So my father heard that they were hiring former local men to take care of the trees.*

*He returned. Our village had been destroyed, so he moved south to where he learned they looked for workers and landed in an area near Genigar, southwest of Nazareth. He applied for work and was hired to dress the olive trees, which he enjoyed. Finding a small house to rent, he sent for us. So we moved to where we are now.*

*Father had learned to take care of the few cars in the area and became a mechanic on the side. So he was able to scrape enough money together to buy the house we rented. The new owner of the orchard lived in a big house in Genigar and would come out to see how the trees were doing and talk with father.*

*We later acquired a small car, which father fixed up so it would run. Our family grew. I and my brothers and sisters didn't have the opportunity to go to school beyond the first few grades. Our parents were sad that they couldn't provide us an education. And of course, our happy life in Irgit had disappeared. My father and mother both died in their sixties. I think they died of a broken heart.*

*My siblings all left for other parts of the world: Lebanon, Jordan, Egypt, and Canada. I stayed, married, and had children, as you know. God has protected us. We have our Melkite Church and made many friends. Now we have some schools, and I was determined that Najid and our other children would have at least a high school education. So when I heard of a large high school in a nearby town, teaching all children—whether Jews, Christians, Muslim or Druze—I enrolled Najid and Sami. The younger ones will go there too. And now Sami is in the new university there. Of course Najid went on to university in Haifa, because he was such a good student.*

Rafiq stopped while Sami looked at him for more of the story. It grew quiet. Ashley started to put her notes away when Rafiq added that he had learned later that the Zionists had forced people out of more than five hundred Palestinian villages in 1948 alone. He didn't know how many since then. "That is why so many Palestinians have left the country."

"You haven't mentioned whether these villages were Christian or Muslim."

Rafiq answered softly. "Mixed, but mostly Muslim. It didn't matter. We have lived for centuries peacefully together with Jewish neighbors and many who are Muslim. We still do, although most of our Jewish friends live elsewhere now, some in new settlements in the West Bank where they have moved because the government is helping them."

# Chapter 33

Rafiq reminded Ashley of Najid—his mannerisms, the way he talked, and smiled. She wanted to ask them to Skype him in so she could both see him and share some of her adventures. But they had talked just that morning, and he would be sleeping in Seattle. So she picked up his picture on the bookcase and gazed at him. Her pulse quickened. She now understood why he seemed to be such an extraordinary man.

Only a few hours had passed since she left the hotel. Being Sunday afternoon, she confirmed with Sami that his parents would usually take a nap. Though a Muslim work day, Rafiq always took the day off for church and rest. On Friday, the Muslim day for attending the mosque, he worked. And on the Jewish Sabbath, he usually was busy either in the orchards or in his mechanic shop. So Ashley insisted they rest as usual.

She tried to digest the stories of Farah and Rafiq, but she needed time to think things through. Why had she never heard these stories at home?

"Do American girls play football, Ashley?" Sami wanted to know.

"Oh yes, but we call it soccer at home. I know we're different from the rest of the world. We have a different kind of 'football.' Most girls don't play that game. It's very rough."

"Would you like to play 'soccer' as you say, in the square? Girls are just starting to play it here."

"Let me get out of this dress and into some jeans, and I'll join you. Oh, would that be OK, to wear pants?"

"Sure, Ashley. You Americans can get away with wearing almost anything, or nothing." Sami chuckled at seeing Ashley's eyebrows shoot upward.

Minutes later, Talib and Hassan dribbled the ball toward the goal, passing it back and forth. Hassan broke for the goal to receive Talib's pass. But just before he could reach it, Ashley streaked out of the goalie's box, intercepted the pass, and flew toward the opposite goal, keeping the ball in front of her. Sami stayed wide, running with her. Talib and Hassan turned and tried to catch up with Ashley, but not before she passed the ball to Sami, who scored easily. She turned to the younger boys, breathless, but with a broad smile. The younger boys looked shocked and spoke in Arabic.

Sami laughed. "They can't believe you, Ashley. They've never seen a girl run so fast and pass so well."

Ashley loved soccer. It had been a long time since her high school team competed for the state championship. For the rest of the hour, the boys played at full speed. Ashley lacked the stamina of the past and couldn't keep up. Perhaps it was the accident and operation, but she did not want to make excuses. She and Sami lost the game five to four.

# Chapter 34

After dinner, Ashley learned that Rafiq and Sami had planned a visit the next day to family friends, Faisal and his wife, Almas.

"They live just an hour's drive away near a town called Zubuda in the West Bank," Sami explained. "Faisal needs some help caring for his olive trees and wants my father to come. You must come to meet our friends."

Ashley remembered her recent experiences in Bethlehem, both the bad and the good. She would be safe with Najid's father and Sami. It would be a chance to meet their friends and visit a farm.

"I'd love to come, Sami. But are you allowed to travel to the West Bank and return to Genigar here?"

"We can because we live here in Israel. But Faisal and Almas can't visit us."

"Why not, Sami? That seems strange."

"It's Israeli law. Palestinians living in the West Bank aren't allowed to enter Israel."

"Will we have any trouble crossing over or back? Maybe having me with you will complicate the situation."

"Yeah, Ashley, you're going to cause big trouble."

"I hope not!"

Sami chuckled. "No. They'll stop us at the checkpoint, but that's just the usual so they can get some excitement in their boring day. They don't see many blonde American ladies wanting to get into the West Bank. They'll probably wonder what you are doing here. It may be more difficult going through the wall later."

Sami didn't explain further, leaving Ashley puzzled. What did he mean by difficulty going "through the wall"? But he had gone into the kitchen, so she shrugged her shoulders and began clearing the table of dishes.

⁎

As they approached the northern border of the Palestinian territory, Ashley grew nervous. At the checkpoint leaving Israel, the border guards inspected all their passports, visas, and papers. They asked Ashley the purpose of her visit and noted from her passport that she had previously been in the West Bank at Bethlehem. Sami helped her understand what they wanted and translated the Hebrew interrogation.

"What group is she with? What is their political agenda? Why is she without her group now? When does she plan to return to Israel? Who is she going to visit? Why?"

The grilling lasted fifteen minutes. One soldier looking over his colleague's shoulder kept staring at Ashley. She felt uncomfortable, her voice beginning to tremble as she explained why she had come to the border. She began to stare back at him until he finally averted his gaze. Ashley sighed as they drove away. Sami and Rafiq seemed to take it all in stride and continued talking in Arabic as though this happened every day.

At the Palestinian guardhouse they were waved through after a cursory look at Ashley's passport.

Rafiq immediately turned off the smoothly paved highway to continue on narrow, winding back roads, which Rafiq seemed to know well. Ashley remembered the best highways in the West Bank were reserved for Israelis. She could see a checkpoint above them on the main highway, guarded by an army tank with armed soldiers who would have stopped them if they had continued on it.

Sami gestured toward them with a smirk. "In our democracy where everyone is equal, it just happens that some are more equal than others."

Finally, they arrived at the olive groves surrounding Zabuda. Ashley pointed to some spectacular white towers high on the hill above the town on the other side of the orchards, surrounded by a wall. She had a quizzical frown.

"Israeli settlements," Sami explained. "Remember, you're in the West Bank."

As they drove down a small road, a high concrete wall loomed ominously behind the bungalow. They wheeled into the driveway to meet Faisal and Almas, in their early fifties, a farm couple that reminded Ashley of Oklahomans.

After introductions, Rafiq spoke to them in Arabic, and then Faisal jumped into his old Ford Pinto, inviting the visitors to come right away. The car seats, covered with brown blankets with occasional rips, smelled dusty.

"Tea will have to wait," he explained with Sami's translation. "We'll be traveling to our olive orchard. It will take about thirty minutes even though it's only a few meters away, just across the wall. We have to drive to the checkpoint." He looked at his watch. "It's already eleven."

"Where do we go to get through the wall?" Ashley asked by Sami's translation as they drove down the dirt road.

"About fifteen kilometers north of here," Faisal replied.

"You have to travel thirty kilometers to get to your orchard? And then thirty back when it is just across the wall?!"

"We do now, Ashley. I used to walk across the road. Actually they built the road years ago, dividing the property. The house and trees used to be all on one piece of land. The road was no problem however. But the wall—"

"Why did they put the wall along the road dividing your farm?"

"I don't know why except, several years before they built it, they came in and put an Israeli settlement on the hill up there—those tall white buildings. They eventually needed a wall to separate us from the new European immigrants. To keep some of us 'terrorists' out."

"Who thought up that idea?" Ashley asked.

"It was Sharon's idea before he ever became Prime Minister of Israel. 'Take the high ground.'"

"Couldn't they put in an opening for farmers like you to get to their olive groves without having to drive around each day?"

"They could but they don't."

*There must be another side of this wall issue,* Ashley thought. *How would the Israelis explain it?* She hoped to make some Jewish friends so she could understand their thinking. It seemed so strange and unjust for Faisal. The wall separated the families from their own land, with Palestinians on both sides. It didn't follow the border between Israel and the West Bank. So how could it be for "security?"

Faisal slowed as he neared the checkpoint. An Israeli soldier with a rifle approached. Ashley raised her smartphone and took a quick picture through the front windshield. The guard, who looked like a teenager, took the paperwork and passports of each person in the car and handed them to another soldier, a young woman, who took them into the small office and sat down at a computer. Several minutes passed. She came out and spoke to Rafiq.

"She wants everyone out of the car," Sami reported.

"Stand here," she ordered. Ashley stood with the men. The first soldier frisked the two older men. They ushered Ashley inside the office where the female soldier patted her down and inspected her purse. She took Ashley's cell phone and placed it in a drawer in her desk.

"Why are you taking that?"

The soldier gave no answer and walked out.

Ashley followed her, teeth clenched and trembling inside. She spoke to Sami. "Would you ask her in Hebrew to return my phone?"

Sami did, but received no reply or recognition. Instead the male soldier said something to Sami, who angrily protested in Hebrew. The soldier raised his rifle and pointed it at Sami. He forced Sami inside the guardhouse.

Ashley climbed back into the car, shaking, and her face white. "Why ... what is going on?" Her teeth chattered. "Why did they take Sami away? Is this what you go through every day?"

Faisal understood some English. "No. They know." He pointed to himself. Ashley understood that they knew him from his frequent trips to the farm.

They sat silently in the car, waiting. Ashley wondered what Sami did to cause them to take him away. *Why did they take him into the building?* Twenty minutes passed with no sign of Sami.

A car appeared from behind the guardhouse with darkened windows and drove on through the checkpoint. They've taken Sami away! She felt faint. *Why wasn't Rafiq doing something? She wanted to ask them, but needed Sami to translate. Maybe it had something to do with her cell phone and taking the picture as they had approached. She shouldn't have come. She must have caused it. Sami had just defended her.* Ashley breathed a silent prayer for him.

After thirty minutes, Sami appeared with teeth clenched and eyes narrowed. His fists were white-knuckled and he looked like he was ready to explode. "They treat you like an animal!" He spit out the words through clenched teeth.

"What did they do, Sami?" Ashley asked with a grimace, raising her hands.

He took a deep breath and exhaled loudly, cheeks puffed out in anger. "They took me into a back room. They made me take off my clothes, including underwear, and then walked out the door into the office with all my stuff. I could see through the crack in the door. The female soldier joined the guy in the office, where they went through all my clothes and my wallet. They left me standing naked all that time in daylight with open windows."

Ashley stared at the soldiers through the car windows, and then looked at Sami. It seemed so hard, so inhumane. She shook her head. "How can they treat you like that? ... What should I do, Sami? They have my cell phone."

Sami asked Faisal, and after a short conversation in Arabic, he turned to Ashley. "He says there is no way now, but we should get it back on our return trip."

Ashley watched as Faisal and Rafiq strolled into the orchard, gazing up at the olive trees as they discussed something. She and Sami meandered down a small road that looked like a tractor path. He seemed distracted, jaw jutting forward, silent. Not the usual light-hearted and talkative Sami. They found an old wooden shed with open cracks between the unpainted wall boards and a sagging tin roof. Through an open door, an ancient tractor with metal treads appeared rusted. It smelled of oil and old machinery. Ashley discovered a faucet on the shed wall over a stained sink with dirt in it. She tried to wash her hands, but no water came out. They walked to a nearby bank and sat down. Ashley waited quietly for Sami to open up and share his feelings. She knew he needed to vent some of his anger.

"I've been humiliated before by soldiers, and always obeyed as a schoolboy. But this was different."

He pounded his fist into his other hand. "Ashley, we are not 'terrorists.'" Sami's voice cracked. "We are not 'dirty Palestinians.' We are people just like they are."

Ashley fought tears, swallowing several times, and looked away. She sighed and picked up a small stone, throwing it hard against the shed wall.

"Why?" Sami continued. "What have we done to deserve this treatment? Can you understand why some of our young people who have no jobs pick up stones to fight back?"

Ashley remained silent, shaking her head. A tear trickled down her cheek. She herself had now experienced a tiny bit of what it was like to be a Palestinian. These daily occurrences never made the papers at home.

They walked slowly back down the two-rut road with weeds growing in its center, silently, not paying attention to the cheerful songs of birds. Rafiq and Faisal appeared out of the orchard. Ashley looked at the two men, who obviously enjoyed each other's company and smiled. She spoke, hoping Sami would translate.

"You have a lovely grove of fruit trees, Faisal. Do you water them often?"

"No, we don't. I used to, when they were younger. But now we don't have much water. It's turned off most of the time. Our friends on the hill up there behind their wall use about eighty percent of it—some for their swimming pools."

They all returned silently to the car. Rafiq drove on the return trip. The soldier with the rifle appeared to stop them and spoke to Rafiq, who shut off the engine of the car. Ashley could see through the window the woman soldier who had taken her smartphone, sitting at her desk. Faisal referred to her as a "Sabra."

"Sabra?"

"It means a person born in Israel, not an immigrant," Sami explained.

She held a cell phone to her ear. *It must be an interesting conversation*, Ashley concluded, as they waited and waited. She wondered whether it was her phone. The soldier with the rifle stood in front of the car. The Sabra looked at the car but continued her conversation.

Sami scowled and looked at his watch. He started to open the door, and Rafiq shouted at him. Ashley noted the soldier had pointed his rifle directly at the door as Sami opened it. Sami closed the door. He turned red in the face and punched the door. He said something in Arabic, words that needed no translation. Another five minutes passed, fifteen minutes altogether since they stopped.

"Do you usually have to wait like this on the return trip, Faisal?" Ashley said to distract Sami with translation duties before he exploded.

"Sometimes they seem to enjoy having you wait, but usually only five minutes driving home. They know we are worried about your cell phone," Faisal replied, turning to the backseat. "So she's probably in there talking to her boyfriend and watching us sit here getting angry. The trouble is that we can never do anything about it. There's no one to complain to."

"I did take that picture of the checkpoint with the soldier walking toward us with his rifle. Maybe that has something to do with our waiting."

"Oh!" Faisal laughed when Sami finished his translation. "They don't like pictures. That explains the long wait."

"What will they do to me for punishment, Sami? I shouldn't have taken the picture. I feel terrible causing all the trouble."

"Don't worry, Ashley. I'll go to jail with you and rip up the whole place," Sami sneered, "No, you'll be OK. Don't worry about it. We're just getting our punishment by waiting."

Finally the Sabra appeared, walking slowly, and handed Ashley's phone to Rafiq through the driver-side window. She said nothing and walked away. The soldier with the rifle stepped aside. Rafiq nodded to him and drove away.

Ashley turned on her cell phone to check her pictures. The last one was gone. She showed Sami the now final picture. There he stood with his little brothers, Talib and Hassan, the victorious football team. He smiled ... at last.

# Chapter 35

The trip back to Genigar passed quickly except for a short stop at the Israeli border. Almas had dinner ready, rice pilaf with a variety of fruits, olives, and figs. Rafiq explained to her why the trip took so long. She smiled at Ashley, who wished she could communicate directly her appreciation for the dinner and her apologies for causing the delay.

After dinner, Farah spoke excitedly about Nazareth and the Basilica of Annunciation. "And you must go to the Synagogue Church. It's the site of the ancient synagogue where Jesus preached as a young man and they tried to kill him."

Ashley reached Jim by telephone at the hotel in Nazareth. The tour bus would leave at nine on Tuesday morning. "I'll try to be there before then, but it depends on Najid's brother Sami driving me on his way to college. If I'm not there, please go without me, and I'll hang out at the hotel and stroll around the old city. I'll stay close to other tourists."

"We'll wait until ten minutes after nine," Jim replied, "and if you're not here, we take off for Capernaum on the Sea of Galilee. If so, don't go too far alone, and stay in touch. Take care."

Sami needed to get back to classes, and Rafiq to work, so with an early breakfast finished, Ashley said her goodbyes and thanked everyone. *Eight-thirty, plenty of time to get to the hotel to catch up with my friends from Seattle.* Sami soon threaded the Pinto through the narrow streets of Nazareth when they heard a loud bang and a repeating thump.

"Oh, oh. A tire!"

"Do you have a spare tire, Sami?"

"Yes, but not a good one. And I've never had to use it."

She made a quick call to Jim. "We may not make it in time, so please go ahead with your trip. I'll be careful. Have a great one."

With Ashley's help, Sami found the jack and attempted to raise the right rear of the car. It fell off the jack. They tried again. Sami struggled to loosen the lug screws, then the spare tire needed air. Sami found a hand pump in the car and slowly filled the tire.

Ashley gave Sami a hug and wiped away a tear. She realized that she might never see him again, and stood in front of the small hotel watching him drive off.

Walid in dark glasses looked like any resident of Nazareth among the half of the population that followed Islam. He stepped into the narrow street and strolled to a small grove of trees. The old city of Nazareth buzzed with the sounds of tourists and honking taxis. He would be both hidden and able to hear Umar. He speed dialed his friend.

"Asalam alekum, Umar," he spoke in hushed Arabic.

"Asalam alekum. Any good fortune?"

"No. Are you sure she's not in the hotel?"

"Yes. I've been in the car here for hours now," Umar said. "I know she didn't get on any tour-group bus this morning. I have her picture in front of me and saw no one that looks like her approaching any bus. So I waited and saw her come by car to the hotel after the buses left. An hour later she walked out of the hotel and up toward the old city along with other tourists. Pretty blonde—fit her description in every way and matched her picture. She walked up toward the basilica two hours ago as I told you. You didn't see her come out?"

"No, but there is more than one door, so either I missed her or she's still in there."

"That seems unlikely. There's not that much to see."

"I've checked the other churches tourists usually visit and have not seen her anywhere."

"Well, keep looking, Walid. We've got to find her. We missed twice in Bethlehem and can't fail now. The boss will be very upset if we have to follow her to Jerusalem. There's a lot of money riding on this."

After her shower, Ashley had picked up a walking guide to Nazareth and strolled along with a group of tourists uphill to the old city, passing many shops along the way. She wanted to visit the Grotto of Annunciation, Mary's family home. Descending the stairs in the basilica, she reached the grotto and the few remaining stones presumably of Mary's childhood residence. Without the crowds as in Bethlehem, Ashley could ponder the young teenager encountering a frightening angel who told her she would be the mother of the Messiah.

Ashley ambled down the hill and through shops looking for small gifts she could bring home to friends. She would find a small restaurant for lunch. The tourists increased in number, and she mixed freely with them, overhearing some of their remarks about the best places to go for gifts. Most of the shoppers were women and she lost any concern about being alone as she stayed in the crowd.

# Chapter 36

Walid continued walking the streets to no avail and then started looking in the shops. As he rounded the corner of a small narrow street, he almost ran into a young woman carrying a shopping bag, peering into an open stall displaying linens. She did not seem to see him as he jumped to the side to avoid a collision. She shouted "Sorry!" over her shoulder without looking back and moved on. Tourists crowded around that particular shop, so he couldn't see her well as she walked away, but he had glimpsed her face momentarily. His jaw dropped as he fished out Ashley's picture from his pocket near the switchblade knife. "That's her!" he whispered excitedly to himself. "I'm sure of it."

Walid wheeled around, turned the corner again in the opposite direction, and sped up to find her. She seemed to have disappeared as he walked fast to catch up. He should be seeing her. He slowed his pace, turned back to gaze in several shops, and finally saw her reaching for some small paintings. She faced the back of the shop and spoke to the single salesperson, a man.

Walid moved across the street to stand in front of a small restaurant so he could watch from a safe distance. Ashley came out after several minutes, stood on the side of the narrow street, turned her head in both directions, and then looked across the road. Quickly, Walid spun and strode away for a short distance, hoping she hadn't seen him. When he looked back, Ashley had crossed the street almost to where he had waited, and entered the restaurant. Walid pulled out his cell phone.

"Umar," he whispered into it. "I've found her. She's in a restaurant now."

"Are you sure it's her?"

"Yes, I almost bumped into her. I checked the picture. It's definitely her, and she spoke a word of English I didn't recognize."

"Did she see you?"

"No."

"At anytime?"

"I'm quite sure she hasn't seen me."

"Good. What is your plan?"

"I'll follow her at a distance. Maybe she'll go down the street that is dead-end—you know, the one that points right to the hotel, but you can't get through."

"You mean Daoud Street, with all the shops right up to the end?"

"Yes."

"How will you do it?"

"If she actually goes there, I can wait for her when she discovers she can't continue. Then if most tourists have left, I can move out quickly behind her. She will never know what happened. The long knife will do its work, quietly. It won't attract attention like the gun going off. I still have it in my pocket, but don't plan to use it this time. It will be quick, and I will be gone before anyone sees her on the street."

"Let's hope she turns into Daoud Street. Keep me informed, Walid."

Walid waited across the street from the restaurant. After an hour she still had not appeared. *She must have met someone.* He finally saw with dismay that he had guessed correctly. She and another Western woman walked back up the street the way Ashley had come. He followed from a distance as the two women talked, laughing and pointing at items in the open stalls of the market. They stopped at several of them and came out with small packages. The afternoon wore on, and Walid wondered, with the sun almost disappearing behind the nearby western hill, what Ashley would do. Near five, they stopped and Ashley pointed in the direction of the hotel. The other woman nodded, smiled, hugged her, and continued on, alone.

Ashley squinted up at the street sign indicating the cross street: Daoud Street, written in Arabic and English. She turned right, toward the hotel just as Walid had hoped, and strolled downhill, peeking in the shops but not stopping. Walid ducked into a leather shop and perused the belts for men. He could see around the corner of the shop that she continued, obviously expecting to approach the hotel. He lost her for a few seconds in the setting sun. He knew she would round the final bend and realize she'd have to turn back. His heart raced. Sweat ran down his face. He gritted his teeth and pulled a different cap from his pocket, one with a visor. His hands shook as he felt in his pocket for the knife. It had the fastest blade action of any knife he had ever seen and switched from a smooth bone handle to a long blade fifteen centimeters in length.

He pulled out her picture again. *Yes, it's her.* He walked by a shop she'd entered then headed down the street as though looking for some item. He rounded the bend in the road and darted behind a dumpster.

After several agonizing minutes, she finally appeared, rounding the turn in the street. He watched as she walked toward the cul-de-sac with a puzzled look on her face. Shielding her eyes with her hand, she squinted into the glare of the low western sun. She stopped. Empty. No shops. She turned around and started slowly back toward the bend of the street.

His heart pounded. He approached silently from behind. He and the woman were alone, finally. Right hand in his pocket, he partially encircled the knife handle with his fingers, his thumb finding the button that would switch the blade open in an instant. He would wrap her with his right arm and the knife, hold his left hand over her mouth to stifle a scream, and plunge the knife home over her heart. It would be quick, and he would duck through shops to another side street in seconds.

# Chapter 37

The characteristic Skype signal sounded as Rafiq checked the Internet for olive and fig prices. He answered Najid's call and saw him on the screen looking rumpled as if he had just arisen from bed.

They spoke in Arabic, and after the usual greetings, Rafiq smiled, but with a quizzical frown. "Why are you calling now? What is it, seven o'clock in the morning in Seattle? Are you well?"

"I am well, Father. But I couldn't sleep last night and want to find out how your visit went with Ashley. I tried to call yesterday but you weren't online."

"We took a trip to Zubuda to see Faisal and Almas and help with their orchard. Ashley went with us. We had a good time with her. They gave us the usual hassle at the wall."

"Did you like her, and did Mother like her?"

"Oh yes. She seems like a very nice young woman."

"She is a jewel. I wish I were there to show her around."

"She had a good time with the boys, even played football with them. Sami translated for us all, and we had no difficulty communicating."

"I'm worried about her, Father. I don't know why. But I couldn't sleep thinking about her, and that maybe she's in some kind of trouble."

"It's nothing I know about, Najid. Sami took her to the hotel in Nazareth this morning, and he's not back from school yet."

"What is it there, almost five in the afternoon?"

"Yes."

"I want to pray for Ashley. Will you pray with me?"

"Of course, Najid. God will hear, and so will I."

Rafiq saw Najid looking up to the ceiling on the screen, holding out his hands, palms up. "Our Father in heaven, maybe Ashley is in some kind of trouble right now and needs your protection. So please shield Ashley right now from whatever danger could be happening. I may be all wrong about this, but I'm just responding to what I think you have put in my heart. Amen."

"That was a beautiful prayer, Najid. I'll ask Sami to get Ashley on the telephone tonight to see how she is doing, and we'll let you know."

⁘

The wind blew as usual in Oklahoma City, rustling a tree branch scraping the house. It seemed eerie to Dorothy Wells. Frank had left early for work, and she read the paper over her coffee. She felt uneasy. She wondered about Ashley. *Maybe she is in some kind of trouble. She must be in Nazareth now, according to the schedule she e-mailed. There are lots of illnesses associated with travel overseas. Why pray when you can worry.* She chuckled. So she bowed and asked God to take care of her daughter, whatever might be happening. The prayer proved simple and direct. Dorothy possessed a simple faith that God would take care of Ashley, whatever the circumstances. After all, she was in the very hometown of Jesus, and surely nothing would happen to Ashley there. Dorothy returned to her paper in faith that her prayer had been heard.

⁘

Walid's target walked slowly back toward the curve in the street. Just as he anticipated success, crouching silently behind her, knife halfway out of his pocket, a woman shopkeeper with her hijab on dashed around the corner toward Ashley. She squinted into the setting sun, shielding its glare with her arm. "I can't see you well, but I just found the piece you were looking for!"

Walid, in shock, dropped the knife back into his pocket and ducked behind the dumpster. He waited. He could kill them both. *No, not a Palestinian.* He climbed the fence, ducked around the back of a building, and walked to another street. He shook his head in frustration. The chance to finish the job blown by a woman—a Palestinian. He sighed and called Umar.

"Did you do it?"

"No!" He cursed the women and the situation and his failure.

"What happened?"

Walid explained the sequence of events. "I couldn't do it right in front of the shopkeeper. I didn't want to kill her too. She's one of us. It became impossible. I have failed."

"She'll be coming back here, but I can't do it here either, Walid. For some reason, several soldiers and police still surround the front of the hotel. There might have been a threat of some kind. I did see a limousine with a flag on the front earlier. It must be some dignitary they're protecting."

"Do you think we'd have a chance tomorrow, Umar?"

"If our target gets on the bus with the others, no. We'd be finished. We have to find her by herself. They seem to practice safety in numbers ... We'll have to go all out in Jerusalem."

# Chapter 38

Ashley entered the hotel curious about the soldiers and police milling around. She wondered what had happened earlier. But her mind focused on happier things. She had been so pleased to meet a new friend in the restaurant; the woman had been such an enthusiastic shopper. Beverly and she had exchanged cell phone numbers after meeting over lunch. The day had gone perfectly, except for the flat tire and missing the bus. But she had enjoyed Nazareth and had lots of stories to tell about her adventures with Najid's family. Marie appeared in the lobby also bursting to tell Ashley about their trip in Upper Galilee.

The entire team hurried out to a recommended restaurant where each wanted to tell their story to the group. Tales went on for hours. They asked for more details of Ashley's adventures at the wall with the Sabra. She had already told them of Najid's family, the friends in Zabuda, and the problems Faisal and Almas had managing olive and fig orchards just across the wall.

Upon Ashley's return to her room, a telephone call from Sami surprised her. Yes, she'd had a good day in Nazareth with no problems. After inquiring about his day, she thanked him again for their hospitality and the wonderful time together.

The team discussed plans for the next day, Wednesday, and decided to go to the Mount of Beatitudes, the traditional site of Jesus's Sermon on the Mount. This would also be their last chance to swim in the Sea of Galilee, as they had stayed too long in Tiberius and Capernaum to fit that in to the schedule. On Thursday, they would head off to the south, to Jerusalem and the Dead Sea sites.

Their bus driver seemed proud of the farmland of Upper Galilee with its hills and valleys, green with open farms and groves of olives and figs.

"The Mount of Beatitudes near Tabgha has a church there, doesn't it?"

"Yes, but apparently the main attraction is the setting itself—low hills overlooking the Sea of Galilee," Marie answered.

Later, reclining on the grass of the hillside overlooking the blue expanse of the water, Ashley listened to Jim read the first of the blessings Jesus spoke about, for those who are "poor in spirit" and later, "peacemakers." She closed her eyes. *This world needs less arrogance and hate and more people "poor in spirit" who recognize their need for God and for each other. And it needs people who make peace, not just talk about it.*

She lay back in the warm sun and drifted off to sleep. She dreamed she was back at the wall in Bethlehem and that someone with a gun had grabbed her from behind. Ashley jerked awake.

"What's wrong, Ashley?" Marie lay with her hands under her head not far away.

"I don't know. I ... I guess I had a bad dream."

"Do you want to talk about it?"

"No. Let's walk up higher for some exercise and get a better view of the countryside and the water. It looks so inviting." She tried to put the dream out of her mind. She didn't want to talk about it. She had tried to put that Bethlehem experience behind her, and she remained determined to not bring it up, to anyone. Swimming in the Sea of Galilee helped her forget.

The bus climbed slowly as it approached Jerusalem. Their new bus driver, Benjamin, unlike the quiet former one, had introduced himself as Ben, a Sabra born and raised in Jerusalem. He spoke flawless English. "You'll notice we are gaining elevation. Jerusalem sits on a group of hills averaging over twenty-six hundred feet in elevation."

The bus passed through the modern city of Jerusalem, and then approached a dramatic high wall of tan- and rose-hued stones that surrounded the Old City. Ben grabbed the microphone again. "Suleiman the Magnificent, the Ottoman Turk, constructed the present-day wall in the fifteen hundreds after it had been built and destroyed many times over the centuries."

Ashley watched intently as they slowed, driving through the Jaffa Gate up to the nearby guesthouse. It shone softly with beautiful stone walls, balconies and courtyards in the afternoon sun. Flower boxes brightened the outside stairs. The entry led into a lounge with several upholstered chairs and a reception desk. It would become a peaceful haven within the ancient city, bustling with shops and tourists.

# Chapter 39

As they rode on, everyone in the bus enjoyed some quiet and a rest after the intense sun and heat of their hike up to ancient Massada in the desert near the Dead Sea. Ashley closed her eyes and grew sleepy. The dream came back. A man approached her near the wall in Bethlehem. He suddenly pulled a gun hidden partially by his hand. Ashley awakened with a startled "No!" raising her arm and striking Marie in the chest.

"Are you OK, Ashley? You cried out in your dream."

"I'm so sorry. I dozed off. Did I wake you up? I think I hit you!"

"No problem. You seem to be having some frightening dreams."

"I guess I am. It's so real at the time. They keep coming back."

"I know you went through a lot at home before coming on the trip. Do you want to talk about it?"

"It's not the bombing at home. I woke up in the hospital from being unconscious and have only vague memories of the whole situation until after my operation."

"Would it help to tell me what's causing those dreams here?"

"I'm not sure, Marie. I haven't wanted to disturb you or anyone on this trip or cause any delays. I've tried to put it out of my mind, but a frightening thing happened to me in Bethlehem when I was out walking alone near the wall. It seems unreal now, but I know it wasn't a dream."

"If you are comfortable sharing it, Ashley, go ahead. Anything you say will not go beyond the two of us."

"Well ... alright. Here's what happened." Ashley related the whole story at the wall. She decided not to tell about Herodian. Maybe that wasn't a real threat after all. "I don't want this to ruin my trip or anyone else's, for that matter. I've tried to put this behind me. I don't want to think about it. I don't even want to talk about it. But it keeps breaking through in my dreams, and those I can't control."

Marie gazed ahead in her seat and then turned to Ashley. "That experience is certainly enough to cause nightmares. Do you have any reason to believe it was more than a crazed man attacking a young lady, you know, any attractive girl?"

"Not really. I have no enemies or stalkers that I'm aware of and certainly not in this part of the world."

The discussion continued. Ashley told of the cab driver that spirited her away so fast.

"It looks like God's provided at just the right moment," Marie observed.

"Definitely. I'm so thankful for that cabbie. I hope I paid him enough. And thank you for listening, Marie. It helps to share the load I've been carrying."

Marie nodded. "Let's stay together from now on. You know, the buddy system."

Ashley chuckled. "I haven't used that since age six in swimming lessons. But thanks. Now it sounds pretty good."

# Chapter 40

Marie and Ashley followed the rest of the team out to the bus after breakfast in the guesthouse. The tour group had decided to visit the Holocaust Museum. Ben told the story as he drove into the modern city, starting with the pogroms in Russia and Poland. Ashley recalled again the Jewish families having to leave their Russian village in *Fiddler on the Roof.* Then he explained Kristallnacht, the night of broken glass in 1938, the anti-Jewish rampage in Germany that killed many Jews and destroyed hundreds of their businesses.

"You soon will see the horror of the concentration camps at the museum, and the suffering of six million Jews." Ben paused. "Then you will understand why we say, 'Never again.'"

Touring the complex with its images and videos of Auschwitz and Treblinka, both in what had been Poland, nauseated Ashley. Human beings were stripped naked and lined up for slaughter like cattle in Chicago stockyards. "I can't look anymore, Marie. I'm getting sick. Let's go outside."

They found a crowded cafe. Marie maneuvered Ashley outside, locating the only empty chairs at a small table where an elderly bearded gentleman with a yarmulke sat sipping his tea.

"May we join you?" Marie inquired.

"Please do," he said, pulling out the nearest chair.

Marie introduced herself and Ashley. "And you are—"

"Rabbi Yusef. You would call me Joseph," he said, shaking hands. He spoke perfect English.

Ashley perked up as the waitress came for orders. She thought tea might settle her stomach. "Are you the rabbi here at the museum?"

"No," he said, laughing. "I retired some years ago."

"You have obviously seen the pictures of Auschwitz, probably many times. I ... I couldn't handle them. They made me sick."

"I was there."

Ashley's jaw dropped and her eyes widened, staring at their new friend. "You ... really? You were in Auschwitz?!"

"Yes, as a child. Both of my parents died there in the gas chamber."

"Oh no! I'm so sorry." Ashley paused, squeezing the rabbi's hand. "I've never met a survivor of the concentration camps. How did you escape?"

"We didn't. My uncle and I somehow lived until the Allied armies freed us."

Rabbi Yusef then related his story, detailing his childhood in Germany, his experience in the camp, and then his release with his uncle. They had immigrated to Israel in 1948 just after it achieved nation status.

Ashley sighed, and both women sat back in their chairs after being on the edge of them during the story. Their tea had grown cold. Ashley had so many questions to ask of this rabbi who had lived through the modern history of the Jews.

"You have been through so much that I'll never understand," Ashley said. "It's such a privilege to hear your story. May I ask you a question or two?"

"'No problem,' as you Americans say." He flashed a sly smile.

"Are you orthodox in your faith?"

"Yes, I am. And many are here. But we've always had a secular government."

"What do you think about Israel getting help from the United States?"

"We appreciate it. Three billion dollars a year allows us to do what we do, particularly with military and security issues."

"Do you have any disagreement with the U.S. policy toward the Palestinians?"

"Yes, I do. I would like America to support us exclusively in our fight with them. They are terrorists and use rockets to try to get rid of us. In the past, suicide bombs. Only the wall has finally brought the suicide bombings to a halt, as well as our soldiers. There is no other way. We have to cement our gains, literally. It has allowed us to take much of the West Bank that belonged to us in King David's day."

"Do you want your government to take over all the occupied territory?" Ashley inquired.

"We won't rest until we have the entire land promised us, at least to the Jordan River. We have too many Palestinians in Israel proper. And too many in the West Bank. Some are leaving, but not enough of them. They have too many babies. If we were all one country, they could take over with time. We have to cleanse the land of Arabs. You can't trust Palestinians."

"Do you think the Jewish settlements in the territories will last?"

"Yes. We need more of them to control their terrorism. Look what happened in Gaza when we pulled out: Hamas. We'll gradually strangle them with settlements, the separation wall, and exclusive roads. Eventually they'll leave or die out and we'll take over the West Bank."

"Really?!" Ashley's heart raced, thinking of Fatima and her family, and then Sami and Rafiq's family. What would Najid say if he were here? The rabbi seemed so certain in his views, so hard.

"Do you know that some Christian churches in America do support Israel exclusively, whatever your government does? It's part of their theology."

"I've heard that is true. But I don't understand it. Do they really think supporting Israel will hasten Messiah's coming? I've heard that they predict a Jewish slaughter at Meggido. I think you call it Armageddon. That's not very popular here." He smiled with a wink.

Marie laughed nervously and touched Ashley's hand. "I think we'd better not keep the rabbi any longer." She left ten Israeli shekels for the tea for all three of them.

Ashley sensed Marie's discomfort with her questions. "I'm sorry for being so forward in my questions, Rabbi Yusef. I wish you God's blessing! Shalom."

"I enjoyed your questions, Ashley, and meeting you, Marie. Here is my card and e-mail address." He reached over the table, handing it to Marie. "Feel free to write. You'll find English on the back. Shalom."

With the team back on the bus heading to the Mount of Olives, Marie turned to Ashley. "Feeling better?"

"Oh, yes. When Rabbi Yusef told his story, I forgot about my stomach."

"Did he answer your questions to your liking?"

Ashley put her hand to her chin, looking out the window at a busy intersection. "I suppose he did, Marie. I ... respect him for all he has been through in a lifetime of stress. But I wonder if he has any Palestinian friends." She paused. "It would have been so much fun to have Najid here to share these experiences together. He would have loved the old Rabbi Yusef, even with his hard views."

# Chapter 41

Ben let the team rest for a bit as he drove back from the modern city toward the old one. They seemed subdued by their museum experience as they wound up the hill to the top of the Mount of Olives. The panorama proved spectacular, with the Old City in the foreground, surrounded by its high stone wall. The Temple Mount crowned the view, topped by the dramatic golden Dome of the Rock shrine, the site from which the Prophet Mohammed was said to have ascended to Heaven.

"When you're ready, we'll take the Palm Sunday path down to the Garden of Gethsemane that you see below." Soon they ambled down the trail as the sun high in the July sky bore down on everyone. They enjoyed the shade of the trees approaching the Garden of Gethsemane below.

Ashley stared at the olive trees in the garden, some trunks fully five feet in diameter.

"These trees may well have been here when Jesus agonized under them," Jim said.

Ashley and Marie strolled the paths in the garden. Beautiful and quiet, Ashley visualized Jesus on his knees, knowing his trial and a painful death awaited. She thanked him quietly as they walked.

Walid looked around Umar's apartment in the Muslim Quarter of the Old City. Dark and dingy, Umar didn't have a wife to brighten it up. Walid had started a close vigil on the guesthouse not far away in the Armenian quarter. He had taken off his visored cap and his Muslim hat. He exchanged his shaded glasses for dark ones. He wore a long shirt with baggy cotton pants.

Umar had laughed. "You look Pakistani."

"I don't care, as long as it hides me. The problem is her. So far they are always together with their group. I guess we'll have to be patient until we can find her alone or somehow separate her from everyone else. She'll be here in Jerusalem for several more days, according to the schedule the boss received. Wherever she goes, one of us has to be in the background somewhere near but far enough away to avoid suspicion."

On a walking tour in the late afternoon, the group passed through the Armenian Quarter of the Old City, entering the larger Jewish quarter. A column of young men strode by in their black suits and white shirts, with broadbrimmed black hats. Their long sideburn braids swung forward and back with each step. Each proceeded head-down, reading from his book and chanting while hurrying along the street.

Ashley looked at them and then turned to Ben with a quizzical frown.

"These guys are Hasidic Jews, a branch of the ultra-Orthodox community. I won't go into all the other Jewish groups, but there are lots of divisions and subdivisions."

"What about Zionism?" Ashley ventured. "How does that fit in with Jewish beliefs?"

"That's a political movement that brought us back to the land and established Israel as a nation." Ben swept his arm around toward a nearby synagogue. "For some, it's part of their religion. For others it's against their faith. For most of our founders in the 1900s, Zionism was strictly political and not religious at all."

"Now we're approaching the Temple Mount. We'll bypass that for now to go through the Muslim Quarter, the Souk. We share this large piece of the Old City with them. It's big. Follow me so we don't lose you."

Ashley noticed more confined alleyways and shops only ten feet wide, open to narrow and sometimes covered walkways. Colorful bazaars filled with jewelry, clothes, beautiful scarves, and wall hangings seemed to fascinate all the women of the group. "Souk" must mean market, Ashley realized. In adjacent areas, from connected stone houses people gazed down through open windows.

Amid the crowd, Ashley glimpsed a man with dark glasses looking at her. Her mind flashed to Bethlehem and the wall. She shuddered. He quickly turned away. She mustn't start seeing bad men in every venue. No, she wouldn't start getting paranoid—it could be anyone. She dismissed the thought.

# Chapter 42

Ben introduced several university students the next morning, all wearing yarmulkes, who would each take two or three people to wherever they wished to go in the Old City. David chatted with Ashley and Marie. "What would you like to do today?" He seemed like a fun young man, ready for anything, slightly built, with dark hair and eyes that sparkled.

"I'd like some local culture and food for lunch," Ashley replied. "Oh ... and shopping. How about you, Marie."

"Sounds good. David, what do you recommend?" Marie asked.

"I'll take you for some falafel and salad with pita bread. Good little restaurant in the Jewish quarter. Then we can go shopping in the Souk."

He walked his charges to a place with outside tables. He pointed to the back wall. "That man standing behind the vat of hot oil is deep frying falafel, the traditional Arab patty made from ground chickpeas or fava beans."

Several pieces with a colorful salad and pita bread soon filled their plates. They found a table and indulged in a few bites when a middle-aged, bearded gentleman in a white shirt and dark pants stopped to greet David. A yarmulke sat precariously on the back of his bushy hair. Ashley wondered how it stayed in place. He seemed very friendly and interested to meet the two women.

David jumped to his feet. "Rabbi Cohen, I want you meet two American friends, Marie and Ashley. I'm helping them shop today."

Marie smiled. "David here is introducing us to your Middle Eastern delights."

"Great. It's good to meet you," he said, nodding. "Any friend of David's is a friend of mine."

He sounded so American to Ashley. "I've been hoping to meet people who live here, so I am delighted you stopped by. Would you join us for lunch?"

"OK, I will. Let me get something to eat and I'll be back."

"Who is he, David?"

"Rabbi Cohen is my rabbi. I think you call it your 'pastor.'"

"Do you take a day off after the Sabbath, Rabbi Cohen?" Ashley popped the last bite of falafel in her mouth as the rabbi sat down.

"We do, Ashley. So this is my day off, to enjoy meeting people like you." He began to eat.

"Where are you from, Rabbi? Your English sounds American."

"I am one. Well, maybe I used to be one. I was born in New York and came to work in a kibbutz in Northern Israel as a young man. I never left."

They shared stories, learning of the rabbi's journey into theological training. Afterward, he'd worked for several years in the kibbutz. Marie shared her interest in various belief systems in college before becoming a Christian.

Then Ashley explained her background and church where support for Israel and Zionism became very much part of their beliefs. "In fact it is central to how we think about the future and the Messiah."

"Really? I've read about the evangelical branch of Christians in America, some of whom are 'Christian Zionists.' It seems like an oxymoron. Also that they have an organization to promote Israeli interests. Is that true?"

"Yes. It's a national organization called 'Christians United for Israel.' It's quite large. I've been raised in Oklahoma to believe all of what it stands for, and now in Seattle, our church also would be classified in the Christian Zionist group."

"Is that what you personally believe, Ashley?"

Ashley looked into the face of this rabbi, whose piercing brown eyes penetrated right into her brain. Her heart sped up. What could she say, now that she had seen the wall from the other side? That her heart had been touched with the plight of Palestinians who had lost everything at the hands of Zionists?

On the other hand, she loved the Jewish people. She appreciated them for their great suffering, perseverance through history, and contributions to society.

Well, maybe she didn't love the soldiers at the wall and checkpoints. Not for what they did to Faisal and Almas near Zubuda. Nor for the government that dispossessed Najid's family of their home and lands forever. But she liked the people, like David here, and Ben their driver, and yes, Rabbi Yusef. Ashley had always been glad that the Jews, oppressed for centuries, had finally found a homeland, a place of safety and protection. Yet look what they did in Bethlehem to Fatima's family and all those who lost their livelihood in Jerusalem because they could no longer enter the city. *Have the oppressed become the oppressors?*

Her mind whirled as she struggled to contain her thoughts. She finally gazed into the street outside and shook her head. "After all the experiences I've had here, Rabbi, I don't know if I believe in Zionism or not." She looked back into his steely gaze. "Do you think we should believe and support it?"

"It's not for me to tell you what to believe."

"OK then, what do you believe?" Ashley's heart raced, wondering how badly she had offended the rabbi.

"What do I believe about Zionism?" He smiled. "In a nutshell, here it is. If you want to know why, I can tell you that too, if you have the time."

"We do. Please go on."

"OK. First, I am loyal to the Torah, your Old Testament. And the Torah teaches that Zionism is not Judaism. In fact, the founding principles of Zionism are counter to Judaism, which teaches us to value the stranger in our midst, not persecute him."

Ashley stared at the rabbi, eyebrows raised, hardly believing what she just heard.

"Second, the state of Israel does not represent the Jewish people. The bulldozing of homes and displacement of people—violence offends me." He shook his head. "These are not religious imperatives. Settlers in the West Bank, mostly secular immigrants, displace local people. These acts are not right or just. Zionists have no right to do such things. Yes, we have suffered. But does our government then turn on others with injustice? Do we subject them to our will? Do we take away pieces of their land and call them our settlements until there is nothing left for Palestinians?"

David nodded as the rabbi spoke. Marie looked shocked and her lips trembled, but she said nothing. The rabbi stirred his tea and waited for Ashley's response. They had heard just the opposite from the old rabbi yesterday, the one who had endured the holocaust as a child. Now this. Ashley certainly had no question now about what Rabbi Cohen thought of her church's position on Israel's policies. But why did he feel so strongly? The rabbi continued as though reading Ashley's thoughts.

"Judaism teaches that we must not take land that is not ours to take—and yet we do it in the name of Judaism. That's wrong. There are many of us who protest, nonviolently, but they trample on our rights. Judaism opposes aggression. The Torah does not sanction bloodshed by those who try to remain true to it." He stopped and gazed intently at Ashley for several moments.

"Most people don't realize that Zionism is criticized fervently by many Orthodox Jews at their own peril. The secular establishment who often substitute Zionism for Judaism have no spiritual basis for ethnic cleansing. Our recent prime minister, Ariel Sharon, said in 1998 of the West Bank, and this is an exact quote, 'Everybody has to move, run, and grab as many hilltops as they can.... Everything we don't grab will go to them.' That's not religion—it's real estate."

He paused again, leaned forward, and cleared his throat. "Look," his voice rose, "the politicians suppress the truth and will not report the voices of observant Jews. So the world doesn't know. It equates 'Israel' with 'being Jewish.' You Americans may never see our objection in print. It is not politically correct. Or if you do, it's 'anti-Semitic.'" He held up two fingers of both hands. "You'll never hear what large numbers of Jewish people in Israel really think about Zionism."

That night Ashley went to bed with her thoughts churning in a whirlpool of conflicting ideas. Drawn first one way and then another, her mind circled ceaselessly. She had come to learn the truth of what she had always believed and to walk where Jesus walked. But now what was the truth? What would Jesus think of the conflict? He'd had his own trouble with religious leaders. She tossed and turned, unable to sleep for hours into the night.

# Chapter 43

Back in the Christian Quarter, David guided Ashley and Marie up the Via Dolorosa or "way of sorrow." They followed it up the incline of the eleven stations of the cross, ending in the Church of the Holy Sepulcher. "Consecrated in AD 335 under Constantine, this complex building contains the twelfth station, said to be the site of Calvary and the cross where Jesus died." David had it down pat.

"How do you know all this Christian history?" Ashley teased. "You know a lot more of our history than I know of yours."

"If you grow up at the center of the world where the three major religions converge in one Holy City, you learn."

Once inside, Ashley's ears buzzed as robed priests of Roman and Greek churches spoke impatiently to manage the crowds that lined up to touch various stones, including the Rock of Golgotha. Ashley felt bewildered. She tried to stand still to pray, but kept being jostled by people surging this way and that.

And amid the chaos, Ashley suddenly felt an odd sensation of being watched. She tried to shake it, but it wouldn't budge. Her spine tingled and her heart began to pound. She looked around but didn't see anyone she recognized. Glancing up, she caught one of the priests watching her. He looked away to give directions to the crowd. Ashley drew in her breath. *Paranoia wins*, she thought. *Again.*

After lunch with the whole group, the bus trip north of the Old City wall didn't take long. Just long enough for Jim to explain that Gordon from the UK discovered the Garden Tomb in 1867 as an alternative to the Church of the Holy Sepulcher. Even if Jesus didn't actually die there, it gave Protestants a picture of what the tomb resembled.

As they entered the gate, Ashley sighed. "Ohhh, it's beautiful. Let's sit down on a bench, Marie."

As they gazed at the pathways and plantings, including shade trees and the natural rock walls of the garden, the sounds of an American tour group singing softly drifted up from a rocky cliff side below them. Tears welled as Ashley gazed at the cliff above the tomb site. They finished the visit by waiting in line to walk into the empty tomb carved out of the rock cliff, with three burial niches lining the walls. A large circular stone stood to one side of the opening. Ashley's spirit finally found a moment it longed for, that indescribable divine connection.

The next day, during lunch in the Armenian quarter close to the Jaffa Gate with David, they discussed their plans: leisurely shopping in the Souk, the Muslim quarter today.

"But tomorrow I'll be by early so we can spend enough time at the Temple Mount," David said. "I'll be with you until you go alone up to the top. I can't go there. But it will be OK. You will be with a lot of other tourists. You can't go into the Dome of the Rock anymore. That's too bad. I've heard it's quite dramatic."

"Why won't you be with us on the top of the Temple Mount?" Marie wondered.

"Jews aren't allowed to go. It constitutes one of the holiest Muslim sites. Prime Minster Sharon forced his way up there in 2002 with soldiers, starting the second intifada. You know, the war that went on for months in the West Bank. So you'll be on your own for your time on top."

# Chapter 44

Ashley awoke early. Their last full day in the Holy Land. After breakfast, she and Marie followed David through the Jewish Quarter to the Western Wall.

They rounded the corner of a large building, pausing to read a sign in English and Hebrew. It explained the history of the temple area and Wailing Wall, that the huge stones at the base of the Western Wall are the original foundation stones of Solomon's Temple. Jews from all over the world have prayed before them for hundreds of years, mourning their temple's destruction and believing in its future restoration. Finally the sign quoted the Sages: THE DIVINE PRESENCE NEVER MOVES FROM THE WESTERN WALL.

Before them was a large open square with a fence on the right side. Women crowded behind it. The men stood in the square below next to the wall, praying. They all had yarmulkes or other hats. Some inserted prayer notes in the cracks between large square stones that each stood over four feet high. Smaller stones stacked above them, towered up forty feet.

David explained: "These people are praying. They are 'wailing' in the view of foreigners, until the temple is restored with its ancient glory. I had my bar mitzvah here in the square when I was thirteen."

"Can anyone pray at the wall?" Ashley asked.

"Well … yes, if you have your head covered. Oh, and if you're a man."

"Why aren't women allowed down at the base of the wall with the men?"

"I don't know, Ashley. Tradition, I guess. We always segregate the women from the men."

They watched as men bobbed toward the wall and back or up and down. Ashley turned and gazed at the square filled with people. Behind the square some large apartment buildings seemed empty. She asked David about them.

"When we captured the West Bank in the 1967 War, we controlled this area and the wall for the first time in hundreds of years. So we cleared the area of houses and apartments in what is now the open square."

"Were they Palestinian homes?"

"Yes. And now the Palestinians want to have this surrounding area, East Jerusalem, as their capital for their new state. It actually is part of the West Bank. So our government is still building settlements right here. If you look over there, you can see new buildings going up for Jewish settlers. We are still destroying more homes to build high-rise buildings. The Palestinians don't like this. They are gradually losing their homes. But Arab workers are glad to have jobs, even if it means building homes that will displace their people."

"What is the crowd doing just beyond the new construction?" Marie asked.

"I hear bulldozers," David said. "I suspect they are taking down Palestinian houses and the crowd doesn't like it."

"Are they paid the value of their homes?" Ashley asked.

"I'm not sure. But they are being forced to move. The end result of the Zionists' beliefs, Ashley. They are gradually taking the West Bank and East Jerusalem, piece by piece."

Ashley grimaced, watching for several minutes as the crowd grew and moved away from them toward the sound of the bulldozers.

"It's time for you and Marie to check in over there to the right of the square at the base of that long wooden ramp. They'll check your passports, and then you can explore the Temple Mount with the mosques. I can't go up there, as I mentioned."

Walid decided he would join the demonstrators just beyond the square. He watched the two women leave their Jewish escort at the bottom of the ramp leading up to the Temple Mount. *Always together. No point in following them up there.* Umar had been sick and up most of the night, so he went home to his apartment. Walid realized that according to their schedule, he'd have to get Ashley alone somehow. It was now or never. He must not fail again.

With David waiting at the checkpoint, the two ladies showed their passports, walked up the ramp to the top, and came out on to a broad stone square, expansive in area. They approached the largest mosque in Jerusalem, Al-Aqsa, just ahead and to their right beyond the museum. Its dome, covered with silver according to Ashley's guidebook, appeared black. They looked to their left, and there, elevated further with stair access, stood the magnificent Dome of the Rock shrine, startling in its beauty with its golden dome.

They meandered around the famous shrine and admired the marble and mosaic tiles inscribed with Arabic calligraphy from the Qu'ran. The exquisite patterns defied description. Ashley's book depicted the interior, a large, carpeted, plain room with stained-glass windows. A low fence surrounded the large rock, the very top of the mountain. Knowing it probably wouldn't work, they took scarves out of Marie's backpack, covered their heads, walked up to the door, and spoke to the guard. He didn't speak English, but waved them off with a shake of his head.

"Bummer!" Ashley said as they walked away. "I wanted to see the top of Mount Mariah."

# Chapter 45

How did you find the Temple Mount?" David inquired.
"More spectacular than the pictures show," Marie answered. "Would Muslims actually keep you from going up?"

"Oh yes. It would be dangerous for me to try. But also, the temple contained the Holy of Holies when it existed two thousand years ago. We think the rock at the top is that site, forbidden for us to ever walk there. Only the high priest may, once a year. It is the holiest place on earth to us, and to Muslims, the center of the world."

"David, to think we walked up there gives me goosebumps. We experienced history."

"What are 'goosebumps,' Ashley?"

Ashley laughed. "That's the first English expression you haven't known. You are amazing, David. It's those little bumps you get on your skin when something really delightful happens, like hearing a song you love."

"Oh yes! I get them during the Passover remembrance."

Ashley peered from the bottom of the ramp area across to the crowd that gathered past the new construction and around the corner beyond her sight. "Let's wander over to see what's going on."

"OK," David said, "but don't wander too far. Stay back. I have friends who may be there who can explain to you what is going on. But be sure we stay together."

The crowd of young men seemed restless, even agitated, shouting and holding signs up in Hebrew and Arabic.

"What do they say, David?" Ashley asked.

"You've probably heard of *Nakba*, or 'catastrophe'. Another says 'shame', and 'stop!' That one with blood dripping down it says, 'Remember Rachel Corrie.'"

Ashley stood and stared at the crowd, lost in her imagination of a young American Jewish woman, crushed in Gaza for standing in defiance before an Israeli bulldozer about to destroy someone's home. She shook her head in disbelief that it really happened.

"She's now a symbol of resistance here," David said. "A real heroine."

"Let's walk around the corner to see what's happening there," Ashley suggested.

As they rounded the corner, the crowd began to flow in behind them, and the three visitors were quickly surrounded. Ashley felt the pressure of the crowd surging and pushing her forward.

Then she noticed an armored bulldozer approaching a house. Two couples, one of them appearing to be grandparents with three small children behind them, held out their hands to the bulldozer operator, pleading with their hands and faces. They stood in front of a small stone home with colorful flower boxes. Several Israeli soldiers appeared with automatic rifles and motioned them to move off to the side. They refused to move. The caterpillar clanged forward slowly, large blade down, driver in a thick glass and steel cage. More soldiers appeared with metal shields and began to push the Palestinian family aside. The bulldozer arrived at the front of the house and crunched the front wall. The house shivered as it collapsed.

Suddenly rocks flew from the crowd toward the soldiers. They fired into the air. But the rocks continued. Everyone shouted and pointed to new troops that advanced on the crowd to the left. Those soldiers fired. The young men closest to the soldiers fled toward the two women and David, now in the middle of the crowd. Two of the young men fell, one bleeding from his mouth.

Then Ashley heard a pop, and tear gas canisters flew overhead spewing gas over the crowd. It settled on them. Ashley's lungs instantly burned. She coughed. Her eyes stung and watered. She could hardly see or breathe.

The crowd swelled and pushed her away from the soldiers. She rushed to keep her footing. Unable to see clearly, coughing, stumbling, and trying to regain her balance, she finally fell forward. The crowd surged around her; some stepped on her arms, almost trampling her in their hurry to flee from the bullets. Suddenly a strong hand reached down, yanked her arm, and pulled her to her feet. Ashley couldn't see her rescuer, but heard him shout, "Keep moving" in broken English. As they ran he held her arm in a strong grip. Her vision cleared slightly. She looked for Marie and David. They were nowhere in sight.

# Chapter 46

David had seen the Israeli troops coming and shouted to both women to follow him to the rear of the crowd. Marie heard him and pushed her way through to follow David. She struggled to keep up with David, running, walking, and pushing.

Marie repeated over and over, "I'm sorry, excuse me." David finally grabbed her arm and pulled her with him as they dashed toward the Temple Mount and safety.

"Where is Ashley? Didn't she follow us?" David shouted.

"I don't know! I thought she would follow me. But where is she? Maybe she didn't hear you."

"Marie, stay right at the base of the ramp over there! I'm going to look for Ashley!"

With that he sprinted after the crowd, which had now largely passed and headed out of the square and down several streets in the Jewish Quarter. The Israeli troops finally stopped pursuing the crowd as it rapidly disappeared. Marie saw vans arrive. Soldiers had handcuffed six young men and herded them into the vehicles along with the two casualties carried on stretchers.

David ran full out and quickly covered the distance between him and the crowd as it dispersed in every direction. He recognized a friend from school. "Have you seen a blonde American girl running this way? She would stand out in this crowd."

"I saw a girl like that running with a tall Arab guy who had her by the arm. They were ahead of me and turned right into one of the small streets toward the Muslim Quarter. I don't know where they went after that."

David thanked him and streaked down the street, turning right into the Souk. He rushed up many streets and alleyways looking for Ashley. He inquired of the shopkeepers. No one had seen Ashley. He spent the next two hours searching and asking if anyone had seen the blonde American. Finally he found an Israeli policeman and reported Ashley missing.

"We'll put out a missing person bulletin." The officer pulled out his radio and started to report what David had told him.

Marie stood patiently by the entrance to the Temple Mount ramp and waited, worried about Ashley, wondering what had happened to her. *I should call her cell phone*, she thought. She did. It rang and rang. No answer.

Surely if she fell and injured herself, David would find her. An hour passed. Marie prayed for Ashley. Then she worried about being alone as the afternoon wore on. She could find her way back to the guesthouse near the Jaffa Gate. But David knew where she waited and had told her to stay there. Surely by this time he would be back with some kind of news about Ashley. More time passed. Soon it had been over two hours since he sprinted down the square to find her. Where could he be, and when would he come with news of her friend? Marie prayed again that Ashley would be found and be OK.

Finally David appeared, out of breath, looking haggard and spent. He shook his head. "She has totally disappeared."

Marie found a small bench at the base of the ramp in the check-point area. "Sit down, David. You look exhausted."

"I am." David crumpled onto the bench and leaned forward, elbows on his knees, holding his head. "I looked everywhere for her, talked to so many people. Only one had seen her, with a tall man, heading into the Muslim Quarter."

"Did you go there?"

"That's where I've been the whole time. Up one alley and down another. No one could give me any help. I did find a policeman and reported Ashley missing. He put out a report on his radio. What do you think we should do?"

"Let's find a police station and ask them."

"I know of one close to the guesthouse," David replied.

David and Marie hurried toward the Jaffa Gate. Marie prayed silently as they went. The police station bustled with people milling around on the stone floor of the main room. Three desks stood in front of several doors. The stone walls contained small windows pro-tected with iron grates and a large Star of David. Everything seemed like utter confusion to Marie. They waited for several minutes in a line to get to a woman sitting behind a desk. She spoke rapidly in Hebrew, frowning to the people ahead of them. Finally David inched up to her desk.

"We lost a friend in the demonstration today," David reported in Hebrew.

"Do you know how many 'lost friends' we're tracking right now?" she snapped back.

"A policeman took the information I gave him and called in a missing person report."

"Alright, what's the name of your friend?"

"Ashley Wells."

The police woman scanned her computer and after a few key-strokes looked up. "Yes, we have her on our list. Blonde American young woman."

"Do you have any leads at all?"

"Young man, we have no idea where she might be. And further-more, our officers are on patrol all over the Old City looking for several people who instigated the demonstration today. Come back tomorrow and perhaps we can help." With that she looked beyond them to others who waited behind Marie.

David explained to Marie what the policewoman had said. "There's not much help here, at least not tonight. I might as well take you back to the guesthouse. We'll find Jim. I think I'll give Ben a call. Then we can decide what to do."

# Chapter 47

Several team members sat in lounge chairs in the front room of the guesthouse, resting after coming back from their adventures. One of them, Betty, spoke. "Did you know about the riot today? We watched it from the ramp going up to the Temple Mount."

"Yes, we were in it," Marie replied as she rushed in to join the group. "Ashley's missing." She shocked herself by saying that word to their friends.

"She's missing?!" The group gasped.

Marie related the story briefly as the others listened with mouths agape. David added how he had tried to find her, guided by a friend, looking everywhere he could in the Souk. "Where's Jim?" he asked.

"He hasn't shown up yet with his crew," one of them replied.

Marie glanced at David talking on his cell phone. She raced upstairs to their room to be sure Ashley had not somehow come back. Hurrying back down the stairs, she entered the front room just as Jim and two of the team came in the door. Marie told the story to the new arrivals just as their driver Ben entered.

Jim took charge as they all found a place to sit, except David who stood behind Marie. "David, would you get the evening supervisor to come join us? We need all the advice we can muster."

The supervisor, Alim, joined them and heard the story of Ashley's disappearance from David as they walked down the stairs.

"Ashley needs our help," Jim began. "And she also needs God's. So let's pray. *Oh heavenly Father, you know where Ashley is and what is happening to her right now. Keep her from harm. Help her to come back to us, or help us to find her. Be her rescuer. Amen.*"

Marie wiped away a tear.

Then Jim looked up. "You heard from Marie and David what happened today. Is there anything else that we need to know? Marie, you've been with Ashley more than any of us. Can you add anything?"

Marie wondered how much of what Ashley had confided in her she should tell. Would it help in finding her? She began with the easy part. "I just checked our room. She's not been there. I called her cell phone several times. It's not working." She closed her eyes, visualizing Ashley explaining her frightening dream. Marie would never disclose anything she learned confidentially. She hated gossip. But now this information could be of help in finding her friend.

After several moments, with every eye fixed on her in the silence, she began, "Ashley had not planned to speak of this with anyone, but being together when she had a frightening dream, she shared it with me, in confidence. I would normally not divulge anything like this, but in the hope that it could possibly help in locating her, here it is."

Marie told of Ashley's dream. "Ashley had been nearly abducted at gunpoint near the wall in Bethlehem, saved by a taxi driver. She had not wanted to disturb or delay the team, so she kept it to herself. She didn't want it to ruin her own trip either, and tried to forget it." Marie paused. "But she couldn't control her dreams. I wonder whether her disappearance now is related to that attempt in Bethlehem. I suppose it could be a coincidence."

The team seemed stunned. Jim spoke quickly. "If I'd known that I would never have let Ashley out of my sight! What is going on? Is someone out to get her?"

"That is possible, Jim," Ben spoke quietly. "But let's not jump to conclusions. I would check the emergency rooms in town to be sure she's not injured and waiting to be seen. I know where she would most likely be taken, probably Hadassah on Mount Scopus. I'll call around."

"Would you, Ben? Thanks."

As Ben left the room to make the calls, Jim turned to Alim. "You have had years of experience here, Alim. What seems most likely to you?"

Alim nodded. "Yes, I have seen people lost for a time, but they usually find their way back to the guesthouse by asking for directions or help. Ashley has been missing for several hours. The Old City is not that big that she couldn't find her way back to the Jaffa Gate, which is well known, and then to here by now. It is only beginning to get dark. So I doubt that she just lost her way."

"David, what are your thoughts at this point?"

"Hmm ..." David hesitated. "Blonde young women attract attention here. If she were lost or injured, particularly if she is conscious, she would be here now, or at least have called and let Marie know what happened. Someone would help her. Oh, here comes Ben. Any news?"

"No. She is not in either of the emergency rooms that medics use."

"Then we have to assume that my friend's story is probably accurate. There were no other blonde girls in the crowd, or I would have noticed them. So she must be in the hands of the man who gripped her arm and forced her into the Muslim Quarter. We know only that he was Arabian looking and tall. I know the Souk, and I looked everywhere on the streets and alleys, talking to shopkeepers. Of course, he could have taken her into any house or apartment."

Everyone remained silent. Jim shook his head as he stared blankly at the wall across the room. Finally he spoke. "All the evidence points to an abduction of Ashley by a man taking advantage of the demonstration—someone who may have been after her in Bethlehem. We can't seem to get any help from the police tonight. So what can we do?"

The group brainstormed every idea they could think of to look for her but Jim shook his head. "We don't want anyone else lost in the dark. It might even be dangerous for either Ben or David to wander around now in the Muslim Quarter. And the police are too busy. I doubt the American Embassy could be helpful tonight."

Alim spoke up. "I know the area better than any of you. You may not realize, but I am Muslim. I could put on my taqiyah, my cap, and check every contact I have in that quarter to find Ashley. I'm not afraid."

"Alim, we would appreciate that very much."

No one had any appetite for dinner. The team sat with Jim, waiting. David and Ben left their cell phone numbers to call with any news and went home. Several went to their rooms to pray or rest, only to return to the front room. Minutes and hours ticked away. Shortly after nine, Alim walked in. They all jumped up to hear the news. It had been nearly three hours since he left.

He shook his head. "Nothing."

Everyone seemed deflated, like a collapsing balloon. As long as Alim looked, they had hope. Now it seemed gone.

"I checked with many of my friends in the Souk, and no one had seen Ashley, or heard of her. News travels fast there, so if anyone had seen her we would know."

"Thank you, Alim. You have done everything you could." Jim then looked at the team. "You all have been great. You're hungry and tired. I would suggest you snack on whatever you have until we can get some food in here."

"I'll call it in, Jim," Alim said. "They deliver, and it's not far away, just outside the Jaffa Gate."

"Thanks for that too." He then spoke to his team: "Everyone, feel free to stay here or relax in your rooms. We'll meet here in half an hour. Dinner should be here then. Seems like there is nothing more we can do tonight."

# Chapter 48

Ashley had regained her equilibrium after her fall and near trampling, then she scrambled with the demonstrators and her rescuer to escape the soldiers with their rifles. Her right arm hurt where he held it tight. She remembered a fellow runner stepping on her right upper arm at just that spot. She scanned the mob for Marie and David again, but saw only young Palestinians running. As the crowd thinned and scattered, Ashley had turned to the tall man with dark glasses holding her arm. Short of breath, her heart raced. They slowed to a walk. "Thanks for your help. You can let go of my arm. I'll be fine now."

He didn't seem to hear her or perhaps couldn't understand English. At least he didn't respond in any way. She tried to stop to repeat that she would be OK, feeling suddenly cold and shaky. He dragged her forward, by her sore arm, forcing her to continue. Ashley raised her voice. "I'm OK now. Please let go of my arm!" She pulled her arm forward to free it.

He shook his head and said something that sounded Arabic. He grabbed her arm with his right hand and dropped his left one. Then Ashley felt something poke her in the back. In thickly accented

English she heard "gun."

Her jaw dropped as she whirled to look at him, wide-eyed. Her mind raced back to Bethlehem and the wall. A tall man, severe look, this time with a white Muslim cap and dark glasses. But he looked like the guy at the wall in Bethlehem. Ashley trembled. She tried to jerk her arm away, but he held it tight and pressed whatever he had harder into her back. She almost screamed, but realized he could shoot her in the chaos and no one would come to her aid. She fought to wrestle out of his grasp. The shouts of the remaining crowd drowned out the sound of her struggle.

He pulled her close and shouted into her ear, "gun!"

She was determined not to panic. She would keep her head. Ashley suddenly turned toward him and tried to knee him in the groin, but hit only his thigh. He struck her with some hard object on the back of her head and shoved her forward.

Ashley screamed in anger, and then leaned back to resist his pushing her forward. The crowd, still moving forward, didn't seem to notice. The man still forced her to walk fast. She dug her feet into the pavement as though skidding down a steep hill. Her lips tightened as she was overpowered. The man veered her into a small street heading into the Muslim Quarter, where Ashley recognized the narrow street and the first of the shops.

He seemed to change whatever he held to her back, as the object poking her felt less sharp. Maybe he *was* concealing a gun. He found the head covering she stashed in her backpack and forced her to put it on. He tucked the gun under his right arm without releasing his grip on her arm and adjusted her hijab to partially cover her face. She glimpsed the pistol out of the corner of her eye. He quickly hid it under a scarf, and she felt the barrel press into her back. They turned into small streets without shops, just apartments and occasional row houses.

Ashley stuck out her jaw defiantly. She would not cry. Her heart raced, and her face turned red. She refused to give this terrorist the pleasure of seeing her fear. She drew a deep breath and gritted her teeth as they walked. No one on the street seemed to be aware of her plight.

Ashley trembled at what might lie ahead. Sexual assault seemed worse than being beaten. *Is he going to kill me? Why me? Why did he drag me away?* She realized she had become a target. Not a random crime that took advantage of a demonstration gone awry. But why?

She had read of obsessed men stalking women. Had he been the one to follow her up that rocky incline at Herodian outside of Bethlehem? She had seen his eyes gazing at her. Same eyes behind those dark glasses. As the puzzle pieces connected together in her mind, it all made sense. For some reason he had pursued her in at least three places. Had he seen her elsewhere also? Her mind raced. She fought tears of anger and frustration. She must not cry. She had to remain alert and strong.

Ashley thought of Marie and David. They would be frantically looking for her. She searched with her eyes and even stole a backward glance over her left shoulder, but they were not following. She knew Jim and her friends would make every effort to find her. But how would they know where to even look in the complicated mass of buildings that comprised the Old City and the maze of the Muslim Quarter? Ashley shook her head, losing hope of escape.

Out of the chaos, from somewhere in the back of her mind, floated the old song her grandmother Millie sang about God's eye being even on the sparrow: "And I know he watches me." Ashley prayed silently, *"Father, you are watching. You took care of me in Bethlehem. Please, God, help me now!"*

# Chapter 49

They turned down several alleyways before Ashley's captor shoved her through an entryway and up a flight of stairs. Unlocking an apartment door, he pushed her in and locked it with the key from the inside. Dropping her arm he motioned with his pistol for Ashley to sit on an overstuffed chair. He punched in a number on his cell phone with his thumb while still pointing his gun at her.

"Umar!" The rest of the short conversation she couldn't understand. Surveying the room, Ashley noticed some well-worn pillows on a worn rose-colored sofa and a number of pictures of people and scenes of Jerusalem. The kitchen off the living room contained a propane stove and a scratched white refrigerator. Everything appeared old and dark. The one window covered with a steel grate looked out into the narrow street and across it to other buildings nearby. They looked like apartments. A hall led to the back.

Finishing his conversation, he searched her backpack and removed her cell phone. With the pack, her captor pushed her down the hall and into a small dingy bathroom with no window and shut the door. An old bathtub seemed too small for most adults. Her mind flew through many scenarios as she locked the door and used the toilet, a porcelain base on the floor with a hole and a tank above with chain for flushing. She had read of Turkish toilets. Her face in the mirror looked dirty. She washed her hands and face in the basin, but left on the hijab. She was trapped and uncomfortable. There seemed to be no escape.

Ashley stepped out into the hall. The man set the gun down on a small table behind him, making sure she saw it. It had some protrusion on the barrel at the end. He spoke ominously in English, "Quiet." She then recognized the extension on the gun as a silencer, but maybe he meant her to be quiet, not the weapon. Ashley's eyes widened. A silencer. She had seen them in gun shops in Oklahoma. He could kill her almost silently. He probably would if she screamed.

He shoved her silently into a small bedroom, windowless and dark. He flipped the switch, lighting a spare bulb hanging from the ceiling, gestured toward the bed, and left. She heard the lock click in the door. After a minute of silence, Ashley moved toward the door. Locked in. Taking off her hijab, she lay down on the dirty pink spread covering a single bed. Exhausted. She stared at the ceiling. Her hope of rescue was now gone, barring a miracle of God. What did her captor plan on doing with her? Ashley cried silently and let the tears flow freely.

---

Walid opened the apartment door at the knock and spoke in Arabic. "Umar, asalam alekum!"

"Asalam alekum. You sound happy."

"I am. I can almost see the check for thousands of dollars. And we can punish the Americans and Israelis who persecute us."

"Do you mean you found the American girl?"

"Umar, I not only found her. She's here! In my mother's apartment. In the bedroom now with the door locked!" Walid continued, telling his friend the whole story of finding and capturing Ashley. He related watching her ascend the ramp to the Temple Mount and waiting for her to come down, not imagining she would ever join the demonstration. It proved almost too good to be true and made it easy to catch her. Then having her here and his mother away working until ten, everything turned out perfectly. "But we have to make plans to take care of the problem."

"So what are you suggesting 'we' do?"

"If you want to get in on the reward, you have to be part of the action, Umar."

"Alright. I'm in. Now tell me your plan."

Walid checked his watch. "It's five o'clock now. When it's dark, you and I will walk out to the nearby Damascus Gate to get the car. It's in a guarded lot fairly close. We'll drive to the Gate, and I'll leave you there in the car, ready to move it if needed since you can't park there or drive through it."

"So I'm in the car waiting."

"Yes. I'll force her to put on an old Afghan Chadri of my mother's so she'll be covered from head to toe and look like an old lady. She's a fighter and kicked me. To be sure she's quiet, I'll have my gun with the silencer so she can see it, but hide it under a scarf when we are walking. We'll use the streets without shops. Without many lights, no one will notice us."

"So what do we do when we get her in the car?"

"We'll tie her hands, maybe her feet. Then we drive down the Jericho Road into the desert. I know a side road we can drive on without lights. The moon is well over half-full to the east, so we can see. Not even the Bedouins live on the hillsides in that area. Bring your pistol, and the two of us can finish off the infidel, bury her with my shovel I have in the car, and come home. No body to discover. No way to find us."

Walid waited for several moments for Umar to speak. He felt a strange heaviness himself. Finally he heard a subdued, "OK."

Somehow "finish off the infidel" dampened his enthusiasm for the money as he thought of his beautiful victim.


By eight p.m. and after eating, Walid and Umar crept silently out of the apartment to walk to the Damascus Gate. She wouldn't know they were gone.

"Are you sure you are going to be able to keep her from crying out or screaming when you bring her to the car?"

"The gun speaks English, Umar. She knows I could shoot her with the silencer on and no one would know. She'd just fall quietly. Remember, I know a way to the gate that avoids any shops that might be open. Besides, it's dark."

# Chapter 50

Walid's mother wiped the glass cabinets of the jewelry shop again since strangely no customers appeared. At eight p.m. she wondered why the Souk remained so quiet, empty of tourists. Probably because of the day's demonstration and shooting. Her shopkeeper boss smiled at his employee in her hijab. She knew his customers enjoyed her friendly manner and that she earned every bit of her salary and more.

"It's as quiet as Saladin's tomb tonight, Salma. You take the rest of the evening off, and I'll see you tomorrow. No sense in both of us staying here until ten."

Salma strolled the short distance to her apartment, stopping at her favorite open stall for some halal beef and a few vegetables. She climbed the stairs and on opening the door immediately noticed the smell of food. "Walid, are you here? You should be home with your family." She called out again. No answer. She didn't know whether to be puzzled or angry at her son, or both. She looked in the bathroom and saw the towel had dropped to the floor. She tried the bedroom door. Locked. Someone had locked it and left the key on the small table.

"What is going on? Walid, are you in there?" she called.

From behind the door, a woman's voice called out something she didn't understand. Walid didn't answer. She waited a minute for them to dress, and opened the door.

A beautiful young woman stood looking at Salma, fully dressed. No Walid. She looked European, not Semitic, and had long golden hair. She had obviously been crying and probably sleeping since her hair appeared uncombed. But the bed looked as though it had not been used, except for the pillow. Her eyes glistened, wide-eyed, staring at Salma. Something seemed very wrong. Trembling, the young woman nodded to Salma and bowed slightly, greeting her in Arabic.

"Asalam alekum. I'd like to explain to you, but I don't know Arabic."

Salma had learned some English in the shop and recognized a few words. She realized this woman spoke English only. She returned the greeting and then asked, "Walid here?" in English.

"No." The woman shrugged and raised her palms.

Salma understood that she didn't know where Walid had gone. She noticed bruise marks on the young woman's right arm. *What is this all about? She's not much more than a girl. Something bad has happened to her. Walid must have put her here. Why, and what happened that he locked her up? He must be coming back before ten, when she would normally arrive home. Why would Walid do this to a girl? What does she want to do?*

At that moment, the young woman used her hand, motioned toward the apartment door, and then pointed to herself saying, "Go!"

Salma understood immediately. She directed the young woman to follow her. They hurried down the stairs and out into the narrow street. Salma didn't know where she wanted to go and shrugged with hands up, pointing first one way toward the Damascus Gate, and then the other way toward the center of the Souk.

"Jaffa Gate!"

"Ah, ha!" Salma nodded and pointed toward the shops. The young woman burst into tears and quickly enveloped Salma with a huge hug. Then she scampered away like a frightened gazelle.

At that moment Walid strode from the opposite direction on his return from the Damascus Gate. He saw his mother and the girl from a distance. He broke into a run. *No! She's released the infidel!*

Salma blocked him. He almost knocked her over. She grabbed his arm. "Mother, let me go! I have to get her! She's bad. I can't let her go. Quit hanging on to me!" He struggled to free himself.

"Walid, you should be ashamed of yourself! I don't know what's going on, but that's not the way Mohammed, peace be upon him, would want you to treat a woman."

"She'll go to the police and report me. You have no idea what I'll lose. I'm sorry, Mother." He jerked his arm violently, causing Salma to fall, and dashed after the girl. He saw her stop momentarily. A shopkeeper pointed west toward the Jaffa Gate, and she turned the corner. Walid had never seen a woman run like that. Her head covering blew off. She sprinted like a football forward flying toward the goal. Walid tried to catch up, but he could not close the forty-meter gap. He noticed a few people on the street, staring, first at her blond hair flying, then at him. She seemed to be headed toward the police station near the Jaffa Gate. She turned to see him. He slowed down and ducked into a side street. He'd failed. He'd been seen by too many people. Possibly even the police. Disaster loomed.

⁂

Salma picked herself up, shook her head, and limped back up the stairs. Her hip landed on the street and she was in pain. She kicked the door open. Her son had become a wild man, locking up an American young woman in his mother's apartment then chasing her down the street. He had no respect for age and knocked his own mother down. She could have broken her hip. She slammed the apartment door and screamed after him, "You're no Muslim! I hope she gets away!"

⁂

The guesthouse front room might well have been hung in black crepe. The team gathered around some pizza, but no one seemed hungry. A heaviness permeated everyone on the team. Jim sighed deeply and suggested they give thanks for the food. All heads bowed. Someone sniffled. Jim felt so helpless, so despairing of finding Ashley. The whole "trip of a lifetime" came crashing down in tragedy. What could they do in the morning? The whole team would be flying home, leaving at five a.m. Without Ashley. He would stay behind. They had just discussed how Ashley had survived the bombing at home and an armed kidnapping attempt in Bethlehem, and now this.

Suddenly Jim heard someone running, and a disheveled Ashley bolted through the door, gasping for air, and collapsed on the table.

Her whole team jumped up. The place erupted. To Jim it seemed everyone, including the guys, cheered through laughter and tears. They all leaped up to hug Ashley and each other.

"Are you OK, Ashley?"

"Yeah, Jim," she managed, trying to catch her breath.

The guesthouse rocked with joy for the next hour as they ate and heard Ashley's story. Then they quieted to thank God for Ashley's return unharmed.

Finally Jim suggested that Ashley accompany him and Alim to the nearby police station at the Gate to report that she had been found. The Israeli policewoman had a phone to her ear and talked to a man bending over the desk while she searched her computer screen. After waiting for several minutes, Alim translated for Ashley as she reported that she had escaped a kidnapping with help from an older woman. The officer found Ashley again in the missing person file on her monitor and typed rapidly. Then she asked a number of questions: What happened, where, when, who captured her, what did he look like? Alim translated into Hebrew. The police woman picked up the phone, and soon a male detective appeared and ushered them into a room where her interrogation continued in English. Finally the last question, "Where can we contact you tomorrow?"

"We are flying to the U.S. from Tel Aviv tomorrow," Ashley said.

"You can't stay another day?"

"No. But you can contact Alim, who will call my young guide, David. He can provide some information."

"That will have to do then. Our follow-up can be by phone. Local police and Mossad will be on this tonight. We'll try to find the older woman first. That shouldn't be difficult. We want to catch the terrorist. But we can't make you stay, since you are only a witness and victim. Here is my e-mail address and phone number." He handed Ashley his card. "Let me know anything else that could help. I'd like your contact information." She wrote it down for him.

Ashley sighed deeply, closed her eyes and shook her head. "It's over. Thank you for your help. I do hope you find him. I don't even know his name." She suddenly felt faint.

# Chapter 51

Arriving at the airport four hours prior to their flight seemed ridiculous to Ashley, until she saw the long lines of travelers waiting to get through multiple security checkpoints. She, at least, felt safer for it. The Israelis didn't seem so concerned about checking small packages, shoes, or underwear, but they did quiz Ashley repeatedly, looking on computer screens for any hint that she might be linked to a threatening organization.

As the jetliner lifted off, Ashley felt relieved but also saddened to be leaving this fascinating country with its many contradictions. She had learned so much, asked and answered so many questions. She felt emotionally spent and physically exhausted. After she'd slept a while, Jim came back to chat with her, taking the empty seat between Marie and Ashley. He seemed intent on getting more information.

"I feel responsible for all you've been through, Ashley. It seems like you've been singled out for punishment on this trip, and I'd like to know why. Do you have any ideas? Are these attempts to harm you all related?"

"I think they are. I've come to the conclusion that the person at Herodian who followed me up the spiral road is the same guy who almost kidnapped me at the wall in Bethlehem. Then, I had the best look at the terrorist who captured me yesterday. Same eyes, same height. I think they are all the same guy."

"Anyone with him?"

"No. I never saw anyone else, although he did talk to a guy named Umar in the apartment. But I didn't see him, being locked in the bedroom. And of course, I met the older woman, who freed me. I think it was her apartment. It didn't look like a guy's place. And everything looked old. I think she might be his mother. He showed up just as she pointed me to the Jaffa Gate. She tried to stop him, and he knocked her down when he chased me. I saw her on the ground when I rounded a corner. Can you imagine? Knocking an older woman down, maybe your own mother? She rescued me. I owe her a great deal, and all I gave her was a hug."

"He obviously didn't want you to get away. It must have been terrifying for you, gun and all."

"Yeah. I never ran that fast playing soccer. He couldn't catch me. I think a few other people being around stopped him."

"OK, Ashley, assuming one guy was after you in all these places, the question is why. Why did he single you out for kidnapping?"

"I have no idea. I suppose there are several possibilities. A stalker, maybe."

"Do you think he's crazy?"

"I suppose you'd have to be a little crazy to kidnap people. But he seemed intentional, like he had a plan."

"How about anti-American?"

"I suppose. But it seems unlikely. I could be from anywhere in Europe or North America. He wouldn't know."

"Religious?"

"That's possible." Ashley nodded. "Maybe he could be angry that I didn't wear a hijab. But mad enough to kidnap me?"

"What about for ransom?"

"He doesn't know my family. I would think he would kidnap someone known to have family money."

"How about being a hired gun?"

"Who would hire him to get me? I am just a graduate student from Seattle."

"That's right," said Jim, "a student who almost got killed in a terrorist bombing in Seattle." He paused. "Don't you think it's kind of ironic? Did it ever occur to you that the Seattle bombing may have something to do with the kidnapping? It's seems like an obvious question."

"Hmm, I never thought of that possibility. But again, who and why? I can't imagine ... unless whoever did the bombing somehow thinks I'm a threat. I don't recall anything around the time of the explosion so how could I be a witness against anyone?"

"Yes, but they haven't caught the bomber yet as far as I know. It would be all over the news broadcasts if they had."

"But Jim, if the bomber is really out to get me, I'm just as much at risk going home as I have been here." Ashley's eyes stared out the window as she thought her nightmare may not be over.

After Jim returned to his seat, Marie looked over at her younger friend who had been through so much in the last few months. Ashley closed her eyes, head back on the pillow, and shut the window cover. She didn't move for several minutes. Then she opened her eyes and gazed at Marie. She smiled a sleepy smile and reached over to squeeze Marie's hand. "We have learned so much together on this trip of a lifetime. You have been a wonderful traveling companion."

"I can't imagine what you've been through. One thing about you really hit me. You question lots of assumptions. I'd be interested to know how this trip has changed any of them for you."

Ashley smiled. "You told me when we started that I had a lot to process from the stuff I had been reading, from Najid, from our church beliefs. You were right. So I just tried to meet lots of people to get different stories and ideas, some Jews, some Arab Palestinians."

They chatted about how she had experienced Muslims of all stripes, from her kidnapper to Fatima's family. She'd learned the stories of Arab Christians, families like Najid's and Faisal's, the wonderful young Jews like David and Ben who had become like brothers to her, then the rabbis who shared totally opposite opinions about Zionism—they had particularly challenged her to think.

"And what about all the conflict that is going on in this land?"

"Marie, I've just experienced a little bit of it. The dynamism of Jewish Israel, their tragic history, and their present confidence are all amazing. But then to hear the stories of so many families being displaced from their homes and seeing a family from children to grandparents pleading with soldiers to not bulldoze their home in East Jerusalem ..." Ashley's voice broke and she paused. "I've seen some of the magnificent buildings of stones, the stones of history, the dead stones. What has affected me most, though, are the living ones."

"So how do you put all this together, Ashley?"

"I haven't. You were right. I have a lot to process when I get home."

# Chapter 52

**M**r. Appleby, Washington calling," his assistant shouted from the other room. Gordon Appleby, wading through the morning's e-mail on his computer, picked up the secure telephone. Putting his feet up on the desk, he took the call reluctantly. Probably they had more work for him to do. *July in Seattle is the time to play, not work twelve hours a day.* He had postponed one hiking trip with his family already. Being an FBI agent didn't prove quite as fun and exciting as he anticipated it would be when he graduated from law school ten years ago.

"Appleby here."

"Gordon, we have some new information on the Seattle bombing." His boss's voice rose as the words tumbled out.

Gordon bolted upright in his chair pulling his feet off the desk. He'd encountered nothing but dead-ends in the investigation over the past month. Somehow a terrorist had slipped through the security net in the United States and totally disappeared. The country remained frightened that their vaunted FBI had not been able to come up with a suspect. Gordon and his colleagues had continued, frustrated with no leads.

"Yeah. We've been contacted by Israel's Mossad in conjunction with the CIA. It seems that your injured young lady—"

"Ashley Wells?"

"Yeah, that's her, took a trip to Israel and is only now returning. Her friends reported her missing last night in Jerusalem, for only eight hours or so. Mossad got right on it from her description of events. Seems some woman in the Muslim Quarter heard a blonde Caucasian girl and an older lady talking on a certain street. A guy came up, the blonde ran, and the man knocked the old woman down to chase the girl. She got away."

"Are they sure it was Ashley Wells?"

"Yeah. She came into the police station at the Jaffa Gate and answered questions, apparently. And Mossad doesn't usually make mistakes. Israeli intelligence is reliable."

"So, what happened?"

"They tracked the older woman down through informants. Turns out she's the mother of the guy who apparently abducted Ashley."

"So did they find the creep?"

"Yeah. Got him locked up. Name's Walid something or other. He admitted abducting the girl. They think from the little he has revealed so far that he's in touch with other radical Islamists and that money is involved."

"Not surprising. Is there more?"

"Yeah. Apparently she thinks the same guy tried to get to her in Bethlehem, twice. So if true, he was serious about it. Could be a stalking, but Mossad doesn't think so. Mostly because of his connections and the money."

"So have we confirmed a financial connection leading to Ashley specifically?"

"Not yet. They first checked whether she posed a threat to someone there. And that seemed unlikely to Mossad. But they think they are getting to the bottom of this. Turns out Walid had hinted that he's not alone and that the money might have come from America."

"So they suspect that Ashley could be a threat to someone in this country, and that he paid Walid to eliminate her in Israel?"

"You got it. That's what they're working on now. They are trying to get the identity of his partner or partners out of Walid. They'll let us know of further developments. They'll try to trace the story back to the United States."

"So Ashley likely will be in danger here?"

"Right. That's why I called immediately. They are due to land soon, U.S. Airways from Tel Aviv."

"Sir, we'll be in touch with her when she gets off the airplane."

<hr />

Gordon Appleby, in his casual shirt and slacks, waited at the entrance to the C Concourse in Sea-Tac airport, shoulder holster and pistol well hidden. He could have shown his card and walked to the gate, bypassing security, but that seemed unnecessary.

He had not met Ashley. So he watched for some young woman, blonde, who looked like Ashley's picture. He didn't want to alarm her or the rest of the team. Their plane had landed, according to the big screen. As he scanned the expectant people, he shook his head at how much of his job consisted of waiting for someone or some bit of information. With a continual stream of people meeting their families, Gordon kept a close watch. Then he saw her, laughing with a tall gentleman as they walked out of the concourse. Suddenly her eyebrows rose and she rushed ahead toward a young man who looked Arabian. They grasped hands and began to chat and smile broadly. Gordon sprang into action, moved forward, and interrupted their conversation.

"Are you Ashley Wells?" he asked, inserting himself between her and the Arab as the man backed away.

"Yes." Her smile quickly faded. She looked frightened.

He pulled out his laminated card, *Gordon Appleby, FBI*, and put it away as soon as she had seen it. "I presume you know this gentleman?" he said, turning toward Najid. He suddenly looked familiar.

"Oh yes, Mr. Appleby. We're good friends. He's a Fulbright Scholar at U Dub. You don't need to worry about him. In fact, he was thoroughly checked by the police after the bombing here in Seattle. I thought by you guys too."

"Oh yeah ... of course. Now I remember. He's your friend that we investigated fully. We met in jail. You're Najid, right? I'm sorry, I should have recognized you. Thanks for understanding what we needed to do to investigate things fully. I'm sorry you were caught up in it." They shook hands.

"Yes, sir, I remember you very well. You don't forget a man who is well over two meters tall and gets you out of jail."

Gordon chuckled. He ushered them over to the wall, out of traffic. The tall man approached with a worried look on his face. He looked first at Gordon and then at Najid.

"Are you OK, Ashley? Are these friends of yours?"

"Oh yeah. Jim, this is Najid, my friend from the U whose family I visited in Galilee. And," turning to Gordon, "this is Gordon Appleby from the FBI."

Appleby showed his card to Jim. "And you are?"

"Jim Swain." Jim extended his hand. "A pastor, and team leader on our trip to the Holy Land."

Gordon shook hands with both men. "Can we sit down somewhere privately and talk? I would be happy to have you two gentlemen join in the conversation with Ashley. It will be a few minutes for your luggage to come. Perhaps you could tell your families that you will meet them at the luggage carousels on the lower level."

Gordon watched Jim returning to their table off by itself in the wide causeway outside an airport bookstore. People walked by, but the four could speak without being overheard.

"I apologize to you, Ashley, for startling you." Gordon nodded to Ashley. "We have information that you should know, and these gentlemen, if you agree, should hear it because they may well be part of your protection."

Ashley's face blanched and her eyebrows shot up. "What do you mean, 'protection'? I'm home now. Safe. Right? But go ahead. Najid and Jim are great friends now."

"Ashley, there is some evidence that you may be perceived as a threat to someone here in the United States. Mossad, the Israeli intelligence people, already have a man in custody who admitted he abducted you in Jerusalem. They don't have the whole story as yet, but they think that he has accomplices. Also they think he did this for money."

"That makes sense." Ashley sighed. "I wonder how they caught him so quickly. I'm so glad they did! I never found out his name, but I think he was the same guy who followed me twice in Bethlehem. He seemed determined to abduct and do something to me. I just don't know why."

"We know his name's Walid. Mossad is investigating, and they think that money came from the United States."

"You are suggesting that someone here in the U.S. paid for a hit man in Israel?" Jim asked, his eyes wide.

"That's exactly what Mossad is checking into as we speak."

"So that means that there still could be someone in the United States who wants to harm Ashley?" Jim interjected.

"Yes. That is our concern right now. And that's why I'm here this afternoon."

"So how would someone like that know that Ashley went to Israel, and how would they find her there?"

"That wouldn't be too hard. Was the trip publicized?"

"Yes it was, in our church. But not the names of those going," Jim replied.

"Was the itinerary on your website?"

"Yes," Jim admitted.

"There you are. If they found out somehow that Ashley would be on the trip, they would have her itinerary."

Jim looked stunned. "I'd never thought that could be dangerous."

"So Jim, the terrorists who did the bombing here in Seattle may perceive Ashley as a threat to them. Maybe they think she saw them at the synagogue."

Ashley stared into space, trying to recall. Her memory for the event seemed so fragmentary. "Like I told investigators before, I don't remember much that happened immediately before or after the blast. I was with Najid and I can't even remember what we talked about."

They glanced at Najid. "I reported all I remember to the police, right after the bombing."

"Yes, Najid, we have that information, and despite jailing you, we appreciate what you did."

"That's alright, Mr. Appleby. The police did their best to learn what happened."

"So, Ashley," Gordon continued, "the point of all this is that you need to be careful and alert. You should always be with someone when you are out and about. There's safety in numbers. Let your friends know if you are going to be away and where you will be. Keep in touch with them electronically, cell phone, text messages, e-mail, and through social media so if you suddenly become silent, they will be alerted and can contact us."

"Can't you protect her, Gordon?" Jim asked. "I mean not you personally, but the police or FBI?"

"We wish we could, Jim. I will tell you that we did have some intermittent surveillance on Ashley after she got out of the hospital. One of our people. That has been part of our investigation to identify the bomber, but not for her protection. We simply don't have the manpower to do that. Besides the law allows only protection of key prosecution witnesses in a trial who may be or have been threatened by the defendant's side. It really comes down to Ashley using her good judgment. Being out past midnight may be especially dangerous."

"I planned to celebrate our return with friends." Ashley shook her head. "I'm trying not to let fear control my life."

"I am sorry, Ashley," Gordon said. "But you need to know and be alert for anything that looks suspicious. In the meantime we and the police will be doing everything we can with this new information to find the bomber, whether here in Seattle or anywhere in the United States. We've had a tight check on international flights and borders ever since the bombing, so it's likely he's here in the country somewhere."

Gordon handed Ashley and the two men his card so they could reach him day or night. He said goodbye and walked away. The three sat there. Najid looked at the floor. Jim grimaced and shook his head, sighing deeply.

Tears formed in Ashley's eyes. "I prayed I had left all the trouble behind, in Israel."

# Chapter 53

Robert Bentley had counted the days. He knew from the Internet that the U.S. Airways flight had landed, bringing back the tour group to Seattle. He paced the floor in his apartment wondering whether or not Ashley Wells returned with the rest of them. Neither cable nor local TV broadcasts mentioned anything about the bombing victim not returning from the Holy Land. They would have if she had disappeared. He'd contact Imam Jabril in the morning to get any news. He could always query his contact in Israel by secure e-mail. Robert tossed and turned all night, unable to sleep. He would have to wait for the answer to Jabril's e-mail. He hated waiting, but had to confirm that Imam Jabril's contacts in Israel had succeeded in their mission to get rid of this woman. She could put him behind bars for life—or worse.

The clock moved so slowly. Robert would drive over at five-thirty in time for morning prayers, and then they could talk. No, he would walk. It would be good to get out. Besides, he didn't want neighbors to identify him now with a red Corvette convertible.

Robert, bowing on his knees with the imam, looked over during the prayers and noted the spot on the man's forehead where he had pressed it to the ground in prostration before Allah for many years. He didn't share that intense desire to pray like the imam, but he did share the desire for revenge against the policies in the U.S. and Israel. He would never lose that hate.

He followed the imam to the kitchen after prayers, for the early morning tea. They carried steaming cups outside in the quietness of an early July morning to avoid any sensitive discussion that could be picked up by the prayer room bugs, if they existed. The backyard had to be safe. It would be difficult to plant eavesdropping devices there since the telephone and power lines came from the street in front. Settled in plastic chairs in the back of the Islamic Center, Robert began, "They're back."

"Who's back?" Jabril asked.

"The tour group from Israel. You know, the group that Ashley Wells traveled with."

"Oh yes. The problem my contact there worked on."

"But I need to find out now whether he succeeded."

"We'll probably know in a few days."

"Look, Imam. I need to know now! My life is at stake here! I'm paying for you and your man over there, lots of money. I want you to go to your computer now and find out with your secure e-mail what happened in Israel!"

"Alright. I haven't checked e-mail this morning. I'll send an urgent message asking him." Jabril walked back into the house.

Robert shook his head. His future hung on the answer. The one bit of news that could free him from the dark cloud hanging over him, and the imam acted like it was just an ordinary morning to drink tea. How long would it take to get an answer back? Who was he writing to, and would he know now what happened to the woman? Robert sighed and began to sweat. Five minutes went by.

Suddenly the imam broke into a run from the house toward Robert. His face appeared ashen. His eyes stared from under his bushy eyebrows. "My friend sent me an urgent message! Oh, Allah! We're in trouble!"

Robert blanched. He held his breath in panic. "What—what

happened?"

"All he wrote in Arabic was 'Mission failed.' Then he wrote 'Mossad closing in' without finishing the sentence."

"Oh, no! Did he say anything in English?"

"No. He must have sent it in a hurry as he saw police or intelligence agents coming. Or maybe he just heard they were coming somehow."

"Who's Mossad?"

"Israeli intelligence. Like FBI."

"What does that mean, Imam? Are we in danger?"

"They work back. They must have captured the hit man and discovered my friend who sent the message and received the funds I sent. Mossad has ways of getting information out of people. I don't know how. But they always seem to get what they want. I had wired half the money you gave me."

"So what does that mean?" Robert looked wide-eyed at Jabril and trembled.

"It means Mossad has his computer now, including the messages to and from me. My friend sent that last message two hours ago. They probably have the FBI already tracing my address as we speak. I've got to get out of here."

"What about me, Imam?"

"You have no electronic or telephone messages to the Islamic Center or to Jerusalem, so they have no way of tracing this back to you. The only thing is the bank. They could follow the money trail ... particularly if my friend is forced to tell where he got the money. But he won't tell. And I use a false passport with a different name to set up accounts to wire funds. He doesn't know who you are. But he can't stop them from reading his e-mail. But no, he won't, how do you say, 'sing'?"

With that, the imam disappeared into the house. Robert waited, frozen over what to do. Within five minutes, Jabril ran with his laptop and a carry-on bag through the backyard toward the alley. He slapped a very small pistol on the table next to Robert, who soon heard a car start and take off, tires squealing.

Robert stood numb and motionless, thinking. Ashley Wells. Still alive, in Seattle, to identify him to the FBI. All his plans had failed.

Robert grabbed his hair in his fists. What would happen to him with the FBI on his trail? What did they know? What would they learn from coming to the Islamic Center? Where would the imam go? What would happen to the center? What about Ali? He hadn't seen him since the bombing. Ali and the other brothers didn't know where Robert lived. Good thing he hadn't shown up at the center. But what should he do now?

He finally realized the FBI could find him at the center. Robert picked up the pistol, bolted out to the back alley, and walked hurriedly out to the next street, heading home at just under a run. He needed time to think this through. He would never go anywhere without the loaded gun in his pocket.

As he sat on the edge of the bed in his small apartment, Robert took a mental inventory of his situation. First, he had kept a low profile at the community college and elsewhere. And Ali, his friend and accomplice, had no idea where Robert lived. The people who helped obtain the C-4 never really saw him or heard his name. Now the imam had left, heading who knows where in the U.S. or Mexico. Probably not Canada. That would be both too obvious and difficult to get through the border. No one else besides those two knew anything. Except Ashley Wells.

He had gone over and over this in his mind so many times. Why hadn't she gone to the police already if she recognized him that day in the church? The fact that he wasn't aware of them following him suggested that maybe she hadn't recognized him after all. If that was the case, then he needn't have tried to get her eliminated in Israel. He had been so caught up in the excitement of the bombing, and then covering his tracks, that he had not been thinking clearly. All he lost was a lot of money. *But the FBI now knows it came from the United States. So that directed their search back here. And with computer information, they would settle on the Islamic Center and Imam Jabril. Jabril thinks his friend won't sing. But with the guy's computer and financial records, it won't matter.*

Robert stared at the floor. Maybe there was no point in going after the woman now. His attempt to neutralize her as a threat would probably fail. It would jeopardize him further. He should just stay away from her so she wouldn't see him again. But on the other hand, perhaps she still posed a danger to him. He must try something.

He could move from Seattle. But where would he go without attracting attention with his red convertible? *You don't live in a stupid little room and drive that kind of car.* Perhaps he should sell it and move. But every major transaction, every move with official documentation, leaves a paper trail to follow. No, he must lie low, use buses mostly, make all purchases in cash, and stay away from any place he might see Ashley Wells. Robert put his feet up to go to sleep. It would be lonely, alone in his apartment. He couldn't even see Jenny at the community college. She might know Ashley from church. But fortunately Jenny didn't know where he lived. What had his life come to? Hiding, alone. He had become a jihadist hero to radical Islamists around the world. But they didn't share in paying the price.

# Chapter 54

Two of Ashley's housemates had welcomed her home, met Najid, and went into the kitchen to cook a homecoming dinner for Ashley, inviting Najid as well. He carried her two bags upstairs and came down to find her lying on the couch, smiling at him.

That began hours of conversation about the trip, her wonderful time with Najid's family and how much she would have liked to have him with her. She avoided telling him about her troubles, not wanting to spoil their time together. She had so much to tell, and she was happy just to be back with this amazing man. She smiled and then yawned as her eyes closed. Jet lagged, she just made it through dinner without falling asleep.

"I'll see you tomorrow," Najid said as she climbed the stairs to her bedroom. Ashley slept for twelve hours.

She called her parents the next morning to let them know she had arrived safely at home. When asked if she had a good time in Israel, she simply shared a bit about the famous churches and some highlights, the Western Wall and the Garden Tomb. She didn't mention the abduction, realizing they had not heard of it, nor of any ongoing danger. Apparently she had escaped so quickly that the abduction didn't make the news. So they didn't need to know any of that now. Her parents had had enough to worry about after the bombing without concerning themselves with something more that may never happen.

# Chapter 55

Najid appeared at the door. He looked at her with a startled look, speechless. He handed her a single long-stemmed rose in a water tube. She thought she had looked a mess when she got off the plane yesterday, so she took special care to look her best when he came. She threw her arms around his neck and hugged him. He stood there, a bit red in the face, smiling down at her. "Ashley, you're, um, you look a lot better than yesterday. It's ... so good to have you back home."

Ashley grabbed his hand, put the rose in a vase, and led him to the table for lunch. Her housemates disappeared. "Can't you stay?" Najid called to one of the girls running up the stairs.

He didn't notice the quick wink she flashed to Ashley. "We've already had lunch. But thanks, Najid."

Ashley brought a salad and sandwiches from the kitchen and sat down around the corner of the table next to him. The sun shone though the large window, brightening the yellow table cloth and red roses from her roommates and now Najid. The neighbor's silk tree dominated the view with its striking light red blossoms, hiding much of their 1920s house and porch.

"I prayed for you every day while you traveled, Ashley. Obviously you needed miraculous help at times, from the little you've explained so far. You remember the ten lepers that Jesus healed? Only one came back to thank him. So I want to thank him now." Najid looked up, eyes open, and smiled. *"Thank you, Father, for keeping Ashley safe and free from harm. You answered our prayers. And thank you for this lunch together."*

Ashley gazed at this remarkable young man, thinking back to their first meeting in the zoology grad student lounge. She kept smiling at Najid, forgetting to eat.

"This salad looks good," Najid said. "Pomegranates. I haven't had them since I came here. Should I have some?"

"Oh! I'm sorry," she said, pointing to the salad. "Please ... start." Ashley flushed. "I ... was just thinking."

"About what? You have been through so much in the last three months."

"Yeah ... about everything. Meeting you. Dragging you to the synagogue just in time to get bombed. You in jail. Me in the hospital. Meeting your family. Having so many experiences with so many different people. I mean the good stuff. That's what I'm focusing on. Not the abduction. Najid, I met so many interesting people."

"Good for you."

"But I haven't put together all that I have learned. There are people in each religious group that have views so contrary to each other. I need to talk it through with you. That's how I process things, by talking. And asking questions. I have collected so many different ideas and impressions and beliefs. Many are a lot different from what I held in Seattle before I left."

"Give me an example."

"OK, two rabbis ..." She stopped and laughed at herself. "Sounds like the old joke of two guys in a bar. OK, we talked to two Orthodox rabbis, one who survived the holocaust in Auschwitz as a child. He loves Zionism. It's part of his faith, and he wants more settlements to take over East Jerusalem and the West Bank to eventually drive the Palestinians out completely. He likes America's money and support but doesn't understand why Christians in the United States would get behind Israel like they do. Particularly since that view of the end times often involves killing Jews at Megiddo."

"So who is the other rabbi?"

"He's also Orthodox and also believes in the truth of the Old Testament. He's the rabbi for the Jewish student, David, who guided us and hunted all over the Muslim Quarter for me. Wonderful guy! Anyway, this rabbi hates Zionism. He believes taking homes and lands by force violates Judaism."

"So then what do *you* think, Ashley? Did you get your questions answered? You know, how the Jewish people feel about the support Israelis get from Christians in the United States?"

"Not really. In any kind of scientific experiment, you need enough subjects in your control and experimental groups to make any differences statistically significant. My sample size was too small." They both laughed.

"I met some wonderful Muslims like Fatima's family who endured so much loss since 2002. They accepted Fatima's following Jesus as long as she remained a cultural Muslim to the world and didn't become a 'Western Christian.' I'll never forget them. But then there's that other Muslim guy, my abductor.

"We loved our guides, David and Ben, guys who were so kind— both Jews—particularly David, who risked his life trying to find me. But then we had bad experiences with Israeli soldiers at checkpoints or the bulldozer guy representing the Israeli government."

"So you found good ones and bad ones of both Muslims and Jews. What about Christians?"

"Well," Ashley chuckled, "again my sample is too small. I wish I could have gone to your church and met your friends there. But if your family represents Christians who have suffered along with other Palestinians, then I have found people who love God and believe in peacemaking. Same with Faisal and his wife in the West Bank. On the other hand, I didn't like some of the religious stuff we experienced in the Christian holy sites."

"So you found it complicated?"

"Right!"

"Good for you. It is."

# Chapter 56

It had been several hours of talking since lunch. Ashley wandered into the kitchen to get some tea. She found Najid standing and looking out the living room window when she returned. She didn't want him to leave. The hours of the afternoon had flown by.

"Would you like to take a walk after tea?"

"Let's do. I think we need to talk about your being tracked down in Jerusalem and what to do now, here in Seattle." He sipped his tea.

Ashley averted her eyes and didn't respond at first. It had been so wonderful to talk about her trip. The abduction was past history. She didn't want to talk about it or deal with it anymore. But now it seemed, the menace continued. Was there someone here out to get her, even in Seattle? When would this end? What should she do?

She knew Najid remained concerned for her safety and that made her care for him. Care? Did she really mean 'love'? She shocked herself at the admission. Yes, she did love him. She had never met any guy like him. He helped her forget everything for a while. And now he wanted to discuss the blackness again. She stirred her tea and raised her eyes to Najid.

"I don't know what to do now that I am back. Even if the FBI or police had me under their surveillance for a few weeks, they can't be with me all the time when I'm out. Gordon Appleby told us that."

Najid seemed lost in thought. Finally he broke the silence as they finished drinking. "Let's go."

They strolled out into the summer afternoon to Ravenna Park, staying in the open areas and avoiding the wooded ravine, although she had enjoyed jogging there many times before the bombing. She took Najid's arm, and he seemed pleased, tightening his arm against her hand. She had never touched him like that before. She sensed some tingling. It felt so good. And she felt safe with Najid.

"So Ashley, if the police can't protect you when you are out, what will you do? You don't want to be ... what is the word?"

"A recluse?"

"Yeah. I learned that recently but forgot."

"You're right. I have too much to do to stay at home completely. I know I need to be cautious, but I refuse to give in to fear or evil. I *need* to protect myself, but I also need to trust God. He sent Salma for me in Israel. It's the only way I can get through this. But maybe a plan will help. I do need to study for the MCAT, and I can do that at home."

"MCAT?"

"Medical College Admissions Test. It's what you have to take to get into medical school. I plan now to take it at the end of summer so I can apply this fall."

"So you're not taking any classes this summer?"

"No, and no lab assistant duties either, just like you. But I do need to work on my thesis as well. What does your schedule look like now?"

"I am taking a class this summer and working on my thesis too," Najid replied. "But I have a flexible schedule for the most part."

"So getting back to my problem, I think I can get my housemates to help. Two of them are also grad students and can be with me going to and from the library. Maybe some other trips too, like shopping and church."

"Here's a bench, Ashley. Let's sit down." They had reached the park in an open area just off 15th Avenue. Najid grasped her hand. "You probably won't understand this, and I don't know how to tell you in the American way, but you have experienced my family and will realize that human beings are pretty much the same in Israel or here. We have the same feelings and desires, whether we have been treated badly or well."

Ashley silently searched Najid's face.

"You have been so welcoming to me, a stranger. You have been kind. And now we have been through so much together. You have met my family, and they think highly of you. They didn't want you to leave."

Tears welled up in Ashley's eyes, and she wiped away a couple of them running down her cheeks.

"Oh, I'm sorry that I made you cry!"

"No, Najid! You just touched ..." She placed her hand over her heart.

"Ashley, I would do anything I can to keep you safe. I'm not sure what that would look like. See, I know that phrase, 'What that would look like.'"

She laughed as she wiped her eyes with her sleeve. "You're getting pretty smart! Too American."

"So let me help you. I have the time and I'm flexible with my schedule. Here is my suggestion: We get in touch every morning by phone. You tell me what your schedule is for the day and whether one of your friends at the house is going to the campus or somewhere else with you. If you want to go out, and you need someone to go with you, I will come and we can go together. I don't want you out alone. If you need to work at the library or go shopping for food, I need to do those things too, and we can go together. OK? Isn't that what you say all the time, 'OK'?" He smiled. "You protected me from the bomb. Now let me protect you."

"You may be putting yourself in danger, you know. It happened before. I must be bad news for you."

"I can handle bad news once in a while."

She laughed and shook her head. "Najid, you amaze me. I've never met a guy like you who can handle trouble so calmly."

"Well, you'd never met a Palestinian before."

"OK." Ashley laughed, and leaning toward him, she grabbed him around the neck pulling him close, and kissed his cheek.

# Chapter 57

Gordon Appleby had worried about Ashley most of the night after meeting her at the airport. So his early morning tennis match would take his mind off this frustrating case. His smartphone rang just as he started to serve the first game of his second set at the Seattle Tennis Club. He groaned as he peeked at his Caller ID. His phone read "FBI Washington."

"Sorry," he called to his partner as he jogged off the court. He ducked into the dressing room and sat down on a bench next to a row of lockers.

"Appleby here."

"Gordon, we have more information on the Ashley Wells situation."

"Give me a few minutes to get to the office and the secure phone." He ducked outside, shrugged to his partner and dressed quickly.

With no one in his office, Gordon left the door open. He picked up the phone. "What's up?"

"Mossad has amazing ways to get guys to sing, and Walid

warbled all the right notes. They found the big man there, got into his computer, and think they discovered the contact in Seattle."

"Did they follow the money?"

"They tried to trace the money, but ran into a roadblock. The funds wired to the big man's account in Jerusalem came from a Seattle bank but under a name and account number that's apparently an alias. Seems the guy in your town had several names and false passport numbers. But we know that because we have his real identity from the guy's hard drive, which Mossad hacked into in Jerusalem."

"So, don't keep me in suspense. Who is it here in Seattle?"

"Name's Jabril. Goes by Imam Jabril."

"Oh, we know him well! He's shifted over the past year to become radicalized and has been preaching jihad to some young guys. He operates from an old house that we have bugged. They call it the 'Islamic Center.' We haven't been able to pin anything on him or any of his followers yet."

"You do now. That's why I'm calling. He's an accomplice. He may have heard from his friend in Jerusalem and could be planning to skip town. We need his computer and any information he can provide. We could be getting close to the real jihadist. Though I doubt it's the imam himself."

"So what are my instructions?"

"Get a search warrant and local police to bring the guy in from the Islamic Center. And do it quickly before he gets away."

<hr />

Armed with compelling "probable cause" for the search, Gordon easily convinced the judge to issue a search warrant. He and several police officers raced to the Islamic Center. They inched toward the building carefully, stationing officers on each of the four corners of the old house. Gordon approached the front door and knocked, pistol in hand. No answer. He shouted at the door, "FBI, open up!" Still no answer. He glanced in the windows. The front room looked empty. Hearing no sound, he kicked the door in and, with another officer, searched the big room, kitchen, and the bedrooms both upstairs and down. Nothing suspicious. A desk in a small bedroom downstairs would be the most reasonable place for a computer, but no luck. With the police they turned over every piece of furniture, and they looked under each bed. They searched every drawer and cupboard including in the basement. Finally Gordon checked the garage near the alley and found the door open. He assumed it must have been a fast getaway.

Gordon quickly phoned his boss from his insecure cell phone. They'd have to choose their words carefully as usual on the public airways. "Looks like the bird got the word and flew away. We have looked everywhere in the place, and found nothing. Apparently took his laptop with him. We couldn't even find any paper files of interest. We've come up with nothing, nada, zip."

"Did you find anyone to talk to?"

"No. Quiet as a tomb. It's Saturday. All the activity was yesterday. Too bad we didn't have the overseas information then."

"Yeah. We'll put out an all-points bulletin for the guy, with his picture. I hope you have one."

"We do, in the office. I'll e-mail it to you."

"Did you have any information about his car?"

"Unfortunately not."

"So until we find him, it looks like the investigation here has hit another dead-end for now. We've put in a computer search on the 'Watch List' database with what we know about the case so far and come up with nothing. We've checked again with the mining company in Montana, who insist they know of no material missing. They admit that the tracer found at the site came from batches they received from the manufacturer. But they keep careful records and everything seems accounted for."

"So where does that leave us, boss? We can't let this slip by us."

"It'll take more time, Gordon. We'll have to wait until we get our hands on the preacher."

# Chapter 58

As summer progressed Robert couldn't decide which he hated more, boredom or fear. He constantly wondered what the FBI and police would be doing to find him. The goons in Israel had failed in their hunt for Ashley Wells. He had failed through them. And now the tables were turned. The hunter had become the hunted. He still wanted to be the hunter. But how? It would be too dangerous. He detested the isolation and inactivity. Holed up in his room. A world-famous but anonymous jihadist. No one knew who he was ... except her.

He did like to cook and eat. So he'd go the supermarket nearby on Broadway, but not until late in the afternoon when lots of shoppers stopped there coming home from work. He fit in easily with his baseball cap pulled down over his eyes, looking like any other student from the community college. He'd found out where Jenny shopped, and it wasn't that market. He went into the kitchen to check the cupboards and refrigerator. They seemed depleted of his provisions, so he scribbled out a shopping list which grew long. Robert checked his watch. His one outing of the day wouldn't start for several hours. He lay down on the couch and tried to sleep. His mind wouldn't let him.

The last week of July provided Ashley the best weather Seattle had to offer: sunny and warm, in the eighties during the daytime. She loved the prolonged twilight that lasted until almost ten-thirty at night. And the colorful gardens. She put aside her data and the first draft of her nearly completed thesis. Looking down the long table in Suzzalo library, she gazed at Najid as he concentrated on his smartphone. Ashley smiled.

She had never felt so safe with a guy. He seemed to handle everything with equilibrium. She'd never seen him angry. But he must be restless too. He wasn't reading his journals right now or writing. Maybe he was surfing the Internet. Others studied nearby, and she didn't want to disturb them. She walked over to Najid and tapped him on the shoulder, motioning him to follow her out into the hall.

"It's so nice outside, Najid. I'm having a hard time writing anymore. It's early afternoon and only Monday, so we have all week to work. Are you still in the middle of something?"

"No, my mind is wandering. I've had enough also. Let's get out of here. Do you have something in mind to do?"

"Yup. I've heard of Volunteer Park on Capitol Hill. It has an Asian art museum and a conservatory with tropical plants—as well as a great view of downtown Seattle and the waterfront. Besides, I've read of a nearby supermarket there that has international foods. We could take a bus from the Ave and start with the art museum and conservatory."

"I can understand *art museum* but *conservatory*, what's that?"

"A conservatory is a house made of glass so the light can come in to make plants grow. They can keep it warm so tropical ones grow even in the winter time. The same word can be used for a music school, just to confuse you more." Ashley's eyes twinkled as she smiled up at him.

Najid gazed at the huge old trees of Volunteer Park as he strolled hand in hand with Ashley toward the conservatory. They dwarfed the olive trees in Galilee. Najid shook his head. "These trees are no good. No olives or any fruit!" He watched her chuckle as they continued walking.

The unusual tropical plants fascinated Ashley. Najid recognized a couple of them. Then it was off to the Asian Art Museum. Najid had never been in such a place. Ashley shared what little she knew of Asian art as they admired the delicacy of the paintings and objects.

Walking down the steps, they spied the waters of Elliott Bay far below, with the Olympic Mountains behind them, still sprinkled with a dash of snow on the very tops left from the winter storms. And then the city itself came into view as they stopped. Ashley pointed out the waterfront with its ships and the Space Needle off to the north. The bay sparkled with thousands of reflected lights from the sun, still high in the Western sky.

They stood together in silence as they gazed out at the late afternoon scene in Seattle. He pulled her close with a sudden hug. His heart raced.

Finally he spoke. "Should we go to the market?"

Ashley sighed and nodded. "Yeah, let's do. We can walk down to it. We can get something to eat there also."

They strolled hand in hand though the Capitol Hill neighborhood, first by the mansions of old Seattle near the park on the top of the hill and then smaller houses and apartment buildings as they approached the market on Broadway. Ashley had taken the bus before and knew the area a bit, that the main street through the many shops and stores led south to the Seattle Central Community College.

"This is the business community of Capitol Hill on Broadway," she explained to Najid, "and south of that" she pointed, "another hill, hospitals, sometimes called Pill Hill." Her eyes lit up as Najid frowned.

"Pill Hill? What is that? I don't know *pill.*"

Ashley laughed. "Those are the little white medicines that you take when you're sick. Didn't you ever take aspirin?"

"I guess I have. I don't remember. My mother used to give me some awful liquid stuff in a spoon. She tried to pronounce the English name. It sounded like 'castor oil.'"

# Chapter 59

People and shopping carts filled every aisle in the supermarket. It was surprisingly busy, Ashley thought, especially for this time of the day. After grabbing a bite to eat at the market café, she began a search for some items on the special sale list she brought. Najid followed as she pushed the cart.

"I think I'll keep you as my guard, Najid," she said with a wink. "Yes, guard or guardian can be used. Sometimes we say 'guardian angel,' meaning someone sent by God to keep us safe. So I thank God for my guardian angel."

Ashley rounded a corner to walk down another aisle and almost crashed into the grocery cart of a young man coming up the other way. "Excuse me," she said instinctively as she stopped. He looked startled and stared wide-eyed at her for a moment. Ashley stood still, frozen in time, and stared wildly at him. That face, enclosed by a hood … those dark eyes, and the distinctive red birthmark above the left brow.

In an instant a memory revived, recalling one that seemingly had been erased: first the scene in the back of the church where she saw him and sensed an unknown recognition, and then another memory card with a picture of a street, and across it a hooded man with his face partially hidden, but bearing a distinctive red mark. Time stood still. She couldn't breathe. She couldn't move.

Robert Bentley's face turned white, his dark eyes wide, as he silently stared at Ashley. He stood motionless for an instant before a muffled "Oh shit!" escaped from his mouth. He suddenly wheeled around with his cart, and she saw him walk slowly back down the aisle, deliberately examining items on either side.

Ashley turned back around the corner to find Najid looking the other way at some juices. She struggled to control her trembling hands and her shaky voice. She whispered, "I saw him. I saw him."

"Who are you talking about, Ashley?"

"The bomber! I know it's him! I know it's the guy! I recognized him. Same eyes. Same red mark. Dark-blue baseball cap this time. He knows who I am. Oh Najid! What should we do? He may come after me!" Ashley shook, her face felt cold.

"Go back to where we ate, to a place where there are many people. I'll be back."

"Don't leave me, Najid!"

"Go, Ashley! He hasn't seen me, at least my face."

"But he may have a gun. What are you going to do?"

Najid raced around the cart and disappeared down the aisle after the guy in the dark-blue cap. He saw him turn to the right and speed up with his cart. It contained several food items. Najid followed him at a distance, keeping back and almost out of sight.

The bomber glanced back quickly and kept going. He picked up his pace, almost running as he approached the checkout stands. Then he suddenly turned into another aisle, and halfway up that one abandoned his cart. He looked around again. Najid realized that the bomber could not see him tucked behind the corner of the tall shelves. *Where did he go?* Najid whispered to himself in Arabic. His heart pounded. *Oh no! Ashley!*

He ran toward the café section and saw her at a distance, approaching a table with several women. *She's OK, but where's the bomber?*

Najid hurried to the front at the checkout stands, looking wildly for his man. Then out of the corner of his eye, he saw him in the parking lot. Najid scurried around the carts neatly stacked into each other and out the door. He saw the man scurry fast past a line of parked cars. Najid followed from another lane, keeping his eye on the bomber, but hidden from his sight. Najid soon blended into others walking on the sidewalk. Cars crowded the street. He saw the bomber turn left into a quieter lane lined by apartment buildings. His man again looked back, but Najid ducked behind other walkers. The bomber turned again, this time to his right. Each time he turned to another street, he looked around. Najid kept his distance, hiding when his fugitive turned a corner.

The man began to run, at first a jog and then faster. Najid wondered whether the bomber might have seen him. He dropped off the pace putting more distance between them, walking rapidly. Turning a corner he came to a short block, and the guy had disappeared. Did he have a gun, and was he hiding, intending to use it? Najid looked around, reasoning that he would not turn back toward Broadway and the supermarket. So he walked carefully to the next intersection surveying all the apartment building entrances.

He knew Ashley would be wondering what had happened, but he had no time to call now. His heart raced. He had lost his man, the guy the FBI has been searching for. He had to find him. As he crossed the intersection, a jogger came by running up the hill. Najid swung in behind him, and soon noticed his prey heading the same direction a block ahead, running. Staying behind the jogger, Najid had no trouble keeping up, and used him for cover. The bomber finally slowed to a walk, taking several more turns down side streets. Najid kept back, determined not to lose him again. This continued for what seemed to Najid at least half an hour. Finally the man stopped. Najid watched from behind a large laurel bush. His prey scanned the street in both directions. He shoved his cap back and waited. Najid studied his face. A car drove by. The fugitive walked across the street and up to a front porch.

He looked around again, in both directions. Finally reaching into his pocket, he opened the door with a key and disappeared inside.

# Chapter 60

Ashley had approached a group of three women sitting at a table. She looked ashen and couldn't stop shaking. "May I join you?"

They looked up, surprise registering on their faces. "Ah ... sure," one of them said, shrugging her shoulders. "Sit down." She smiled.

"I'm sorry," Ashley replied as she sat down. She took a deep breath and leaned back in her chair. Her hands shook. She fought tears, blinking several times and swallowing repeatedly.

Another of the women put her arm on Ashley's shoulder. "Are you in trouble?"

Ashley sniffed and reached in her purse for a tissue. "I may be. But I'm also concerned for my friend. I don't know what's happening or where he is." She looked at her watch—eight-thirty. "I'm afraid to call him right now."

"Whatever is going on, you are safe with us. Would you like us to stay with you for a bit? We're just having iced coffee and chatting."

"That would be wonderful. You're so kind." She scanned the area for any security guards and didn't see any. "Thank you."

"Is there anything we can do to help?" another of the ladies asked.

"You've already helped." Ashley sighed deeply. "Why don't you go on with your conversation and I'll just sit here for a while, quietly. I need to think."

"No problem," one woman said. "We'll pretend you're not here so you have time to collect your thoughts." And they resumed their conversation quietly.

Ashley closed her eyes and remained silent, remembering the confrontation with the bomber in detail. She shuddered inwardly. He hadn't come after her with a knife or a gun, and it had been several minutes now. But he could be hiding and still shoot her.

She felt somewhat safe with the ladies. *But where is he? Had he left the store? Is he hiding somewhere? And where is Najid? He took off down the aisle after the man. Are they fighting? Is Najid OK? Is he trying to catch the guy? Maybe he's armed and Najid's in trouble.*

Ashley sighed deeply, closed her eyes, and began to pray under her breath. As she opened her eyes, Ashley saw one of the women looking at her.

"Hi," she said, extending her hand. "I'm Ann. You look calmer. That didn't take long."

Ashley took her hand and smiled. "I'm Ashley. Yes, I feel better now. I guess I should give credit where it's due. I prayed to God."

Her new friend glowed. "We understand. Ashley, this is Mindy and Pat."

They shook hands all around. Ann continued, "Pat and Mindy have to get home to put their kids to bed, but I have time to stay with you for a while. Is that OK?"

"I'd love it. I really appreciate all of you." Ashley stood up. "Thanks, you guys."

"Tell me about yourself," Ann said. "You talk like you're not from Seattle."

"You're right. I'm from Oklahoma."

"Ah ha! 'Where the wind comes sweeping down the plain.'" Ann smiled. "That's my favorite musical of all time."

Ashley nodded. She knew every song in "Oklahoma" by heart. Ashley learned about Ann, and then began to tell her story. The minutes rolled by as they shared at first tentatively and then more deeply. Ashley told of the bombing.

"Oh!" Ann jerked upward, her hand covering her open mouth. "I knew you looked familiar. I saw your picture in the paper just after the synagogue collapsed. Oh, my goodness!" She stared at Ashley. "Weren't you in Harborview Medical Center?"

"Yes. I had surgery, but I'm fine now."

"And they haven't caught the bomber yet, I understand. He could be anywhere in the world by this time."

Ashley shrugged. "I can't talk about it."

"Is that why you're so upset?"

"Yeah, it's related. But also I've lost my friend, Najid. I don't know where he is. He may be in danger. He told me he'd be back." Ashley reached into her purse, not knowing whether it would be safe to call him. So she texted a question and waited, staring at her phone. No answer.

"When?"

"I'm not sure, Ann. It's nine-thirty now and will be getting dark by ten or so. Your family is expecting you home. Why don't you go? I plan to stay here until Najid returns."

"Do you think he will come?"

"I think so. If he doesn't, I'm calling the police."

"Maybe you should call now?"

"I think I'll wait. He's reliable and resourceful. He'll be back; I'm sure of it ... unless he has met with some kind of trouble."

"I'm not leaving, Ashley, until I know you're OK." Ann pulled out her cell phone. "Honey, I'm a bit delayed at the store, so I'll be home later than planned. Love you."

The women talked further. Ashley worried about Najid. The guy could have a gun. Najid could be lying somewhere, injured or dead. He wouldn't keep her waiting if he could call. She should text him again. But maybe it would be dangerous if his phone even beeped. She would just wait. She checked for messages again. Nothing.

Ashley did talk about her trip to the Middle East without mentioning the abduction. Ann seemed eager to hear the stories. She knew little of the area and didn't seem to know why the West Bank got its name or who lived there. She had heard of Palestinians and assumed they were all terrorists, and how could you negotiate with such people? Ashley tried to explain by telling several stories of Palestinian families she had met. Ann stared at her wide-eyed. She had never heard such things, or about walls or checkpoints. Time flew by.

Ann glanced over Ashley's shoulder, listening to the stories. She suddenly screamed, "Ashley, someone's coming fast!"

Ashley jerked her head around, panic on her face. She leaped to her feet and ran into Najid's arms, laughing and crying all at the same time. They hugged for several moments. Ashley grabbed his hand and led him to the table. Ann's eyes stared, raising her eyebrows.

"Ann, this is Najid, my friend." Ashley looked at him. He looked sweaty, his shirt wet under the arms. She had to hear what happened, but that would have to wait. At least he seemed OK. He smiled and shook hands with Ann.

"Ann here has taken care of me for the past two hours, Najid. She has been wonderful. I had never met her before."

"Good." He placed his hand over his heart. "I appreciate your care of Ashley. Let's celebrate with some tea!"

Ann shook her head and started to laugh.

"Oh, you don't like tea?"

"No, no, Najid," she sputtered. "It's … it's just the whole thing tonight. Some things in life seem unbelievable until you experience them. The tea at ten-thirty on top of everything else that's happened to you guys just struck me funny."

Najid chuckled. "OK. What drink would you like? I'm buying."

He soon brought back one decaffeinated coffee and two herbal teas from the counter. "Ashley, are you alright?"

"Oh, Najid! I'm fine since Ann and her friends were here. But I've been worried sick about you. But what about you? What happened?"

# Chapter 61

Najid told the story beginning with his tracking and then losing the bomber in the store. At the end of the account, he explained why he'd waited so long behind the big bush, with a dead cell phone. He needed to find the address number on the house and couldn't see it until he got close. So he waited until it grew dark and it seemed unlikely that the bomber would be looking out through the window. With that, Najid pulled out a slip of paper from his pocket and showed it to Ashley. "That's the address of the bomber."

Ashley sat spellbound, pondering Najid's story. She gazed at Najid and couldn't speak. Tears welled up again, and she wiped them away. Ashley sighed deeply and wilted. "It's almost over."

Then she leaped to her feet. "We've got to call Gordon Appleby! The FBI needs to know! What am I doing sitting on this information, now that we have the guy's address? Ann, would you take us home quickly? I'll call Appleby as we go."

"Follow me!" Ann shouted as they ran for the car.

Ashley speed dialed the number.

"Hello. Appleby here. Who is this?"

"Mr. Appleby. This is Ashley Wells, with Najid. We just got some important new information for you that could be very helpful."

"Stay right there. Are you home?"

"I will be in ten minutes."

"I'm on my way!"

Over the next few minutes in the front room of Ashley's house, Gordon Appleby listened to her and Najid tell the story of meeting the bomber in the store and the adventures that followed. He peppered her with questions until he seemed satisfied that Ashley knew that the guy she saw was indeed the bomber. Najid's details of the guy's escape lent further confirmation. The FBI would want every detail. Najid handed him the slip with the bomber's address.

Appleby suddenly stood. "You two are amazing. And Najid, I have rarely seen such bravery and smarts outside our organization. I've got to get to a secure phone now, arrange a stakeout, and work out plans for a search and seizure immediately. The vulture may fly away soon."

# Chapter 62

Gordon Appleby began arrangements with Seattle Police while he drove to his office. Within minutes, they parked a dark, unmarked car across the street from Robert Bentley's apartment, with two officers charged to prevent his escape.

Gordon raced to his office and called his boss in Washington D.C. on the secure line.

"Appleby here. Are you awake?"

"Appleby, this better be necessary. It's, let's see, two in the morning, and I'm in the middle of a great dream."

"We may have found the culprit in the Seattle bombing."

Gordon heard his boss stirring as though getting out of bed. "OK, I'm awake and at my desk." He heard a chair scraping the floor, and a brief silence. Then, "You found the bomber? Give it to me!"

"We may have." Gordon related the story Najid and Ashley had told him. "It sounds real and bona fide. I think we should investigate the lead."

"Get a stakeout on his residence right away."

"Done. The police have it in place as we speak."

"Yeah." Then silence for several moments. "We are getting closer on this end by following the money trail of the imam. We haven't found him yet. And with his aliases and accounts, we can't come up with who lined the imam's pockets in Seattle. Maybe we just moved past that ... Get warrants for a search and for the guy's arrest before he can destroy his hard drive."

Gordon called the U.S. Attorney he knew and the on-call federal judge shortly after midnight. He explained all the evidence to date to both of them. By two a.m. he had picked up the signed affidavit drafted by the attorney at his home and driven to the judge's home to obtain both search and arrest warrants for one "name to be determined" at the address given him by Najid.

Meanwhile, the Seattle police had assembled their emergency Special Weapons and Tactics team for counterterrorism operations. They prepared for the possibility of explosive materials as well as guns. Five men stood ready for action by two-thirty in the morning. They met Gordon at the Capitol Hill precinct of the Seattle Police and raced off in an armored vehicle by three a.m.

Gordon radioed the officers in the stakeout vehicle. "Any activity?"

"None so far, sir."

"Good. I'll be there with the SWAT guys in five minutes. You can join us to surround the house, and we'll move in on it."

"Roger. Affirmed."

They moved silently through the darkness. Two regular-duty police officers and three SWAT team members guarded the entire perimeter of the house. Gordon and the remaining two special officers approached the front door and knocked quietly, guns drawn. Gordon's pulse raced. The porch light flickered on. The door opened slightly. An old man in pajamas peered out from behind a safety chain with a shocked look on his face.

Gordon raised a finger to his mouth then whispered, "FBI, sir.

Please unlock the chain and step out quietly." Gordon showed him his FBI credentials. "Please turn the porch light off and do not turn on any lights in the house. Do not make any sound except whispered answers to my questions."

The man complied then stepped out to the porch and quietly away from the house into the darkness, visibly trembling. "What's this about?"

"It has nothing to do with you directly, sir. This is about a young man who we think lives here."

"You mean Robert? I don't know what he's been doing. He stays in his room most of the time now."

"Do you have his last name?"

"Oh yeah. Bentley. Robert Bentley. Pays his rent every month on time, by check."

Gordon showed him both the search and arrest warrants by penlight. "We didn't have his name until now. We have reason to believe he could be involved in a serious crime. This is a search and arrest as part of our investigation. So we are asking for your cooperation in quickly answering a few questions. You are the owner of this property?"

"Yes."

"Are there other individuals in the house that we need to protect?"

"No."

"Do you have a dog or any animal that would make noise?"

"No."

"Do you have any reason to believe Robert Bentley is not here now?"

"No. I heard him moving something heavy across the floor just an hour ago. Woke me up. It sounded like dragging a dresser over to the door on the north side of the room. It's right above my bedroom."

"So there may be a dresser blocking the door. Are there any backstairs where someone could escape, or windows?"

"No. It's a small house, one stairway with just two bedrooms and a bathroom upstairs. There are two windows in his room and also in the empty one."

"Is the door to the empty room open?"

"Yeah." He nodded. "I keep it aired out. There's no one living there now. The bathroom door should be open too. It's directly ahead as you come up the stairs. Robert's door is on the right as you reach the upstairs hall."

"Robert could have explosive material with him and use it. We would like you to wait safely in that vehicle across the street. One of our officers will escort you there before we go inside. Are you willing to do that?"

"Yes. But could I go back in to get some things I can't lose?"

"No, sir. We cannot allow that. We need total silence. Surprise is one of our best means of avoiding injury to anyone or any property. Now we need to move. The officer next to you will escort you to the police vehicle for your safety."


A SWAT officer silently signaled the team on the perimeter of the house by a red light flash that they were going in, guns drawn. Gordon and the two SWAT officers crept silently up the pitch-black stairs to the top, finding the small hall and the open bathroom door ahead.

Through their night vision goggles they saw the right-hand door clearly. The SWAT officer who looked like a football lineman raised his right leg and smashed the door open with a huge kick, pushing the dresser clear across the room. With the loud crash, the three men leaped into the room shouting, "Police! Hands up." They focused an intensely bright light on the far wall and bed, momentarily blinding its occupant. Robert Bentley squinted into the light as he bolted upright and leaped toward his laptop computer. A SWAT officer tackled him, pinned him on the floor, and quickly bound Robert in handcuffs. They dragged him to a chair and turned on the room lights.

# Chapter 63

While one officer guarded their prisoner, Gordon and the other one searched the room for any evidence of explosives or weapons. They found a small pistol only, loaded. Gordon again displayed his FBI identification with his picture, and examined Robert's wallet and driver's license.

Gordon told Robert his Miranda Rights. He had gone through this so many times he could say them in his sleep. "You are being arrested. I have here both search and arrest warrants signed by a federal judge, based on a legal affidavit that states there is some evidence to believe that you have committed a serious crime. We will detain you as a suspect only, in jail, pending further investigation. That will include questions of you. Do you understand … Robert?"

Robert looked down, refusing to look at the warrants and refusing to speak.

"You have certain rights under the Miranda law. They include the right to silence. You should understand that anything you say could be used against you in court. You have the right to counsel, a lawyer, before answering any questions. Do you understand?"

Robert offered no response.

"You can choose to answer my questions now if you wish. What is your name?"

Robert remained mute, refusing eye contact.

"Alright, gentlemen, please escort the prisoner to your vehicle and bring back in the owner of the house with an escort to get a few clothes and essentials," Gordon said. He pressed his radio activation button. "I'm asking the team to come up here with latex gloves and containers for gathering evidence. Contact the bomb squad with a dog to sniff out any missing explosives. We'll ask the owner to leave briefly until that sweep is finished."

They took pictures of everything in the room. With many gloved hands obtaining evidence from Robert's file drawers, scraps of paper, CDs, iPod, smartphone, and most importantly his laptop. The passport picture matched his driver's license one. Gordon noticed a Pakistan visa dated in March. The team labeled everything, including where they found the item in the room. Finally they carried it all down and loaded the plastic containers in the SWAT vehicle with Robert caged in back. They drove to the Federal Detention Center in SeaTac not far from the airport. Robert, heavily guarded, walked with the SWAT officers into a room for pictures and fingerprinting. Then his jail door clanged shut.

Robert stood in the middle of the cell, hearing the footsteps of his guards receding down the echoing hall. Suddenly alone, he stared at his enclosed cell. It smelled like floor cleaners. The light in the ceiling, covered with a steel mesh, would be just enough to read. The toilet and fold-down bed on one side balanced the steel chair and table on the other. He stared blankly, thinking of all that had transpired in one hour, his greatest fear now realized. He grimaced and shook his head.

It had all started with such excitement, such fervor, as he would prove to the West, to the U.S. and Israel, their injustice to the Muslim world. He had prayed facing Mecca. But it didn't seem to protect him.

Maybe Allah wasn't merciful after all. He had been in the company of jihadists, but now he was alone. They offered no help.

He used the toilet and then sat down on the bed. It felt hard, with a thin mattress enclosed in tough plastic, a small pillow, and two blankets. Robert Bentley lay down, unable to sleep. He saw no one. He was in solitary confinement. He thought of his parents. They would soon find out where he was. What should he do? The FBI guy mentioned that anything he said could be used against him. So the best thing was to say nothing. He wouldn't give them the satisfaction of any reply. They would have to prove his guilt. The guy had said something about getting a lawyer. He wouldn't even do that. A lawyer might make him talk somehow.

Gordon collapsed in bed at six a.m. and set his alarm for nine o'clock. The State Police laboratory chief called just after it went off. Gordon's wife had insisted that he sit down to eat.

"What have you found so far?"

"Gordon, we've got enough on this guy's computer alone to hang him."

"Passwords any problem?"

"Not for our people."

"So what have you found?"

"E-mails galore to and from Islamic radicals here and abroad. He came out to Seattle because of a group that frequented the Islamic Center of Imam Jabril. From his online banking evidence, we found the missing link, the check for thirty grand that the imam split, sending fifteen to Mossad's guy in Jerusalem."

"You know if he went to Pakistan?" Gordon asked.

"Yeah, we'll get the CIA going on that. We won't leave any stone unturned."

"Good. We'll send everything here to the FBI lab for confirmation—fingerprints, traces of explosives, anything we find. But we've got enough evidence now for any prosecutor to put this murderer away for life, even if he says nothing."

Ashley slept in after the excitement of the previous night. She boiled a couple of eggs to go with her toast when the telephone rang. Her housemates had left for work.

"Hello."

"Ashley, this is Gordon, from last night. We got him."

"You mean you already have the bomber? In jail?"

"Yep. Behind bars. His name is Robert Bentley."

"I can't believe it!" She exhaled slowly ... and for a moment couldn't speak. "You guys amaze me! Anyway, Najid apparently found the right guy, huh? Have you confirmed it?"

"Ashley, his computer is full of incriminating evidence. This is all preliminary of course, but there's hardly a snowball's chance in hell that he's innocent of the bombing."

"Isn't there a lot more to do? Has he said anything?"

"Yes there is, and no, he won't talk."

"Is that a problem?"

"Not yet."

"Will he get out on bail?"

"I doubt it."

"I assume you can't discuss details with me, but do you think he has any accomplices here that might be looking for me?"

"Ashley, I don't know. It'll take time to find that out. We do know now that you were followed in Israel, four times, with the intention to abduct and kill you."

"Uh ... only three times, Gordon. Twice in Bethlehem and once in Jerusalem."

"You're wrong. It's four times. You were stalked in Nazareth on a shopping afternoon, but you apparently never realized it. I am not sure what happened to thwart that one."

"I didn't know that. Are you sure?"

"Your stalker over there, guy by the name of Walid, has confessed to all four attempts, including the one in Nazareth."

"Oh my goodness! How did this 'Walid' get involved, or even know me?"

"It's a long story, Ashley, but just know that Robert Bentley here in Seattle paid thousands of dollars to have you wiped out in the

Holy Land because he feared you recognized him and would turn him in. Which you did."

"Oh my goodness! It's all ..." Once again, the reality of how and why she came so close to being killed in Israel shocked her into silence.

"Are you still there, Ashley? You OK?"

"Yeah, I think so. It just hit me again how close I came. So there still could be someone out there he paid to track me down here in Seattle?"

"It's possible. For now I'd still be careful."

Ashley hung up the phone and sat down to think. She didn't know whether to laugh or cry. They got the bomber with lots of evidence against him—that was the good news. But did someone out there, here in Seattle, still want her in his gun sight? Most jihadists didn't work alone.

# Chapter 64

Robert heard footsteps rumbling down the hall, echoing off the bare walls. An armed officer opened his cell door and stepped in, followed by the tall FBI guy who arrested him the previous night. Robert had only had a couple hours of sleep.

"Robert Bentley, I'm Gordon Appleby with the FBI. We met last night, as you will recall." He quickly showed Robert his FBI documentation.

Robert remained silent.

"We informed you of your right to be silent and to be represented by an attorney. It would be best for you to have one. Are you agreeable to that?"

Robert stared at the floor without speaking.

"Alright. Let me explain the situation to you. We have evidence from many sources, now including your computer, that you may be guilty of a combination of hate crimes. That puts you in federal court jurisdiction. This is not your usual local or state court system. So you are now in the Federal Detention Center in SeaTac. Do you understand that these are serious charges against you and that the justice system of the United States of America will govern what happens to you next?"

Robert struggled to keep from shaking. Trembling, he would not speak, even if tortured.

"You will be treated fairly and are presumed innocent until proven guilty. I'm going to explain the procedures you will go through. You will be taken to a U.S. district court where the federal judge will talk to you and give you some good advice. This is a preliminary hearing. He will decide whether you could be released on bail. He will review the charges against you and explain the procedures. The government has the legal right to keep you confined here during the pretrial period if it comes to that. You could avoid a trial by pleading guilty in court. Do you understand, or do you have questions?"

Robert shifted his position on his bed and said nothing. His mind whirled. He had lots of questions. He couldn't seem to put everything together. Watching crime shows and court scenes on TV didn't prepare him for this.


The next morning they came for him. The orange jumpsuit didn't bother him, but the shackles and chains on his wrists and ankles did. He stared as he walked into the stark courtroom. The judge peered down at him. The presumed U.S. Attorney with the FBI guy across the room and the armed guards all looked frightening. Reporters with notebooks crowded the area behind the railing. Robert felt nauseated. This was for real. They ushered him to stand before the judge, who seemed to look right through him. The room remained silent as the judge gazed at some papers on his desk. Finally he spoke to Robert.

"You, Robert Bentley, are being charged with several serious crimes. You are in federal court because of the nature of the charges. I will ask the federal prosecutor to bring the allegations based on whatever evidence they have."

The attorney stood to read the charges. "Your honor, Robert Bentley is charged with assault using powerful explosives, second degree murder, and attempted murder with intent to kill." He sat down.

The judge looked at Robert. "How do you plead, guilty or not guilty?"

Robert said nothing. He stood still, head down.

"Do you hear the charges against you? Are you guilty or not?"

Robert's heart raced and he shook visibly.

After several moments, the judge continued. "Hearing no plea, the court presumes the defendant alleges innocence."

The judge spoke again to Robert. "Young man, you have heard the charges. The court determines you will remain in custody without bail because of the risk you pose of either fleeing or being a danger to others. Your case will go to a grand jury, which is normal procedure in the federal court system. A jury of your peers will decide whether the evidence presented by the federal prosecutor will be sufficient to indict you. That means they will decide whether you should stand at trial for the charges against you. If they are not sufficient, you will be freed. If they are, you will be tried in federal court by another jury. If you decide to plead guilty, you can avoid a trial and will appear in court to be sentenced. Do you have any questions?"

Robert shifted his position a bit. The shackles dug into his ankles. He heard all the judge said, but it seemed unreal. He wouldn't give him the satisfaction of a response.

"Robert, I understand you don't want to talk. Listen to me now. You need a lawyer. These are very serious charges. The crimes you are alleged to have committed have reverberated around the world. The United States federal courts have prized evenhanded justice for over two hundred years, to free the innocent but also to punish the guilty, usually with imprisonment. You are at risk for possible life in prison, if not the death penalty."

Robert felt his face blanch. His shackled hands shook. He suddenly felt faint as his heart thumped rapidly in his chest.

The judge continued: "To serve as your own lawyer is not wise. You can hire your own counsel, or we will appoint a public defender for you on standby, to advise you even if you don't want him or her. You need a defense attorney to represent you and guide you, beginning with your appearance before the grand jury. You will have visiting privileges and telephone access while in detention. If you decide to talk or ask questions, let one of the officers at the center know and an attorney will be available." He banged his gavel. "Court dismissed."

# Chapter 65

Conrad Bentley leaned back in his reclining wood chair, set his feet up on his desk, grabbed his early morning coffee, and reached for his *New York Times*. He'd been so busy the previous day he'd skipped the evening news broadcasts. But no deadlines today. So good to stay home. Internet access made it unnecessary to fight the crowds on the Long Island train going to Wall Street every day.

Life had treated him and his wife well, except for their only son. Lorraine and he missed Robert, despite his tirade when he left one year ago. He had never sent an e-mail or called. They had tried to find him on social networking sites, but to no avail. They talked about him frequently, expressing regrets for being too busy for him in earlier years, wondering where he went and when they would find him. They had considered contacting police about his being missing, but Robert had reached legal age and had a right to his independence.

Conrad opened his paper and stared at the headline, SEATTLE BOMBER CAUGHT. Then his eye stopped at the first paragraph in bold print: "Robert Bentley, 22, of Seattle, the alleged synagogue bomber, apparently acted alone. Taken into custody early yesterday ..."

"Lorraine! Come here!" He read on, his mind a blur as he scanned the article, seeing the words "Long Island" and "Pakistan" and "homegrown radicalized Islamist." He couldn't get enough air to breathe. He pulled his feet off the desk and spilled his coffee over his lap, dropping the cup on the floor. Lorraine rushed in.

"What happened? What is it? Are you OK?"

"Read this!" He shoved the paper at his wife and buried his face in his hands. His breath came in quick gasps while she read out loud.

Her voice quivered as she read the story. He looked up to see her face flush down to her neck. Her voice broke as she finished the article and shook her head. She began to cry.

"No, no! This must be a mistake!" He continued: "Robert had issues, but not this. Turn on CNN while I go online." The story was all over the online news sites. Every one had screaming headlines, bloggers' comments, analysis, interviews with police, security experts, the FBI. CNN had information in its news scroll as its anchors interviewed various sources with information or speculation.

Suddenly, Conrad Bentley's cell phone beeped. He didn't recognize the "206" area code.

"Conrad Bentley speaking."

"Mr. Bentley, this is Chad Harris with *The Seattle Times* newspaper. May I speak to you about Robert Bentley? We understand he is your son and—"

Robert clicked off his cell. "Oh my God! Lorraine, the news media knows Robert is our son."

Lorraine wiped her tears with the back of her hand. "Robert, you used to be such a fine boy. You've had trouble, but this? What could have possessed you? We've tried to raise you to respect people. But a rabbi died as a result of the bombing. You're being charged with murder. I can't believe you did it. This can't be!"

Lorraine threw the paper on the floor sobbing. She looked at her husband, still bent over with his head in his hands. The coffee soaked his pants and the cup lay on the floor. "My baby! Our child? What has happened? There must be some horrible misunderstanding. What can we do?"

"We've got to find out more," Conrad said, shaking his head in disbelief. "Turn off your phone, dear. I am going to call the office and tell them not to respond to any media inquiries about our son ... and I am going to reach out to the FBI."

After a couple of phone calls to regional FBI headquarters, Conrad reached the Seattle office where a receptionist answered the phone.

"Who are you?"

"I'm Robert Bentley's father. I'm calling from New York."

"Oh, yes, sir. We've had a hectic morning with calls from the media here and around the world."

"So you do have him?"

"He's at the SeaTac Detention Center south of Seattle."

"Can you give me more information?"

"Sir, I am certain our agents will want to speak with you, but for now here is the number of the center. I suggest you start there. But first, give me your contact information."

Conrad tried the number. After several more minutes on hold, a male voice answered. He acknowledged that Robert occupied a solitary cell in the highest security wing.

"I'm his father, calling from New York. Is it possible to speak with him?"

"No. I'm sorry. We've had many reporters wanting to get to him. I have no way to verify you are not a reporter right now."

"Look! I'm just his dad, for heaven's sake! I want to talk to my son. He's innocent until proven guilty, isn't he?"

"Yes, sir. OK, let me get some information from you so we can confirm who you are." He proceeded to ask several questions that only the family would know.

The hours ticked by slowly as Robert's father tried to work. He couldn't concentrate as he stared blankly at the stock exchange data changing wildly around the world. He talked to several family members who called about Robert. Finally after dinner, the call came. Both he and Lorraine picked up the phone.

"Conrad Bentley? I'm calling from the Federal Detention Center in SeaTac, Washington."

"Yes. I'm on the phone with Robert's mother as well. Can we talk with our son?"

"Unfortunately, no. Officials have been attempting to talk with him all day as part of our investigation. He refuses to say anything or answer any questions. They did ask whether he would take a phone call from you, and he shook his head. In fact, that response is the only one we have had from him."

"Does he have a lawyer?"

"Not to our knowledge. The arresting officers read him his Miranda Rights. He's just been arraigned in federal court today."

"How will he defend himself without an attorney?"

"The judge has strongly advised him to get counsel. Even if he refuses, the court usually appoints a public defender to monitor the proceedings and advocate for him as needed to be sure he is treated fairly."

"So he knows anything he says may be used in court against him?"

"Right."

"He needs a lawyer right away. If we flew out to Seattle, do you think he would see us?"

"I don't know. You are welcome to try."

A few minutes later, Lorraine Bentley walked down the stairs to her husband's office. "I don't know what to think," she said to Conrad. "If he won't even talk to us—"

"He must be scared to death, Lorry. So he won't talk to anyone, even us. Of course we might be the last people he wants to confront right now. I wonder if he would talk even to a defense attorney.

"Whatever he has done, he needs legal help. We have to get a lawyer for him. I'm going to book a flight for tomorrow, for both of us."

# Chapter 66

Conrad and Lorraine Bentley stepped into the large, stark white reception office at the Federal Detention Center. "We spoke over the phone yesterday. I'm glad you flew out today. I'm Officer Greg McKenzie." He shook hands with both Bentleys.

"We're sick about Robert," Lorraine began. "We haven't seen him for a year and have no idea where he lives or what he has been doing."

"Remember to be careful in what you say, Mrs. Bentley. He is innocent until proven guilty."

"We hope he is innocent of the charges, of course. Does he have a lawyer yet?"

"Not to my knowledge. However, yesterday at his arraignment, the judge said he will appoint a public defender if needed."

"Did he speak to the judge or to any of you?" Conrad asked.

"No. He remains silent. Won't talk to anyone. He is eating, however."

"Oh!" Lorraine sighed deeply. "What should we do?"

"Go see him. You are not the first anguished parents we've seen.

Many of them come in wondering how their son could have landed here. Sometimes parents are good at getting cooperation from the inmate. It's to his disadvantage not to have legal help."

Lorraine's heels echoed loudly as she walked down the cement corridor with her husband and Officer McKenzie. She noticed the smell of some kind of cleaner that irritated her nose, and the harsh fluorescent light flickered. They had to go through a metal detector and handbag X-ray.

McKenzie led them to the bars fronting Robert's cell, but did not let them in. "I'll be right around the corner at my desk if you need me for anything."

"Hello, Robert." His Dad extended his hand through the bars. Robert did not take it. He looked briefly at his parents then turned away.

Lorraine erupted into tears. "Robert, we love you no matter what has happened. We came to be with you and help in any way we can. Please don't reject those who love you the most."

Robert remained standing with his back to his parents. The one-sided conversation continued for ten minutes. Finally it became apparent, even to Lorraine, that he would not even acknowledge them. They called Officer McKenzie, and he led them out. They said goodbye to Robert's back.


On the cab ride to their hotel, both Bentleys sat silent and dazed. Finally Lorraine spoke. "I can't believe he is treating us like this when we flew out to be with him! Is there any point in trying to get a good lawyer for Robert if he won't even talk to anyone, including us?"

"I think we should try," her husband said. "I have contact with some financial attorneys here in Seattle who should know the name of a good criminal defense lawyer. I'll work on it tonight in the hotel room. Then let's try to see Robert tomorrow to talk some sense into him." He paused. "I take it back. Let's wait a day for both of us to cool off and for Robert to change his mind when we don't appear tomorrow."

Robert sat over his breakfast of eggs, sausage, and toast, deep in thought. He wished his parents had not come to Seattle. They were trying to run his life again. He'd made his own decisions now and would have to live with the consequences. He didn't need them and would continue not responding to anyone, certainly not to his parents. That would make them return to Long Island.

Robert lay down to nap. It would pass some time. The guards did allow him a few minutes for exercise right at ten, outside in the courtyard. He remained alone except for a dog that seemed friendly and apparently belonged there. On returning with a guard, he found Officer McKenzie and a man in a dark suit waiting outside his cell.

"Robert, this is Mr. Charles Rand, an attorney here in Seattle. He's here to help you and needs to get acquainted."

Mr. Rand reached out to shake hands, but Robert refused and looked away into his cell. Officer McKenzie opened the cell door and motioned for both men to enter. Then he stood in the hall outside the cell. Robert shuffled in first and sat on the edge of the bed, face impassive. Mr. Rand stood, briefcase in hand, and peered at Robert. For several moments he didn't speak, but looked around the cell. Finally he asked Robert if he understood why he, Robert, landed in federal detention here and what to expect next. Robert remained silent and studied the floor tiles.

Rand tried several times to engage Robert in conversation about himself personally, even about sports. He tried fishing and then travel in the U.S. Did Robert know how much experienced lawyers could help to minimize the time convicted felons must serve? Or how sometimes they could get people off the hook completely?

Robert refused to talk, becoming increasingly agitated. He knew his dad had hired this guy, and he wasn't about to knuckle under and accept help. Finally Mr. Rand shrugged. "Here's my card. Call me if you decide you want my help." He left it on the small table.

# Chapter 67

After lunch Officer McKenzie came with an envelope addressed to Robert. He handed it through the cell bars. "We've checked it for hacksaw blades. There's only one there." He chuckled at his stale joke. Robert didn't, but took the letter. He wondered who could be writing him. It looked like a woman's handwriting. There was no return address but it was postmarked in Seattle at six the previous night. Maybe Jenny. She must have read about his arrest. She must be shocked.

Robert tore open the envelope, sat back down on the bed, and began to read. The handwriting looked feminine and graceful.

*Dear Robert,*

*Now that I know your name, we can meet officially. We have seen each other several times now, first at the synagogue, I think, then at church, and finally in the supermarket on Broadway in Seattle. On each occasion one or both of us have been afraid. We've run from each other. I can't live with fear or hate in my heart for another person. I realize the dangers and implications of writing you, and that this letter may not remain private. Yet I feel I must write. So I choose my words carefully.*

*I did recover completely from my injury when the bomb went off. I know the bomber didn't intend to harm me, personally. I just stood in the wrong place at the very moment of the explosion.*

*Then in Israel and the West Bank, on four occasions, a man tried to abduct and kill me. It frightened me. But all attempts failed. Clearly someone here feared I'd report him as the bomber.*

*Robert, I feel heartache for you. You must be very lonely in detention, awaiting the grand jury and the unknown. And very frightened. I'm trying to put myself in your place now, what it would feel like. You probably don't trust anyone now and may be abandoned by your friends. How about your family? I'm just guessing how you might feel.*

Robert turned to page two of the letter. Why did she care how he felt? She couldn't know, but she guessed right. The paper smelled something like mint and reminded him of his family's garden on Long Island. He hadn't received a real letter like this since Boy Scout camp at Alpine. Memories flooded back. Life seemed so simple then. But his interest climbed quickly. He read on.

*A jury will ultimately determine your guilt or innocence. That's not up to me. But I will write from my own conviction. Whatever you have done to me, if you did, I forgive you. I don't know why you might have done what you are charged with. It doesn't matter that I don't understand. Nor does it matter that you have not asked me to forgive you. If I harbor bitterness or revenge in my heart, if I live in unforgiveness, I am the one who suffers for it. It will eat away at my soul, the real me inside. It will eventually consume me.*

*I remember reading of a very special man of Galilee, who stood where I visited recently. His friend came to him and asked how many times he should forgive his brother who wronged him. Seven times? No, he said, seventy-seven times. Then later, when he hung dying on a cross, innocent of any crime, in the cruelest of slow executions, he asked his Father in heaven to forgive those who put him there. They didn't know what they were doing.*

*None of us always understand what we are doing. I know only that I must forgive you, totally and completely, not just by saying it, but from the heart. So with God as my witness, Robert, I forgive you. That also means I am to forget the past and start over with a clean slate when it comes to you. There is no barrier of fear anymore. You are a person I would like to meet, just to be your friend. This is sincere. I am not a plant of the police or FBI, nor do I wish to talk about what happened. I want to talk person-to-person before any lawyers prevent our meeting.*

*You probably need friends right now. I would like to visit you on Thursday. Would you agree that we could just talk and begin to be friends?*

*Sincerely,*

*Ashley Wells*

Robert forgot momentarily where he was. He stared blankly at the wall, remembering a beautiful blonde taking a direct hit from the crumbling synagogue. She fell, bleeding on the sidewalk. He imagined his hit man following her in Israel, four times, terrifying her and failing. And now she forgave him, wiped the slate clean, and wanted to become a friend.

Robert never even dreamed of this kind of forgiveness and reconciliation between former enemies. It just didn't happen in real life. No one would do that. She obviously was up to something.

Robert shook his head slowly and rocked back on his bed, holding one knee up. But now his jihadist friends were gone. No Ali. He wouldn't bother trying to pray toward Mecca. It wouldn't do any good. Imam Jabril had fled with no thought of Robert. He didn't seem to care. The five pillars of Islam made no sense anymore. Nothing did.

He felt totally alone. He wouldn't respond to his parents or anyone. Even if they wanted to help him. He would show them his hate by his silence. They'd understand eventually. He'd make his point.

Robert swore under his breath. He lay back on the bed and tried to sleep. He couldn't even escape his thoughts anymore by getting high on pot. He missed it.

Officer McKenzie came by and tossed some old magazines into the cell. "Thought you might be getting bored."

Robert shook his head. They held no interest for him, and he left them on the floor where they landed. Finally dinner came. He started to hate prison food and picked at it. Everything tasted the same, the meat, the carrots, and potatoes.

Finally as the cell lights dimmed at ten o'clock, Robert drifted off to sleep. He woke up at three a.m. after dreaming about Ashley falling to the sidewalk, bleeding. Now he couldn't get her letter out of his mind. She had written that she had forgiven him and wanted to be his friend. And that she would be coming today.

He bolted upright. What should he do if she really came? She wanted to talk. Did he want to talk with her? He'd be breaking his silence. And she had something to do with his arrest. The authorities probably put her up to this. *She probably has a hidden agenda.*

Robert's thoughts paused a moment. *But, if she has, then why did the letter seem so ... so true?* He realized something in him wanted to believe her, then chided himself for being so gullible. The thoughts tumbled over and over in his mind. He finally decided that he would choose whether to talk to her only when she came. He didn't need to settle it yet. He lay back down and finally slept.

# Chapter 68

After breakfast Robert heard activity in the hall. It sounded like more than one person. He jumped up from his bed as visitors approached. McKenzie had not said anything about visitors. Suddenly she appeared, long blond hair, smiling, accompanied by a tall young man who looked like he could be anywhere from Afghanistan to Morocco. Robert knew who she was, but had never seen the man. Or had he?

McKenzie brought two chairs and placed them just outside the cell. "Your visitors, Robert. Be nice for a change." He gestured to the visitors and then the chairs with a half-smile. "I'll be nearby, just around the corner if you need me. You can stay for twenty minutes."

Robert looked at Ashley, who smiled at him. "I'm Ashley. We come in peace and as your friends, Robert. This is Najid, from Palestine, now Israel."

Robert continued gazing at them both, first one and then the other. Shorter than Najid, he suddenly felt like a trapped small animal. Hate rose within him. Why did she bring him? Maybe for protection. He had almost decided to talk with her. This guy must be her boyfriend. Was he the guy at the synagogue?

The silence seemed awkward. He felt like telling them to go away.

Finally Ashley spoke. "Robert, it is good to meet you when we can talk rather than run from each other. Did you get my letter?"

He still felt trapped. He couldn't say no if he wanted to talk with her. But he didn't want that guy around. He sighed and looked from one to the other, finally nodding.

"Yeah, I did." That broke the icy atmosphere.

His visitors seemed pleased and relieved. He focused on Ashley. She looked radiant. He couldn't take his eyes off her. But he could hardly bring himself to talk with her, let alone this tall stranger who could easily use anything he said against him. He probably would.

"Then you know that I have totally forgiven you for anything you might have done. I hope that we can just talk as beginning friends."

"Yeah, I understand you want to talk. But it has to be alone." He nodded at Najid. "You need to go."

Najid's eyes widened. "How do you feel about that, Ashley? Are you OK with my leaving?"

"I'll be fine, Najid. You can go and chat with Officer McKenzie."

Robert stared at Ashley. How could she say she'd be fine, alone with her bitter enemy? Could he still silence her somehow? But time and events had moved on. Too late. Officer McKenzie appeared. Robert realized he had overheard their conversation, and that he would have to talk softly. The marshal ushered Najid down the hall.

Ashley seemed to understand he didn't want anything said to be heard by anyone but her. She scooted forward until her knees touched the bars of the cell. She didn't seem to be afraid of him. Did she really want to be his friend? Or was it some trick to get him to talk. He'd have to be careful what he said.

"OK, what do you want to talk about?"

"First, Robert, I want to assure you that I am not here to report on you. No one but the Detention Center people, Officer McKenzie and you know I'm here with Najid. The supervisor gave me permission to visit even though I'm not family. When the lawyers get involved, it's unlikely that you and I can meet until after your trial, if it goes that far. So I've come just as a new friend, not a victim or an enemy. The letter explained it."

"But you had something to do with my capture."

"Yes, I was terrified that someone might try to hurt me here in Seattle, like in Jerusalem. So I contacted the police."

"I never hired a hit man to find you here in Seattle. And they'll have to prove I did it in Israel."

"Robert, I felt threatened. That's why I went to the police. What happened at the synagogue was wrong and deserves justice. I realize you feel I'm your enemy. But I don't see it that way."

"Will you be testifying against me?

"Either side could subpoena my testimony, so perhaps yes, although I don't want to."

"They have my computer, so I don't stand much of a chance."

"Robert, I didn't come to talk about your case. And I don't want you to worry about anything being recorded here. I have no other agenda. You can ask me anything you want. That's how friendships are built." She paused. "You must be pretty lonely right now. What about your parents? Are they in town?"

"You've guessed right. Yeah, my parents are here from New York. They visited me day before yesterday."

"Will they help you?"

"I hadn't seen them in more than a year, not since I left home. And no, they won't be helping me."

"So, why did they come all the way from New York if they weren't here to help?"

"I don't want their help. I don't like them or what they stand for. I didn't even turn around to shake hands."

"Don't your parents love you?"

"You'd have to ask them."

"Don't you love them?"

"It's a long story I don't want to go into. But it's why I left and came out here."

"But now, after a year's absence, you ending up in jail, and their rushing out to Seattle to see you—isn't that love?"

"I don't know."

"Is it possible they want to help you?"

"I doubt it. They just want to look like they're caring." He shrugged his shoulders.

"You don't have to explain anything to me, Robert. I'm just a new friend. But it sounds like your anger is working against you. Whatever you have against your parents from the past, it sounds like they really care for you and want to help. By turning them away, you are hurting yourself. A lot."

"How am I hurting myself? I'm communicating my hate to them … to everyone." He grew silent and gazed at the floor. Then he glanced up again.

Tears filled his eyes. Then he shook with sobs. He couldn't stop. He felt like an abandoned little boy in deep trouble with no one to turn to. All the loneliness, the guilt. The pent-up frustration, fear, and accumulated anger of years poured out in a torrent of emotion.

Ashley stood and reached through the bars. He held on to her arms, put his head on them, and sobbed. He finally calmed down, and Ashley sat down, wiping away her own tears, looking deeply into his eyes.

"What do you think I should do?"

"Accept help wherever you can get it, Robert. You know the trouble you are in. You need lots of emotional support and love from your family. Restored relationships are so important, particularly close ones in families."

"You mean I should go beyond talking with them about my legal problems?"

"Exactly. And you can ask them to forgive you for whatever you have done to them. And more than that, you can choose to forgive them whether they ask for it or not. It will take away that horrible burden of hate for them."

"So what happens if I forgive them, and they forgive me?"

"Reconciliation. Previous enemies become friends. Just like us today."

McKenzie appeared. "Time's up. It's been twenty minutes."

"My parents sent a lawyer to see me. I'll call him," Robert said. "He left his card. Ashley, when will you come back?"

"I don't know. I'll try soon, but it may not be possible. But remember your promise to make that call!"

Robert watched her disappear down the hall, taking Najid's arm. He drew in a deep breath.

# Chapter 69

Robert trembled as he waited on the cordless phone for the lawyer to come on the line. "Charles Rand here."

"This is Robert Bentley. I'm calling from the Federal Detention Center."

"The young man who wouldn't talk to me?"

"Yeah. I've changed my mind. You said to call you if I want help."

"Are you sure? Will you answer my questions if I come back?"

"Yeah."

"OK. I can't come today, but will try for tomorrow."

---

Conrad and Lorraine Bentley spent the day asking themselves what they had done to create so much anger in Robert. It had something to do with their putting work and money ahead of time with their son.

The next day as they entered the center, Conrad Bentley watched his wife being patted down by a female employee at the metal detector. It had squealed.

McKenzie opened the door of the cell this time. Robert stood, his back to his parents as they walked in and heard the door close and lock behind them. "I'm just around the corner if you need me," McKenzie reminded the Bentleys.

"Robert. We're here again because we love you," Conrad began.

"I hope you know that, Robert." His mother's voice cracked. "Your dad and I have had long discussions, and we realize now that we failed you, son—that we were not there when you needed us. We're sorry." Robert wheeled around. He wasn't smiling, but he didn't have that hard squinting-eyed expression that frightened them two days ago. He nodded as he looked at his parents.

"Yeah, I understand that now."

McKenzie, listening in the hall, tiptoed away.

Lorraine wept quietly while Conrad enclosed Robert in his arms, patting his back repeatedly. Robert seemed a little stiff but accepted his dad's hug. Then he put his arms around his mom. Conrad sat on the small table, Lorraine on the metal chair and Robert on his bed. Conrad felt like the darkness had lifted a bit, but clouds still hid the sun. They sat quietly looking at each other. Robert gazed at them, and then dropped his eyes.

"What happened, Robert?" Lorraine asked. "You're so different today. We love you—" Her voice broke.

"It's true, Robert. Although I'm not sure I've ever said that to you." Conrad shook his head, thinking about the past twenty-two years of his busy life. It seemed difficult now, but he would actually say it: "I love you, son."

Robert told of Ashley's visit and how she had forgiven him. He described her letter and their subsequent conversation. Then he mentioned that Charles Rand would be coming back tomorrow.

"How did you get Mr. Rand to come back?"

"I called him. He left his card and said to call if I wanted his help."

"So he's on now as your defense counsel?"

"Yeah, I think so. He said he's coming tomorrow." Robert dropped his head. "I'm sorry for treating you and him so badly." He paused, gazing at the floor. "Uh, please ... for-forgive me. And thanks for hiring him for me."

Mr. Charles Rand entered with a quizzical expression on his face. Robert studied the short, bald man with intense blue eyes, opening his laptop computer.

After they shook hands, Mr. Rand began, "Why did you call me back?"

"It's a long story, you know, but after a visit from a friend, I realized I should do it for my own good. So I'm glad you came back, and I apologize for my treatment of you the other day."

"That's OK. It's your life and risk. Apology accepted."

Mr. Rand began by outlining the charges against Robert, and he summarized the legal steps they would go through together. Robert already knew most of them in general. The attorney impressed Robert with the seriousness of the charges. He should talk to no one about the case, including law enforcement officers, parents, or friends.

"You mean I can't see the only friend who has come to see me?"

"Not if the person is a potential witness."

"What if she was a victim of the bombing?"

"Definitely not! You must not see or talk to her on the telephone. She of all people could literally end your life."

Robert sighed. He sank back into the darkness that had only recently lifted with Ashley's visit.

"Are you with me, Robert? This is stuff you need to know."

Robert snapped back to the subject at hand. "Yeah, my mind drifted a bit, but I'm with you now."

"OK." Mr. Rand continued: "First, I need you to be completely open and honest with me. No hiding of any facts. If you are guilty of any of the charges, tell me the whole story. Answer any of my questions fully. Understood?"

"Yes, sir."

That began his attorney's investigation into Robert's past and recent activities. Over several weeks no subject escaped exploration. The sessions included legal education about the process and various defense options, including plea bargaining.

After his parents had returned to Long Island, Robert looked forward to Rand's sessions. He had no other visitors.

# Chapter 70

Ashley believed Robert had not hired hit men in Seattle. But Gordon Appleby did, and felt Ashley still might be a target. She called again to arrange a visit with Robert. But McKenzie informed her that Robert could not see her or anyone who might be involved in Robert's case or might be called on to testify in a trial. Disappointed, she hung up the phone thinking that Robert needed her. But right now he needed his lawyer most of all. He must have accepted one.

She had briefly met his parents before they left for New York. They expressed their appreciation for Ashley's reaching out to their son. "We could hardly believe the change in Robert after your visit," Lorraine added.

Mr. Bentley repeatedly thanked her for persuading Robert to call the lawyer he'd hired. "I can't believe you did this after what he allegedly did to you."

After dinner with Ashley's housemates, she and Najid went

out to walk around Green Lake. The sun shone in the July evening. Ashley took his arm. She loved being with Najid, and he seemed to enjoy being with her.

Ashley guided Najid to a park bench. Najid slipped his arm around her shoulders and drew her close.

"Let's see ... I forgot what I was saying ... oh yeah, what's happening at our church?"

"Maybe a bar mitzvah?"

Ashley couldn't keep from laughing with this Palestinian who seemed to become more American every day. "You silly man!" She elbowed him in the ribs. She had not asked him to attend her church, knowing he might not feel comfortable with its Israeli tilt. "I've been thinking about dragging you there."

"The last time you 'dragged' me to a place of worship it didn't turn out so well."

"Sick humor," Ashley chuckled. "OK, but this time it'll be fun. Our travel team is having a debriefing after church this Sunday."

"What's a 'debriefing'?"

"It's where people talk about their experiences on the trip and try to make sense of them. You hear from others, what they saw and learned. It helps to sort out your own impressions."

"So why would you want me to come? I wasn't on the trip."

"Well, first you could hear what some Americans think about their observations in the Holy Land. I think some of us came back with a lot of questions. Maybe you'd get some insights on why we're so confused."

"Like what?"

"Like Bethlehem, for example. Confronting the wall of separation, right in the city where the Prince of Peace was born. A few short years ago it became a war zone, and now it's a prison for many residents. What do you do with that?"

Najid turned toward her and looked into Ashley's eyes. "Right. What do *you* do with that?"

"I don't know what to do with it. I'm hearing so many different voices. That is why I want you to come."

"You think I can sort out such complicated issues for you?"

"You know, Najid, you and your family and this trip and my

struggles with jihadists have had a profound effect on me. I'm not asking you to sort it all out for me. I need to come to my own conclusions someday. But after meeting your family in Galilee, I'll never be the same. I want you to come and simply tell your story, and that of your family, going back beyond 1948. A story can be an image that says so much more than words alone can express. You and your family are part of the 'living stones' that we encountered. If you came, that picture would show up so much more clearly than my telling about your family. I'm not asking you to draw any conclusions either. Just tell your story."

Najid gazed into the distance beyond Ashley, apparently thinking and enjoying the peaceful lake with people swimming and scullers out in the middle, rowing their long, sleek boats. "Would I be welcome there? I don't want to upset anyone who has strong Zionist beliefs. Or anyone else. That's why I determined not to get into that conflict here in America or tell my family story. It upsets some people, and I don't want to do that."

"But it's real, Najid. It happened. And it's a story we in the United States rarely hear. You are a living, breathing example of what God can do in the life of one who loves others and longs for reconciliation between people who sometimes hate each other. So what do you say? Will you come on Sunday? You don't have to be in the church service."

Najid laughed. "I'll come even for that. For peacemaking." He winked at Ashley. "But mostly for you." His arm tightened around her shoulder as she reached for his other hand and squeezed it.

⚜

Ashley watched Najid's face glow as he experienced such a large crowd at her church, singing a lively worship song. The words projected on large screens and the music leaders playing their electronic instruments and drums seemed to fascinate him. She watched his face as Senior Pastor Tom Evans sat on a high stool, dressed in jeans, discussing a fundraiser for Israel. She couldn't tell what Najid was thinking.

The pastor then taught from the Bible. He referenced Jesus's sermon on the mountain that overlooks the Sea of Galilee. "Blessed are the peacemakers, for they will be called Sons of God."

Ashley looked at Najid, who nodded several times. He seemed to track completely with the ideas.

After the church service and some general visiting, the travel group and Najid walked to Pastor Jim's office for their debriefing. They sat in a circle and talked while Jim finished his phone call. He hung up, smiled, and looked up as the door opened suddenly. Pastor Tom appeared. "I've had a schedule change. May I sit in on your debriefing? I'd like to hear more of your stories. We might have a couple of you share for a few minutes some Sunday morning."

"We're delighted to have you join us," Jim said. Addressing his tour group, Jim welcomed them back together and asked each person to introduce themselves so Pastor Tom and their guest would know who was who. Ashley introduced Najid, explaining that she had visited his family in Galilee and had invited him to join them.

"We're going to share informally," Jim advised. Then several people shared what had impressed them, and what they learned. Finally they all turned to Ashley.

She began softly, "You all prayed for me in Jerusalem, and God heard you and saved my life. I love you guys. But I'm not talking about that today. We all visited many churches and shrines built from the ancient stones in the Holy Land. These are the ones that have lasted for centuries and should endure for many years to come." She took a deep breath and looked at Najid. "I'd like to tell my impressions about the people I met, our Jewish guides, two rabbis, our new Muslim and Christian friends—but I don't have time. It's because I've asked my friend Najid, one of those living stones, from a town near Nazareth, to share his family story. I visited them, wonderful Christians whose family history goes back for many generations on a farm in Galilee. He's a graduate student at the U. Also a peacemaker." She nodded toward Pastor Tom.

Najid proceeded to tell of his ancient church, the olive orchards, and the home that his parents shared happily as children with his grandparents. He explained how in Irgit, a Galilean village, Jews, Palestinian Christians, and Muslims had lived peacefully together on their family farms of mostly olives and figs for centuries until

1948, when Israeli soldiers took over their house and ordered them to leave. He shared all that happened to his family and others after that—the lost farms, businesses, homes, refugee camps. He told of friendships, of walls, checkpoints, and more. He revealed his longing, and the longing of so many good people he knew from so many backgrounds, for an end to the military occupation. For justice, for peace. Not peace at any price. But a just peace and ultimate reconciliation.

Jim sat, chin in hand, slowly shaking his head. Ashley saw Pastor Tom sit motionless, his eyes searching Najid's face.

Najid ended by mentioning Jewish, Muslim, and Christian organizations working together for justice and peace using nonviolent resistance.

Najid looked at Ashley with a nod of conclusion. The group sat in silence.

Ashley looked at Pastor Tom, wondering what he would say. He held his handkerchief. He looked ready to speak, but signaled he needed a moment, swallowed, then finally spoke: "I think we've heard from heaven just now." He paused again, nodding and biting his lower lip. Then he continued, shaking his head. "I've been arrogant, hard, and judgmental against Palestinians, not having any idea what they have gone through over so many years." He shook his head. "Please God, forgive me."

# Chapter 71

Ashley and Najid had found a spot on the sidewalk downtown with thousands of people watching the Friday night Seafair Torchlight Parade. "I've got something to tell you, Najid." She looked up into his eyes, grimacing and gritting her teeth while taking in a deep breath. "My parents will be coming for a visit in three weeks. I know it will be a difficult time for all of us." She finally exhaled.

Najid nodded and remained silent for several moments. "They'll be interested to hear face to face about your trip, and ..." His voice trailed off.

Ashley waited for him to finish, but he seemed lost in thought. "I've explained over the telephone some of what happened. I didn't want to scare them over the phone."

"Yeah," he said, nodding slowly. "That's probably wise."

Najid slipped his arm around her waist and drew her close as a float came by with the Seafair Queen and her court. Ashley leaned her head on the front of his shoulder, quickly changing her mind about further discussion of her parents' visit. She should never have brought it up. She would ruin an enchanted evening.

Moments later, Najid scarcely noticed the huge red paper dragon with many Chinese boys' legs underneath, hurrying it along, crisscrossing down the street in serpentine fashion. It looked fierce with flashing red eyes. But Najid paid no attention to the rest of the parade. His heart raced as he held Ashley. He instinctively wanted to turn her toward him and kiss her. But he could not bring himself to do it in public. So he kissed her hair and reveled in the ecstasy of the moment. He didn't want the parade to end. But soon the last of the horses, floats, and bands passed.

They stood quietly as people walked by, leaving the parade route. Najid enjoyed the soft summer evening as he drew her closer. The red glow over the Olympic Mountains and Puget Sound darkened slowly. The moon rose in the southeast, almost full and glowing brighter as the twilight faded. Moonlight brightened her silken hair. They stood silent, neither one speaking; it seemed to him that time stood still.

The silence broke as cars again filled the street. Najid's mind continued to race. He couldn't put his feelings into words and didn't know what to say to Ashley.

He had never experienced these sensations before, these intense desires. He couldn't get close enough to her. His excitement rose as he pulled her even closer, then cupping his hands around her cheeks. He kissed her. She grasped his hands, squeezing them. He heard her sigh and sensed her tremble against him.

A little boy ran by, and looking up at Najid, tripped and fell. Screaming, his mother picked him up and examined his skinned knees. It broke the enchantment and they strolled silently toward the bus stop hand in hand.

As Najid said good night to Ashley on the front porch of her house, the moon cast a silver glow on her hair. His excitement rebounded. He drew her close as her soft body melted into his embrace, both their arms around each other, hers around his neck. After several moments, she stepped back, silently holding his hands, smiling. He felt confused, somewhat embarrassed, not knowing what to say.

"Ashley ... I don't know what is happening to me. I've never wanted to be so close to anyone like this. I hope I have not offended you." He looked into her eyes and saw her smile.

"Najid, you have done nothing but make me happy. I have never met anyone like you. I love being with you."

She pulled his head down, and they kissed each other.

Ashley's mind raced as she went to bed. She loved him; she knew it. And now he loved her. It had become obvious. He treaded so carefully to not offend her, uncertain how to proceed in a relationship of love for the first time ever, and in a foreign culture. She had no idea what his family would think of his bringing her into their circle. Would she as an American be accepted in his family?

But the main problem would be her parents, not his. And to complicate things, her parents would arrive for a visit soon. She so wanted her mother and father to accept and even love Najid. He would be the most gracious and loving son-in-law they could ever imagine.

Ashley turned over in bed, unsettled. She was an adult now and could make her own decisions. She and Najid could marry despite her parents' objections. But could she risk breaking her relationship with her parents, who had cared for her lifelong? She loved them. How would they handle bringing Najid into the family over their objections? What would it do to Najid or to her? What about children in years to come? Would they be accepted?

She tossed and turned, trying to turn off her mind and sleep. But the nagging, immediate questions kept recurring in her mind: What to do in three weeks when her parents arrive? Would she bring Najid to see them? Would they walk out and refuse to talk to him again? If only they could get acquainted, they would learn to love him. The ethnic and cultural differences wouldn't matter. They could blend and work through those in love and respect. Najid was a loving human being, courageous, unselfish, bright, and loved God. What more could you ask for your daughter? But if you coldly reject someone before you get to know him, how can you ever establish a relationship or friendship? Would Najid ever get over being rejected by them? Would he even want to try to establish a friendship?

Ashley sighed deeply and looked up to imagine the man of Galilee on that hillside two millennia ago. He still spoke to her about the rewards of being poor in spirit and a peacemaker. She turned on her side and finally fell asleep.

# Chapter 72

Ashley, Ashley," she heard her name being called, not knowing whether she dreamed it or not. The call continued as she shook her head, trying to wake up. "Phone for you!" One of her housemates banged on her door as Ashley stumbled across the floor and jerked open the door. "Mr. Appleby's on the line." She handed Ashley the cordless phone.

"Hello." Her voice croaked.

"Appleby here. Sounds like I got you up. Sorry."

"Yeah, but I think I'm awake now."

"We haven't talked for some time now, and I wanted to bring you up to date on what's going on."

"I appreciate your calling. I've wondered what's been happening to Robert. I did visit him once, before his lawyer or the U.S. attorney got involved."

"I heard about that. Apparently you convinced him to cooperate with the legal system and meet with his parents. Good work! OK, now about the grand jury. They met. The prosecutor had plenty of evidence to present to the jury without calling you to testify, mostly from Robert's own computer with all the e-mail, financial, travel, and

Internet information. They needed twelve jurors to indict him, and eighteen of nineteen did."

"So now he goes to trial?" Ashley asked.

"Right."

"And I won't have to testify against him?"

"Probably not. We'll let you know if that changes. The discovery process has uncovered so much evidence that the defense counsel is recommending a guilty plea to Robert, with a plea bargain."

"So what does that mean?"

"The grand jury agreed to the three charges brought by the prosecutor, the U.S. attorney assigned to the case. Second-degree murder for the rabbi who died in the synagogue. Then attempted murder, of you and Najid, as well as of you in Israel. And third, assault with a deadly weapon: the bomb. The plea by the defense is to drop the attempted murder charge, which would be harder to prove, but not impossible, and for a recommendation of leniency by the prosecutor to the judge because of Robert's age and this being his first offense. In exchange, Robert would plead guilty to the first and third charges. It looks like he is going to accept this."

"I imagine the world wants him hung."

"Probably so, Ashley. But thirty years in prison, if that is what he gets, is no Sunday school picnic."

"So what happens now?" Ashley pictured the little boy inside this angry young man, now faced with the steel rod of justice for what he had done. He must be terrified.

"He appears with both lawyers before a federal judge in court, who will take into consideration the guilty plea on two counts and the plea bargain worked out by the opposing lawyers. It will take some time for the court to decide whether to accept the plea. Assuming acceptance, Robert will have to appear again for sentencing."

"And what can he expect, realistically?"

"Probably years in prison. No one can predict how many. It varies so much in the federal court system that there is no average sentence for a given charge. But probably not life without parole, as that is usually reserved for first-degree murder."

Ashley stared vacantly ahead, shaking her head and visualizing Robert standing before the judge, totally at the mercy of the court. In forgiveness she had lost any feeling of hate for what he had done to her. Her strong reaction surprised her—pity and sadness, knowing justice would prevail. "Can I see him now?"

"No, not yet. Once sentenced, he will be shipped off to federal prison somewhere. Then he can have visitors."

"So how soon?"

"If all goes as I suspect it will, he should be in federal prison in three months, probably November sometime. Oh, and by the way, you know we've been searching for his accomplices, whoever helped him acquire training and materials, right?"

"I assumed he must have had help."

"Well, we've discovered he had a friend who guided him for training and getting the explosives. A radical Islamic guy, an imam named Jabril. We have come close to tracking him down in Los Angeles. He's slippery as an eel. But we'll get him. Anyway, you still have to be careful, Ashley."

Najid, his face beaming with a hope-filled smile, hurried to the phone. He had never been on a mountain, certainly not a huge volcano like Mount Rainier. He called Ashley. He could text her but he didn't. He liked to hear her voice.

"Ashley, have you ever heard of FIUTS?"

"No."

"It stands for 'Foundation for International Understanding Through Students.' They are offering a sponsored hike up to Camp Muir on Mount Rainier. Would you like to go with me? They tell you what boots and clothes to take, and you can even borrow a backpack. We'd have to rent the boots."

"Najid, I'd love it! We see Rainier from Red Square on the campus, but I've never been to any of the mountains here." She laughed. "Oklahoma is pretty flat."

"It's over the Labor Day weekend, and we probably should do some running to get in good shape. We would climb from fifty-five hundred feet elevation at Paradise to ten thousand at Camp Muir. That's an overnight station used for climbing the mountain, the most common route to the top, which is more than fourteen thousand feet. But we can relax ... we'll stop halfway."

"How'd you get so smart?"

"It's called reading from a brochure."

# Chapter 73

The bus parked in the large lot at Paradise on the south flank of Mount Rainier. The fifteen hikers, counting their guide from FIUTS, began the climb up the Skyline Trail heading to Alta Vista and then on to Panorama Point at seven thousand feet. They met several climbers coming down the mountain with ice axes, crampons, and ropes, who confirmed the ranger's previous caution about a storm approaching. However, they should be back down to Paradise long before it blew in. Ashley appreciated the bit of survival training their own guide had provided and found comfort in the safety gear in their backpacks—flashlight, thermal blanket, some energy bars, and small snow shovel. She'd made sandwiches for lunch.

Ashley climbed steadily on the trail through rocky screes, following Najid and others. The patches of snow interspersed with late summer alpine flowers soon faded into one vast Paradise snowfield. Gazing into the sky, the summit shone bright in the sun, far above them, and yet it looked close because of its huge size. The dark clouds in the distance only highlighted the mountain in the bright morning sunshine.

The sound of rocks falling from far above resounded as the glaciers groaned and inched their way downward. On a rocky ridge nearby she heard a shrill whistle and then spied a noisy marmot sitting up on his haunches to warn his friends of the approach of strangers. Ashley jogged over to Najid and grabbed his gloved hand. She smiled and gave it a squeeze. He squeezed back as they climbed. Ashley wondered what would heaven be like if earth was like this.

Their guide stopped on the snow. Ashley appreciated the rest as they drank from their water bottles and scanned the snow slope ahead. The guide pointed out some famous places on the mountain and gestured toward the huge Gibraltar Rock above them, Little Tahoma Peak on the right skyline and the ridge extending out to the east above them that looked like an anvil, appropriately named Anvil Rock.

They started climbing again. Ashley noticed the elevation gain as she breathed harder. Najid seemed not to feel it. Most in the group were guys. The three girls banded together and dropped a bit off the pace. Najid waited for them and then stayed with Ashley. She didn't want to admit that she felt tired or short of breath. It had been four hours of climbing, and always one more ridge ahead. Anvil Rock to the right seemed to be so close and yet always receding. The air grew cooler as clouds occasionally shaded the sun.

One foot in front of another, again and again. She'd learned the "rest step," locking her knee momentarily as she ascended. The guide taught them the "kick step," kicking a foothold in the snow to provide a solid platform for the next step up. Finally climbing over yet another of the many undulating ridges she had not seen from below, two rock-built cabins of Camp Muir appeared.

Ashley sat with Najid on the warm rocks, leaning up against the south wall of the larger of the two cabins. She welcomed the rest and the sandwiches. In the cool air, she leaned back against the rock wall of the hut, sun in her face, warming her tired body. "Najid, I'm so glad you brought me. What an incredible experience for a girl from Oklahoma!"

"For me too. We have mountains that feed the Sea of Galilee, but nothing like this with so many glaciers in the summer."

"Would you like to walk over to Anvil Rock, Najid? It doesn't look far. The guide said we have an hour here and can explore a bit, except upward on the glaciers. Let's put on our backpacks and stroll over to the Rock."

Ashley and Najid found a comfortable rock platform to sit on, out of the snow at Anvil Rock. They gazed south, munching on M & M's. Mount Adams, another volcano to the south, had disappeared in clouds. Soon the dark billows blocked the sun over Rainier. A breeze began and picked up speed as the temperature suddenly dropped.

"I think we better get back," Najid said.

Ashley rose to start back to Camp Muir when her left foot slipped off an unstable rock. She twisted her ankle, yelped with pain, and fell forward. A sudden panic poured over her. Najid rushed to her side.

"I'm OK, Najid, except for my ankle. It hurts."

Najid opened her boot to examine her ankle that began to swell. He raised her to a sitting position on the rocks. "Can you walk on it, Ashley?"

"I'm not sure right now. Give me a few minutes, and it should be better." She laced up her boot loosely.

As they sat the clouds rolled in rapidly, soon enveloping them in a thick fog. Ashley tried to remain calm. "The storm is coming faster than we thought. We better get back."

With her left arm over Najid's shoulder, and his right one encircling her waist, she tried hopping to keep weight off her left ankle. Bearing weight on it caused sharp pain. Najid maneuvered her off the rocks onto the snow, turned toward the camp, and supported her from the downhill side.

They moved slowly in the thickening fog. Then everything turned white. The feeling that she stood inside an empty white refrigerator overcame Ashley. There was no horizon to indicate where the snow stopped and the air or sky began. Disoriented and dizzy, she couldn't determine which direction they should go. She couldn't even tell which way the slope tilted. They could be struggling uphill or down, or maybe in the wrong direction. She felt disoriented, not even sensing where her feet were. She couldn't see them.

Suddenly, her stomach cramped with a surge of nausea. She

breathed in hard to overcome it. Droplets of condensing fog beaded on their parkas. The wind picked up and howled.

She glanced at Najid. He also seemed unsure which way to turn.

"I think we are walking too much uphill," Ashley shouted as they struggled forward.

"It seems to me we're going downhill and need to turn to the right. But if I'm wrong, we could get into the cliffs over there beyond Anvil." Ashley's ankle throbbed with pain.

"I can't walk any farther, Najid. Let's stop and figure out what to do." She sat down on the snow.

"We can't stay here, Ashley. I'll shout for help. I can't see anything but white, and I think we are turned around." He shouted "Hello!" several times, but the howling wind carried away any sound.

Ashley shivered as half-rain half-snow pelted horizontally into her face and neck despite the parka hood. Her hands and feet felt frozen, and she feared she could faint from the ankle pain. A sense of helplessness and dread came over her.

"I'm not much good for any decisions right now, Najid," she lamented. Her teeth chattered as the sleet drove hard against her. Cold began to penetrate her body as she collapsed on the snow. She prayed out loud, her words muffled by the wind. *"Lord, we're in trouble here, and we need help!"*

"Amen!" Najid shouted into the wind. "As you prayed I suddenly remembered the stuff in our backpacks! It's time to use it." He reached in, pulled out his thermal blanket, and taking off her boots, quickly wrapped Ashley in it, laying her down in the snow to minimize the direct wind chill. He placed a large rock at her feet to prevent her sliding down the slope. "This shovel might help now."

"Of course! Like the survival shows on TV. You are supposed to stay put and dig a snow cave. We'd be out of the wind and snow."

With that, Najid dug furiously to form a tunnel slanting down so the entrance faced away from the wind. The snow proved plenty deep from last winter's accumulation. After twenty minutes, he had created a two-meter-long tunnel they could both get into well below the surface snow. He eased Ashley in her thermal blanket into the snow cave. Then taking the other blanket, he removed his boots, wrapped the metallic but plasticlike sheet around himself and slid down into the tunnel beside her, removing his hat and gloves. He had brought the boots and backpacks with him to partially plug the end of the tunnel.

As they lay in their cave, Ashley could just see Najid in the gathering darkness, his head partly covered with his blanket, which looked like a hijab. She smiled. The howling wind and sleet above could not get to them now, and she quit shivering. They lay close together, wrapped like mummies.

Ashley looked at him, seemingly amused. "What's so funny?" he asked.

"You in your hijab."

Najid grinned. "It feels so good around my head. Are you better now?"

"Much. You saved my life again. It got us out of the storm!"

"So what did your TV program tell you to do now?"

"OK ..." Ashley hesitated. "As I recall, you're supposed to stay inside your snow cave until the storm passes."

"That sounds good, except that you are not in shape to hike down with your ankle, even if the sun comes out tomorrow."

"Yeah, you're right," Ashley said, "barring a miracle." She paused a moment. "I guess we'll just have to wait to be rescued if I can't make it down. At least we're OK for now."

"So, I guess we go to bed together for tonight, all wrapped up like a cocoon." Najid smiled in the semi-dark snow cave. "It doesn't seem to be wrong to sleep together like this, even though we're not married yet. If we stay close, we should be warm and OK to sleep."

Ashley suddenly turned toward Najid from lying on her back. She laughed. "What do you mean, 'not married yet'?"

"I, I, um, I guess it just slipped out. I didn't mean to shock you, certainly not here. I shouldn't have said that."

"Well, you don't even know if I want to be married!"

"OK. Well, do you?"

"Yeah," Ashley said casually as if he had asked her if she wanted a candy bar. Then she added, "Someday."

"Do you have someone in mind to marry?" Najid sounded a bit worried.

"I guess I do, but he's never asked me." She chuckled.

"How could he ask you if he hasn't had the chance to go to your father?"

"Would he ever ask me if he couldn't go to my father?"

"Oh no! That would not be right. And it would bring on all kinds of trouble."

"So would he want to see my father first? Before he asked me?"

"Yes. That's the way he would do it. He would never ask the girl first."

"What about his parents? Would they accept her without asking?"

"No, but maybe they already have."

"You're saying they would accept her into his family?"

"Yes. They might think she's pretty special."

"So, all that's needed is for him to talk to her father? Then he could ask her?"

"Yes, if he wanted to." Najid laughed.

"Well, does he want to?" Ashley asked with a smirk on her face he could not see.

"You'll have to wait to find out, just in case he could talk to her father."

Both drifted off to sleep, smiling despite the raging storm above.

# Chapter 74

Najid awoke first, struggled out of his thermal wrap, pulled on his boots, and pushed the packs out. He climbed out of the snow cave to a morning of high clouds but clear air. No wind. He heard the thump-thump of a helicopter approaching Camp Muir. It landed near the huts, about one half mile away. Najid tightened his boots and ran, arms waving and shouting. Soon the mountain rescue team jumped out of the army chopper. One of them looked up and saw Najid running toward them. He quickly broke from the group and walked rapidly to meet Najid.

After a quick discussion with Najid, the man returned to the helicopter, pulled out a toboggan with blankets, and three rescuers in bright yellow parkas followed Najid to the snow cave. Ashley crawled out half-awake with Najid's help. The team strapped her into the toboggan and soon lifted her inside the helicopter. During the flight to Seattle, the medics splinted Ashley's ankle. Overcome by relief, she shook her head and smiled, starting to thank her rescuers, but the noise of the chopper prevented conversation. She jerked a hearty thumbs-up to them with both hands.

Ashley recognized Harborview Medical Center. The X-rays showed no fracture. An ankle boot and crutches would keep her comfortable as the sprain healed.

Their FIUTS guide appeared, shaking his head with relief. The team had looked for them. "But the one remaining Mount Rainier climbing guide at Muir advised me to get the group off the mountain as quickly as possible. He led us down using his GPS and compass. They arranged a search and rescue as soon as possible. But they had to wait out the worst of the storm. Obviously a helicopter could not fly with the strong wind and zero visibility."

Ashley and Najid expressed their appreciation to all. She felt embarrassed that she had caused so much trouble for so many people.

Ashley's mind whirled as the team guide drove them home. She gazed at him in the rearview mirror. "We could have become increasingly hypothermic. You had the foresight to put a snow shovel and thermal blankets in our packs—even in the summertime!"

Ashley gazed at Najid in the front seat. She smiled, recalling their conversation in the snow cave. Was it a proposal of marriage or not? Certainly not your traditional down-on-one-knee proposal. All done theoretically, in third person. She chuckled. But one thing she had learned, he wanted to talk to her father. No, he needed to talk to her father.

Sitting in her house with her left ankle up on the couch enclosed with an ice pack, Ashley felt like Cleopatra. First Najid and then her housemates catered to her every need. This had to stop. And it did. By the next day she crutched to the telephone when no one answered it.

"Hello."

"Appleby here. May I speak to Ashley?"

"Oh yes, Mr. Appleby. This is Ashley."

"I just read in the paper of your adventures on the mountain. You keep having them."

"I'm so embarrassed about it. It put lots of people in danger."

"Don't worry now. That's what those rescue guys enjoy doing. Lovely maidens in distress, you know."

Ashley chuckled. "OK."

"What I called about, Ashley, is with another update on Robert and to convey a request. The lawyers worked out a plea bargain that the judge accepted. So Robert is awaiting sentencing, and the judge has allowed him to have visitors now."

"Do his parents know that?"

"Yes they do. But he's asking to see you."

Ashley drew a deep breath and sighed. "It must be terrible, in jail, no visitors, alone, waiting for a severe sentence of years in prison. Yes, I'll go. What are the hours? Should I call ahead?"

"He's not in solitary anymore. So you need an appointment time, and you would see him in a visiting area with a glass between you. Good luck. He's anxious to see you."

After several of her "crutch days," Ashley could walk with her ankle boot. Between writing her thesis, spending time with Najid, and planning her parents' visit, she needed to think about Robert again. So sad to see a young man get to such a dark place that he could kill—actually take a life. Now coming out from there, he faced a life ruined. So young. What help could she be? Why did he want to see her again? She called to make an appointment.

An appointment? Her mind wandered. Why not make one to see Jim also? He had become more than her associate pastor and team leader. He had become a good friend. He seemed to understand Najid and his background now. The visit to Bethlehem and meeting the students in the Bible College, he said, encouraged him to explore his own theology in a renewed way. And hearing Najid's family story had affected him as it did the whole travel team, and even Pastor Tom, their senior pastor. She could confide in Jim her dilemma—her love for that Palestinian man her parents had rejected.

# Chapter 75

Robert wore an orange jumpsuit. It seemed strange to Ashley, talking to him behind glass with headphones and a microphone. What a barrier to human contact, she thought. He looked so pale and forlorn. But after initial greetings, they soon forgot the glass barrier, microphones, and speakers. Robert's eyes watered at seeing Ashley.

"I've gone over and over what you said about forgiveness, Ashley. I chose to forgive my parents like you said. You know, for exchanging money for love all my growing up years. And now, you know, I'm sorry I ever got involved in this jihadist thing. I've hurt my parents like they hurt me. I could ask the judge for forgiveness, but that wouldn't change the facts of what I did and the penalty that I must pay. Justice must be served." A tear rolled down his cheek, and he grew quiet.

"I am sorry too, Robert, that any of this happened. But it did. You can't change that and you have to pay your debt. But you still have a life to live, even in prison."

"I know that. But I want to understand about penalties you must pay and how forgiveness works. All I've ever known is revenge."

That began a long discussion as Ashley tried to answer the many questions Robert posed. "How can God forgive us?"

"Because justice has been served ... on the man from Galilee."

After an hour, a guard came to take Robert back to his cell.

He gazed at her, nodding. "You bring me hope, Ashley. Will you come again?"

"Yeah, I will." She watched as the two men walked through the doorway. Robert looked back, with tears in his eyes.

Ashley strolled into Jim's office at the church, remembering the first time they met before the eventful trip and their many experiences together in the Holy Land that changed them both.

"You became famous again, Ashley. I read about you the other day, surviving at night on Mount Rainier in the storm. You've got to quit these harrowing adventures."

She laughed and shook her head. "That's what Gordon Appleby said. But you know, Jim, stuff happens. Hopefully I can learn from it."

"So, to what do I owe the pleasure of this visit? I don't get to see you at church very often. Too many people."

"I want to get your thoughts, about Najid—"

"That guy planted a bombshell around here," Jim interrupted. "Sorry," he chuckled, "poor choice of words,"

Ashley laughed, then grew more serious. "I'm sorry if he caused trouble. Maybe I shouldn't have asked him to share in our debriefing."

"No, no! We had a wonderful challenge! He's sparked a lot of thought, debate, and theological discussions. No matter what we believe, we need to embrace love of our neighbor and avoid thinking one group has exclusive rights no one else has. I wonder if we have sometimes lost sight of justice and mercy. We need to see all the people involved in the Holy Land as those God loves, who need him and need each other. I couldn't believe the effect his story has had on our senior pastor."

"What effect? You mean ... for good?"

"Yeah. Just like I experienced first in Bethlehem at the college. I had never heard the personal side of what has happened over there. Najid's story cuts to the heart of the injustice ... of years. It was powerful."

"So what now?"

"Well, for one thing, the leaders in this church began some deep discussions of our Zionist theology. How can we support our brothers and sisters of Palestine *and* Israel who are trying to bring peace with *justice*?"

"Wow! I am so excited to hear what's going on. But that's not actually what I came to talk about."

"Yeah," Jim smiled, "but you brought up Najid, who turned us upside down."

"OK, I did. But not for that reason."

"So, what is the reason?"

That began the long story of Ashley's history with Najid, meeting his family in Galilee, his leading the police to Robert, their increasing time together, and their love for each other. She related her parents' total rejection of Najid in the hospital, and their advice to not see him as a friend. Then she told about the conversation in the snow cave involving their respective parents, and Najid's roundabout way of telling her he would like to marry her, but would have to get her father's permission before he would even propose to her. And there lay the problem.

"Why do you think your parents have rejected Najid so strongly?"

"I'm not sure except that he is Palestinian, and of course all Palestinians are terrorists. Besides he's different from my parents, and even though he might be a Christian, they could not trust him. They have no idea what a wonderful man he is. And from such a loving family."

"Do your parents have a Christian Zionist view?"

"Oh, Jim! In spades! They outdo our church here in supporting the Israeli government's positions. I had the same general ideas when I came to Seattle, as you may recall, because that is how I was brought up. Like most Americans, they have no idea from the news outlets here what is really going on in Israel and the West Bank."

Jim put his hands together and lowered his head, obviously deep in thought. Ashley waited. He finally spoke. "I'd like to meet your parents, Ashley. Do they ever come to visit you here?"

Ashley laughed. "Would you believe they're going to be here in five days? I've been racking my brain trying to figure out what to do. Do I share about Najid and how we love each other despite their disapproval? Do I put them all in a room and let them duke it out together? Or do I say nothing, keep Najid away, and make no progress at all?"

"Probably none of the above, Ashley. Let me talk to them. I'll work something out. Let's meet after church. You can introduce us, and I'll take it from there. I would not talk to them about Najid if I were you. At least not until after we have a chance to meet. You and Najid should not be with us here in the office while we talk. He doesn't attend here, does he?"

"No. That's great Jim, whatever you can do. They'll be here for just two days before I bring them to church. Thanks for coming to my aid, again."

"I've got to think about this a bit. I may call you to get a bit more information."

# Chapter 76

Sunny and seventy degrees in Seattle, Dorothy." Frank Wells peeked at his wife before he reclined his seat as the airplane reached cruising altitude. "Their Indian summer's a lot cooler than ours in Oklahoma."

"I'm looking forward to some respite from the heat," Dorothy sighed.

"Seattle is a different place." Frank turned toward Dorothy. She looked so much like Ashley at times. "I wonder if we should have encouraged our daughter to go somewhere else for graduate school?"

"It wouldn't have mattered what we think, Frank. Ashley just does her thing."

"I can't figure her out sometimes. She seems so stubborn once she gets on to some idea. And she is being exposed to concepts out there in Seattle that I don't like."

"She has certainly had her share of adventures between what we read and what she tells us."

"I'm not sure she is telling us the whole story, Dorothy. I don't think we know what really went on in Israel. She seems to be hiding stuff. Maybe things she doesn't want us to know."

"I agree. She hasn't shared much about how she identified where the bomber lived in Seattle either, only that she tipped off the police." Dorothy shook her head. "Some things don't add up."

"And how did she happen to get lost in the storm on Mount Rainier?" Frank asked. "From what we read, a group of international students climbed up to a base camp on the mountain. It didn't mention that Palestinian by name, but I wonder if he persuaded her to go."

"She never talks about him on Skype. But I have my own intuition, Frank. I think she is still seeing him and just doesn't want us to know."

"I think you're right." As an engineer and businessman in the oil industry, he tended to think logically and make correlations. He turned to Dorothy. "Who accompanied Ashley when the bomb went off? That guy Najid. She had hinted at visiting a family in Galilee— maybe it was his. How did she track down the bomber in Seattle? Was he involved? If all that is true, this man brought trouble on Ashley."

"Do you think he has ulterior motives?"

He nodded his head. "He may, Dorothy. We've got to protect Ashley from this Palestinian guy. I don't trust him with our daughter."

Ashley spied them wheeling their carry-on bags as they emerged from the B concourse at Sea-Tac airport. She ran to hug them. Her parents looked tired. After the greetings she'd take them to their motel on 25<sup>th</sup> Avenue near the university. They hadn't eaten since their layover in Denver hours earlier. "I know a restaurant on the Ave that you'll enjoy."

"It looks like Seattle agrees with you, Ashley." Dorothy smiled at her daughter as they drove on I-5 toward the Seattle skyline. Ashley sparkled and looked beautiful, her long blond hair blowing in the partially open window. The blue water of Puget Sound glittered as they neared the city, with the Olympic Mountains as a backdrop. Ashley pointed out some of the tall buildings and then the Space Needle. They neared the Mercer Street exit. Suddenly Ashley looked quickly into her side mirror and behind her as she eased the car into the exit lane.

"I just had a great idea. Let's have dinner at the Space Needle. It's still early,so we probably can get in without a reservation. They have a revolving restaurant at the top that completes one revolution per hour. It's a beautiful day, so we should be able to get a sunset view we won't forget. You up for it Dad? It's a tad pricey."

"Ashley, we've come all this way just to see you. And if that's what you think we'd all enjoy, go for it!"

⁂

Ashley emerged first from the elevator looking high over Seattle to Mount Rainier. Frank and Dorothy stood staring at the huge mountain, glaciers draped down its sides like white banners interspersed by rocky ridges of black. The flat top with its mile-wide crater shone in the afternoon sun.

"It would have been nice to have this kind of weather two weeks ago," Ashley said. "But then I've heard the mountain even makes its own weather."

Led by the hostess, they stepped over the seam in the carpeted floor. Frank noticed movement, a stationary center core, and an outer ring that rotated slowly clockwise. The tables on the ring wound gradually past each window. Being an engineer, his curiosity perked up. As they sat down he placed a cheap ballpoint pen on the window counter, out near the glass.

"Why did you do that, Frank?" his wife asked.

"I want to see how soon the pen returns. Then I'll know whether Ashley is correct."

"Correct in what?"

"She said we rotate once per hour. We'll see whether she tells the truth." He winked at his daughter. Both women chuckled.

They had just finished their salads when the pen appeared. Frank looked at his watch. "She's right, one hour and two minutes."

Ashley pointed out the city lakes as they rotated again north and then east, first Green Lake, Lake Union, and after the Ship Canal, Lake Washington. On the third trip around, as they finished a chocolate mousse, they watched the sun sink. The sky turned red and the water of Elliott Bay a rose color in the September Indian summer. They left reluctantly.

⌁

Over the next two days, as they toured the sites of Seattle and rode a ferry up through the San Juan Islands to Friday Harbor, her parents wanted to know the whole story of her adventures in Israel. Ashley told them everything, except about her visit to Najid's family. They had many questions. Her adventures and survival seemed hard to believe. They had never heard any of the personal side of the people in the Holy Land. Coming out of Friday Harbor on the rear deck of the return ferry to Seattle, they saw an Orca breech, its striking black and white body brilliant in the western sun, with Mount Baker and Mount Shuksan shining in the east behind it.

"I can see why you like Seattle, Ashley." Frank became serious. "But you haven't told us much about your social life here. Nothing about your Palestinian friend. Are you still seeing him?"

"Yes, Dad. I am."

"Does he go to church with you?"

"No, he attends a small Middle Eastern group."

"Oh. Then he's really Islamic."

"No, Dad! I've told you, he's a Christian. He really is! Can't you understand anyone outside of our own culture? Why do you close your eyes to people who don't fit into your particular mold? Why do you close your heart to them?"

"Look, Ashley," her dad said, leaning forward and shaking his head, "we care for you and don't want you to continue seeing him."

Her mother nodded her head. "Sometimes parents see things that their children, in their emotions, don't recognize. We're not stupid. We've been around awhile."

"Mom, you don't even know Najid! You won't let yourself even get acquainted! How can you learn someone's character without even talking to him?"

"We just have more experience than you do, Ashley." Frank stood and paced the ferry deck. "As your father, I have the responsibility to protect you. And I intend to do that. I don't want my daughter dragged off to some godforsaken desert in the Middle East to a Muslim culture where women have no rights. I've read their stories. It ends up in abuse of the young wife in the family. Her kids don't even belong to her. I couldn't bear that for you or  my prospective grandchildren."

Ashley stood up and faced her parents, narrowing her eyes. "I respect you as my parents, Dad and Mom. I love you guys. And I listen to your views. But I am a grown woman now, and it is my life we are talking about, not yours. You have made your choices. I have the right and freedom to make mine. Even if you think I'm making bad ones, you'll have to accept them. You can no longer tell me what I can and cannot do!"

"OK, Ashley," her mother softened her voice. "We understand you have the right to choose. But we don't even know this guy. What kind of man is he anyway?"

"Exactly! You don't know him because you have chosen not to even listen to him!" Ashley stood up, eyes flashing, brow furrowed. "I know him. We have been through a lot together, and I trust him. He's a wonderful man with a great family, and I love him. Do you hear me? I love Najid, and he loves me! There is nothing you can do to stop me from loving him! Or seeing him!"

Ashley let her tears fall as she walked rapidly toward the bow of the ship. Then she remembered that Jim suggested she not discuss Najid with her parents. But she hadn't brought it up. Her father had asked directly. She shook her head, talking to the wind. "Now I've really messed it up."

Frank sank onto a bench, head in his hands. Dorothy wept, shaking her head. "I didn't want this to happen, Frank. Why did you have to bring it up now? We've had such a beautiful trip so far. Now you've ruined it."

"We needed to talk, Dorothy. The visit will slip by without resolving this for our daughter. I will not lose total control of her and let her make foolish mistakes!"

"Maybe we should meet him. We're going to her church tomorrow. But then he doesn't go there, so we won't see him. Anyway, we'll have to talk sense into her sometime before we go, and maybe even meet him just to placate her."

The rest of the trip back in the sunset passed quietly. The blue water foreground and the city skyline with Mount Rainier as a backdrop calmed the Wells family's raw nerves. They talked little except about where to eat dinner.

# Chapter 77

Ashley took time on Sunday morning to call Jim at his home before picking up her parents.

"Hi, Jim. I just want to confirm that you will be meeting my parents after church and will take them into your office for a chat regarding Najid."

"It's all planned, Ashley. Thanks for providing the information I needed. You might have a brunch with your parents before the eleven o'clock service so we can continue a bit into the afternoon. I'll talk to them alone at first. But I want you to have Najid there with you by two. Wait outside the office. I'll come and get you."

"Really? Have him there? I thought you were going to chat with them without either of us present."

"Trust me on this one, Ashley."

"Okaaay ... I do appreciate your help, Jim. I just don't want to barge in with Najid and upset your conversation. You know, 'fools rush in.' This is so important to us ... that my parents begin to understand."

"I've got your back, Ashley. Just have them at church."

Ashley made one more quick call. "Najid, Jim is meeting with my parents after church today."

"Good. I'll be interested to hear how that goes."

"He wants us both there, at two p.m. Sorry for the short notice. I didn't know his plan. He wants us at his office in the church."

Ashley heard nothing on the line. "Najid, are you there?"

"Yeah, I'm still here."

"Well, can you come then?"

"I'm not sure I'm prepared to meet your parents yet, Ashley."

"You mean you won't come?"

"Have your parents agreed to meet me? You remember last time in the hospital, they didn't want to even shake hands or talk with me."

"Najid, I've been having a good time with them. Well, for the most part. But Jim asked me to trust him, and he wants you there."

"Do you think anything good can come from my meeting them?"

"I hope so. That's why I asked Jim for help, to prepare the way for us. I didn't expect him to have me or you in the room for the discussion. But Jim says it's all planned and that I should go along with his plan. I do trust him."

"What is planned, Ashley?"

"I don't know. He didn't tell me. I guess we'll find out later today. You know Jim now, Najid. He respects you. So does Pastor Tom, our senior pastor. Your story prompted a lot of discussions in our church—good ones. None of the leadership had ever personally heard anything like what you told during the debriefing."

Ashley waited for Najid's answer. She knew he would eventually let her know after thinking about it. It seemed now or never to her, as though this would be the turning point of her future, with or without the man she loved.

"OK, I'll come. Where do I come and when?"

"Oh, Najid! I love you! It's the same office where we had the debriefing. I'll come and pick you up at one-thirty."

<hr />

Ashley could hardly concentrate on Pastor Tom's sermon except when he mentioned the study group to evaluate how their church could better help the Christians in the Middle East promote justice and be reconcilers and peacemakers. She noticed her father lean forward to hear. His eyes widened. Finally they stood for the last song and then proceeded out to the foyer after the pastors had walked by. Ashley had explained they should meet with Pastor Jim because he had led the team to the Holy Land.

They waited until the crowd had thinned. Jim came over and Ashley introduced her parents to him.

"It's a pleasure to have you with us today. I think very highly of your daughter."

"We do too, Pastor Swain," Frank said as they shook hands.

Dorothy reached out her hand as well. "I understand you led the team to the Holy Land and did such a wonderful job, particularly when Ashley ran into trouble."

"I did lead the team, Mrs. Wells. We ran into a terrifying situation when she didn't return to the guesthouse. I'd like to tell you more and discuss some things with you. You may have some additional questions that Ashley can't answer."

"I'd like to hear more, Pastor." Her father seemed surprised but willing to meet with Jim.

"Ashley, why don't you get some refreshments over in the gym. We'll have some in the office, your parents and I."

"OK, I'll see you in a bit." She smiled as Jim led her parents to his office.

A woman came into Jim's office with coffee and tea and a plate of veggies with dip, crackers, and cheese. They all sat around a circular table on comfortable upholstered chairs. One remained unoccupied.

Jim reached for his coffee. "I'm so pleased to meet you both. You have an amazing daughter. She inspired all of us to meet with people there, not just see sites."

"We've heard some of her stories, Pastor," Frank Wells began, "but I'd be interested in your impressions as well. We didn't hear fully why the guy abducted her."

"I realize that you don't have the full story, and I'm happy to fill in some of the gaps. My understanding is that the bomber here considered Ashley the only one who could identify him. So he paid for a Muslim radical in Jerusalem to hire a hit man to eliminate her. The guy in Jerusalem operated out of the Muslim Quarter in the Old City. He tried several times to capture your daughter, but succeeded finally in Jerusalem. We prayed intensely for her during several hours, and God used the guy's mother to release her from captivity. That's the short version."

"Thanks for filling us in, Pastor."

"Please call me Jim. You can imagine our relief when Ashley walked into the guesthouse after running from her captor. My job was to protect all our team, and in that I had failed. We had divided up into smaller groups led by young Israeli guides. Ashley got caught up in a demonstration in East Jerusalem."

"She could have been killed, Jim. You know that better than we do," Frank said. "As Ashley's dad, my job also is to protect her. I don't know whether you know this, but the last time we visited Ashley, she had nearly died from the bombing and lay in the hospital bed following emergency surgery. A young Palestinian friend named Najid came to see her. Apparently they work in the same department in graduate school at the university. He was there at the bombing. I don't know whether he had something to do with it or not. Ashley thinks he's a Christian, from some ancient church. I have no idea whether that is true. But I know what Palestinians do to the Jews in Israel. I don't trust them. We're worried that this guy is trouble. And we told Ashley to have nothing to do with him."

"I understand your concerns. We trusted Ashley when she wanted to visit Najid's family near Nazareth in Israel. She seemed safe."

"Oh! We had no idea she visited his family. I guess she didn't want to tell us." Frank, raising his eyebrows, lowered his head and shrugged.

"Would you like to know more about Najid?"

"I suppose so, particularly if he continues to try to see Ashley despite our wishes."

Jim went to the door and ushered in a middle-aged woman. He introduced her to Dorothy and Frank as Jane Smithwick. He explained that he met her when she came to check on Ashley at the hospital one day. A witness of the bombing, she was concerned for the young woman. After the usual pleasantries, Jim spoke.

"Would you tell us what you saw when the synagogue exploded?"

Jane smiled and addressed Frank and Dorothy. "I live across the street from the synagogue and rushed to the window when I heard and felt the blast. It almost makes me cry to think of it. Here was this lovely young lady lying on the sidewalk, bleeding, and a young man kneeling over her, waving his hands and calling for help. He succeeded in attracting attention and soon Medic One came. He got up after they had taken her in their van and began to walk away with his arms bleeding. He looked shocked, overwhelmed. The police quickly handcuffed him and took him away. That's all I know."

"Thank you so much for coming, Jane. You've helped fill in some blanks in our understanding of what happened."

Jim escorted her out and brought in a tall man. He introduced him as Gordon Appleby to Ashley's parents. "Mr. Appleby, an FBI agent, has been involved with Najid from the outset of the bombing. Mr. and Mrs. Wells, Ashley's parents, sir. They are interested to learn what you found out about Najid in particular. And thanks for taking time from your family to come."

"Well, first of all," Gordon began, "you have an outstanding daughter. I can't say enough about her steadiness through all the trauma she's had. She has been incredibly helpful, even to getting the bombing suspect to open up to his parents, to us, and to his defense counsel."

"Thanks, Mr. Appleby," Dorothy said. "Ashley didn't tell us that."

"Please call me Gordon. But you wanted to know about Najid. We arrested him at the scene of the bombing thinking he, as a Middle Eastern young man, may have had something to do with it. We investigated him thoroughly. Believe me, there is not one shred of evidence to suggest that he was involved. We released him as a person of interest after only one night in jail. He has been nothing but respectful and cooperative, realizing we needed to do our job of investigating."

"I understand the suspect has admitted guilt, Gordon?"

"Yes, sir. And Najid had something to do with that."

"How was that?" Frank inquired.

"It's quite a story, but the short version is that Najid and Ashley accidently ran into Robert Bentley in a supermarket. Ashley recognized him as the bomber, was terrified, and panicked. Najid, at his own peril, not knowing whether Bentley was armed—he was—tracked him home. We don't advise people to do that, but Najid cleverly followed him to his residence, unobserved, and then notified us where he lived. Najid's action enabled us to arrest the first U.S. bomber since 9/11, a murderer that we in the FBI had been unable to locate for several months."

"Hmm." Frank frowned.

"Oh, and one more thing. Bentley, the bomber, had hired a hit man in Israel to get rid of Ashley, as you now know. We thought he might have retained a killer here as well. So from the time she got off the airplane, we told her never to be out on the street alone, particularly at night. Najid became her bodyguard in that she could call on him at anytime, and did. So he ended up protecting her for several weeks until we were sure no hit man existed here in the U.S."

"We didn't know that either. Why did you come here to tell us this, Gordon?" asked Dorothy with a quizzical look. "You're a busy man."

"I would have come to Oklahoma to tell you this and put your mind at ease about your daughter and Najid! He is one of the most courageous and brave young men I have ever met. Helpful and pleasant. Delightful guy. What you see is what you get."

"Thanks, Gordon," Jim said. "I know we've imposed on your weekend. Please thank your family for us. You've given me some insights I didn't have." Jim ushered him to the door.

Jim came back with a short, wiry, athletic-looking young man. "Mr. and Mrs. Wells, this is Jerry Farnsworth of the mountain rescue team here in Seattle." After everyone shook hands, Jim continued. "Please sit down. We are interested to hear what you learned about Ashley Wells and Najid Haddad at Anvil Rock on Mount Rainier recently."

"OK. They told us they had climbed to Camp Muir with a group from the U. She suggested they walk over to Anvil Rock during a lunch break. A storm came up while they sat on the rocks away from the group at Muir. She sprained her ankle, couldn't walk. They got caught in a whiteout—you know, where you can't see a thing and get disoriented. It's a weird feeling. No horizon. Can't tell directions or even upslope or down. So they did exactly the right thing. Najid dug a deep snow cave, wrapped Ashley in a thermal blanket they both had, and shoved her in. She shivered with hypothermia and couldn't make any decisions by her own admission. But she soon warmed up. They stayed in the cave all night, and we rescued them easily by helicopter in the morning after the storm."

"So they kept their heads?" Frank asked.

"Yeah. If they had tried to make it back on their own, they probably would never have found Camp Muir or their group in the gale and sleet. Even if she could have walked normally, or if they had stayed on the surface, either way, they wouldn't be here today."

"Did Najid have any mountain experience to know how to dig a snow cave?" Frank wondered.

"Not to my knowledge. He saved her life by not losing his head and thinking what would make sense. She said she had seen survival shows on TV. That may be where the idea of the cave came from. But he accomplished a major feat protecting them both in a howling storm."

"Hmm …" Frank remained quiet for a moment, then replied, "I'm amazed that you would take time out from your weekend to come here and tell us this."

"I have the highest respect for this guy, for saving your daughter's life."

"Thanks, Jerry. You guys are fantastic in your work. Most people don't know you are all volunteers. And thanks for volunteering again today." Jim escorted him to the door, and this time brought in Ashley.

# Chapter 78

Welcome to court, Miss Wells," Jim said with a smirk. "You're the next witness, and I'm the prosecutor. I think you know these people, the jury."

Ashley laughed, glancing at her parents, but still felt a bit nervous. "Okaaay. I'm not sure what I'm supposed to report."

"I'll ask the questions." He turned to Frank and Dorothy and winked. "It's true. She doesn't know what's coming or what just happened. I haven't told her anything."

"Miss Wells, did you visit the Haddad family in Northern Israel, in Galilee?"

"Yes, sir." Ashley glanced at her parents with a nervous laugh.

"What did you find? What are they like?"

She took a deep breath and sat back in her chair. "Rafiq, Najid's dad, looks like him and has a gentle manner, polite. Of course he speaks Arabic, so his son Sami translated for me. Rafiq is soft-spoken, like Najid. He lived during early childhood as a landowner's son in a large house surrounded by an olive grove. But now they live in a small three-bedroom house with six kids, and he is a farm laborer in someone else's orchard."

"What about his wife?"

"Oh, Farah loves her kids. They speak of Najid with such affection and talk with him on Skype once a week."

"How does Rafiq treat his wife?"

"With real tenderness. I could see they are very much in love. They're Christians, you know. She speaks lovingly of Jesus. They attend a historic Christian church, Melkite. They are great people. In a short few days, I grew to love them. Najid has a wonderful heritage."

"What about the other kids?"

"They respect their parents and are all younger than Najid, but full of life. I played soccer with them. Sami, next oldest, got angry at a checkpoint in the West Bank, but only because the Israeli soldiers stripped him naked and left him in a room for fifteen minutes, for no apparent reason. We were trying to get through the wall to get to a friend's orchard. It's a long story."

"Anything else about them?"

"I guess the most amazing thing is the way they get along with both Jewish and Muslim neighbors in Israel proper. And despite being harassed at checkpoints in the wall of separation, and having been displaced from their ancestral home of many generations, they are not bitter. In fact, they want to be reconcilers between the Jewish Israelis and Palestinians, whether Muslim or Christian. Najid has had Jewish friends from his own childhood."

"Thank you, Miss Wells." Jim started to say something else when the door opened. Ashley left.

"Jim … I didn't realize you had a meeting going."

"It's OK, Tom. I want you to meet Ashley's parents from Oklahoma, Frank and Dorothy Wells." He turned to them. "Pastor Tom Evans you know from this morning's sermon. Please come in for a moment and sit down."

Flashing a warm smile, Tom shook their hands and sat down in the now empty chair. "I don't want to interrupt you all."

"No problem, Tom. We were talking about Najid, learning more about him. Would you tell Ashley's parents about his contribution to the trip debriefing the other day?"

"Right." The senior pastor looked from Frank to Dorothy and back to Jim. "Ashley brought Najid to tell his family story as part of the debriefing since she had visited his family in Galilee. It gave us a sense of who this Palestinian family really is, meeting a member of it in the flesh. Najid told the story of his grandparents' expulsion from their family home and lands in 1948 and their years of wandering as refugees when no country really wanted them. It was the first time I had ever heard a personal account of what happened. I am still trying to sort this out. That is why we are embarking on a serious rethinking of our position as a church."

"Do you think Najid told the truth?" Frank asked.

"Everything I know of him seems genuine. I believe he is a true follower of Jesus and has a heart for going back as a reconciler in Israel. You can sense what rings true. We've witnessed his genuine faith. He's a dear brother and a mature young man."

"Thanks for sharing your thoughts, Tom," Jim said. Pastor Tom shook Frank's hand, nodded to Dorothy, and left.

Frank and Dorothy looked stunned. Frank tried to speak, but couldn't. He could only shake his head as he thought about what these people said about Najid. Jim rose and walked quietly to his desk. He reached for a rectangular piece of wood, with rough bark on one side but finished in a light stain on the other. He turned it around slowly three times and after several silent moments, sat down. He said nothing, but gazed out the window. Ashley's parents looked at the finished side of the piece and read the inscription: "Judge not that you be not judged." The room remained silent. Frank sat, head in his hands. Dorothy wiped a tear away.

Frank Wells liked to deal in facts. He could change his views, but only with solid evidence. He recognized they had been set up, albeit lovingly, with Jim inviting all those people to let them know about Najid. Everything they said seemed true.

After a long interval, Frank spoke. "I can see I've been too hasty in my judgments about Najid. Actually I've been wrong to judge at all. I had no idea who he is or his family. I haven't removed the plank in my own eye to see the speck in his. I'd like to ask his forgiveness for rejecting him as a young Christian brother ... if I could." He stopped, reaching for the box of tissues.

"You can." Jim rose and went to the door, motioning Najid to come in.

Najid entered, hesitant with each step. He nodded to both Frank and Dorothy and moved tentatively toward them. He eased his hand out toward Frank Wells, who took it and pulled Najid into a tight hug. "I'm so sorry for how I've treated you, Najid. I have been wrong about you, and I want to ask you to forgive me." He released Najid. Both men blinked water from their eyes. Najid nodded and smiled. He tried to speak, but couldn't.

Dorothy stepped up to him and wrapped his hand in both of hers. "Najid, I'm sorry too, for the way I rejected you in the hospital. You have been a guardian angel for Ashley, and we didn't know it. I love you for it. I can't tell you how sorry I am for judging you wrongly. Please forgive me too." Her voice broke and she swallowed several times. "We'll try to make it up to you somehow."

All three sat down, wiping their eyes. Najid exhaled and finally found his voice.

"Where's Jim?" He scanned the room. They were alone. They began to talk, at first quietly and then more quickly, about Najid's family and the Wells family. Dorothy asked to hear more of Najid's family story, and then about his siblings and parents, their work and interests. Both of Ashley's parents shared a bit of their family histories and their life in Oklahoma. Soon the conversation became so animated they did not even notice the fourth chair had become occupied. Ashley had slipped in silently, listening to the conversation.

Frank leaned back in the chair silently, thinking, while Ashley joined in the conversation with Najid and her mother. Ashley obviously wanted them to accept Najid as her fiancé.

"I know you love Ashley and raised her to have the life that God wishes her to have," Najid said, breaking a long, silent pause in the conversation. "I have grown to love her too. We have so much in common and enjoy each other's company so much that I would like to spend the rest of my life with her. Even though I come from the other side of the world."

Najid took a deep breath and sighed. "I'm just a graduate student on a scholarship right now, and I'm from a part of the world that I realize you have never visited. I'm a foreigner. So I can understand that you would worry about letting your daughter marry me and perhaps live far away. Who am I to ask for such a wonderful lady to be my wife? You have every reason to question the idea."

"I admit I did, Najid," Frank said. "But in the past hour we have learned much about you from third parties who have no axe to grind."

"I'm sorry, I don't understand about the axes."

Frank chuckled. "I shouldn't have used that phrase. It means the people who we just listened to, talking about what you have done to protect our daughter, had no selfish reason to tell us anything but the truth of what they observed about you. So we now feel like we know better who you really are. And that is reassuring. I mean it makes us relax about you. So go ahead with what you were saying."

"OK. I have not asked Ashley to marry me."

Frank raised his eyebrows and sat up straight in his chair. "I thought you said you wanted to marry Ashley?"

"I do. But in my culture, most marriages have been arranged by parents in the past. Now more young people are making their own decisions, but I would never think of deciding such an important step over the objections of her parents. It would just lead to all kinds of problems. I have thought until now that you would never consider allowing Ashley to marry me. So I didn't know how I could ever ask you. I was afraid you would say no. But I am willing to wait for Ashley if you think I have a chance. I want to prove to you that I really love her and would care for her for the rest of our lives together."

Frank looked at Dorothy. Tears rolled down her cheeks. His own eyes watered. "Najid, you have already proven that you love and care for our daughter, even at considerable risk to yourself."

"You mean that I would actually have your permission to ask Ashley to marry me?" Najid asked, eyes wide and sparkling.

Frank glanced at Dorothy, who wiped her eyes and nodded. Frank began slowly, "We don't know where in the world you two will be ten years from now or what you might be doing. But we trust Ashley, and now we trust you to take care of her anywhere as you already have here. So yes, Najid, you have our permission to ask Ashley to marry you." He had a flicker of a smile. "But what if she says no?"

"I'll take that chance, Mr. Wells. But first I need to go shopping."
He leaped into the air and punched it with his fist. He grabbed Ashley
and danced around the room with her.

Ashley broke free, drew a happy face with a wink on a piece of
paper, signed it "Ash" and put it on Jim's desk. She grabbed Najid's
hand and skipped out the door, leading her parents. "I know a great
place for lunch now, for falafel."

"What's that, Ashley?" Frank asked.

"You'll find out, Dad," she said with a coy smile. "I can't wait to
have it again ... with Najid ... when we return to the Middle East."